THE ETHEREAL HAND

Alexander Jacobs

Chapter One

Chapter One

"Wake up, Dakota." Dakota's pupils darted behind closed eyelids, and his pulse quickened as his heart struggled to offer enough blood to bring his oxygen-starved brain to consciousness.

"Dakota, darling, it's time to awaken." A warm hand rested on his arm, and he forced his eyes open, blinking them several times to clear the morning fog. The body hovering above him belonged to a woman whose round, creased face glowed with a generous warmth. Despite himself, Dakota trusted this stranger.

"Who are you?" he asked, finding he could barely whisper.

"I'm your mother," she said, and Dakota examined her with new wonder. "Here, drink this water," she continued, helping him to a sitting position and offering a clear glass. "You're parched, sweetheart." Dakota paused, though, before bringing the glass to his cracked lips. Try as he might, he couldn't recall this woman, and if he failed to remember his own mother, then something was terribly wrong.

"I'm not thirsty," he lied, lowering his head and trying without success to organize his scrambled thoughts.

"But darling, you must drink." The woman's brown eyes hardened, and as Dakota regained a sense of self, his trust in this stranger dwindled. A quivering edge of doubt took hold in the corner of his mind, spreading outwards with the growing realization that he didn't recall how he'd gotten here. He lifted the glass to his lips, but at the last moment, he let it slip through his fingers and onto the bedspread. The water soaked straight through the thick sheets, and the woman straightened.

"I'm sorry," Dakota whispered.

"Don't worry," she said. "I'll get you another glass." She turned and strode towards an opening that appeared in the featureless, glossy walls. Her heavy feet fell in silence on the plush carpet, which reflected an intense red color to the white, glowing ceiling.

After the woman left, Dakota squeezed shut his eyes and spoke to himself under his breath so that his voice didn't even reach his ears. "I am Dakota. I have three brothers and one sister." At that, he stopped. No matter how much he struggled, his memories refused to return. He repeated those two sentences, but his mind collided with an impenetrable brick wall.

The woman returned, breaking Dakota's concentration. Examining her with a clearer head, his certainty that she was not his mother grew. He asked, "Who are you?" The woman approached him with a fresh glass filled with a clear liquid she'd claimed was water.

"Your mo—"

"Don't lie to me," Dakota said, grabbing her wrist and twisting it. The liquid spilled, turning the carpet a deeper shade of red. Dakota rose to his feet, steadying himself against the soaked sheets.

"You're confused, darling," the woman said, attempting to pry Dakota's fingers from her arm. "Let me help you."

"No. You're not my friend." Dakota's legs shook under him as he tried to walk, but a measure of strength returned to his limbs.

The woman pried her wrist free, and she jumped back, saying, "They warned me you were trouble."

"Who told you that?" Now his legs had regained enough strength to push himself free of the bed.

"It doesn't matter," she answered, producing a syringe from inside her sleeve. Not wasting any time, she stabbed at his shoulder, but the needle only hit empty air, for Dakota had sidestepped the lunge, twisting his hips to plunge his knee into the woman's lower back. Despite Dakota's small size, the jab was enough to send her to the ground, and the syringe dropped at Dakota's feet.

Before the woman recovered, he lifted the syringe, pushed the needle into her shoulder, then collapsed onto the bed. Her eyes darted about the room until her pupils grew cloudy, and she looked up with a disconcerting, blank gaze.

"Who are you?" she asked with mild curiosity. Whatever the syringe had contained seemed to have wiped her memory, and Dakota breathed a sigh of relief at avoiding the needle.

"Go to sleep," he ordered, standing. The woman obeyed like an automaton, pulling the soaked covers over her shoulders.

Dakota decided that the woman no longer posed a threat, so he ignored her and paced the room. As his legs grew steadier, his thoughts hardened, bouncing against the mental barrier that prevented access to his memories. He pushed his knuckles into his eyes, forcing himself with all his might to remember.

He stopped pacing. "I remember," he said aloud. His efforts had shattered the mental block, and an icy calm descended over his mind as his natural personality reasserted itself.

A moment later, Dakota plucked the syringe from the sleeping woman's shoulder and approached the wall where a raised section protruded from the otherwise seamless surface. With the flat metal top of the needle, Dakota pried the panel away from the wall, revealing a tangle of multicolored wires.

"A challenge," he said with mild satisfaction. Dakota laid out the wires in his mind, creating a mental picture of the circuit in front of him. Within seconds, he learned all he needed, so he pulled loose two wires to trigger the hidden door.

The red carpet ended at the doorway, giving way to cement floors. Bare light bulbs illuminated the narrow, cold passage ahead, and dripping water sent regular pings echoing off the walls. After carefully examining his surroundings, Dakota chose a direction and walked until he arrived at a monitor. His fingers tapped out an intricate pattern on the display to decipher the digital interface and summon a map of the complex.

"Ah," he said after discovering the generator's location. His mind filled with dozens of different tools he'd be able to salvage from the generator room, but as he walked through the abandoned halls, he became distracted.

A bitter sense of injustice built in his idle mind, and though he'd never experienced genuine anger, his emotions now strayed as close to hatred as they ever had. Someone would suffer for his imprisonment, Dakota decided. The prospect of retribution calmed him, and by the time he reached the generator room, he'd regained his concentration.

Inside the room, Dakota surveyed the available materials, relieved to find portable power units nearby. He had invented these energy storage devices three years ago when he turned seven—though dozens of years had passed since then while they kept him asleep—so he already understood how to create the mechanism that would enable his escape.

Just a few minutes later, Dakota strapped two of the smaller units to his waist, regretting only that his ten-year-old frame could not bear more weight. With a wince, he punctured the skin below his heart, feeding two of the units' wires into his body before activating the devices.

"Onto step two," he said, recalling the facility map he'd seen earlier. He memorized his route, stepped back into the corridor, and followed a series of turns to the administrator's office. Dakota reached out to the steel handle before him, already knowing the door would be unlocked, and pushed the slab of metal inwards.

The cramped office held an array of screens stacked high on three of the four walls, each displaying a distinct data set. If Dakota had more time, he'd have enjoyed examining them, but his business lay ahead. The administrator rested in a gleaming silver chair facing away from the door. Only a narrow wooden desk separated him from the bank of glowing screens.

"You are the administrator," Dakota said with enough volume to enter the man's headphones. The startled administrator spun in his chair, white hair falling from its combed pattern. With a quick survey, Dakota decided the man was in his sixties, just over six feet tall, and in remarkable shape for his age.

"You… you shouldn't—"

"After a thousand years of imprisonment, you dare offer me a command?" Dakota noted the horror on the older man's face. His glasses had slipped to the end of his hooked nose, and he raised his hand to shove them back to his brow.

"No, no. You misunderstand. They hired me to manage this facility." He sputtered, rattled by the cold stare of judgment that was so out of place on Dakota's young face.

"Is that an excuse for your actions?" Dakota asked. "Your words are of no consequence. Allow me to leave this facility, and I will not harm you."

"Harm me?" The man stood, towering over Dakota. His broad shoulders cast a dark shadow, and though Dakota's primitive instincts made him yearn to cower in fear, he'd learned long ago that size held no meaning.

"You're a little boy," the man said as shock gave way to confidence. "A dozen soldiers are stationed down the hall. If you don't return to your room, they'll force you with their guns. You know what a gun is, right?"

"I will give you one more chance to allow me to leave before I force the entry codes from you."

"This is absurd." The man reached into his desk drawer, pulled out a gun, and pointed it at Dakota.

"Do not aim your weapon at me," Dakota said with quiet determination.

"Aim? I'll do more than aim unless you return to your room." The man growled and stepped forward, but before his foot hit the ground, Dakota acted. Drawing as much energy from the power units around his waist as he dared, Dakota gave substance to his Ethereal Hand, knocking the large man back and pinning him to the wall of monitors.

"How… what are you doing?"

"Your masters failed in your education, and I'm afraid we lack sufficient time to explain the Ethereal Hand." Without another word, Dakota's Ethereal Hand delved into the man's mind, breaking apart any resistance easily and freeing the access codes. The man fell to the ground, unconscious or dead.

"I never was very good at that," Dakota said, remembering with admiration his brother Lysander's skill.

Dakota walked to the computer terminal at the administrator's desk, and, using the man's codes, he signaled all the facility's locks to release. He knew he had only a minute to reach the elevator before another employee overrode the command, so he broke into a jog, weaving his way through the empty halls until he reached the elevator platform.

Dakota used the administrator's access code to activate the lift, and the elevator rumbled to life, pulling Dakota to the planet's surface from the subterranean depths. The doors opened onto the street, and he stepped forward, pausing to examine his surroundings.

Massive steel and glass buildings, taller than the crystal towers he recalled from the images his brother had sent him of Stomatus so long ago, lined the street, reaching up to the heavens. Automobiles barreled past, and bright screens the size of houses lit the street, counteracting the diminishing light of the setting sun.

"So much progress," he said with a measure of admiration before striking out in search of a computer terminal. He had a thousand years of human history to research.

Chapter Two

Cayden balanced on the precarious branch. The ground stretched out far below him, mountains no larger than features on a map, and one false step would send him tumbling. He was tempted to cheat, to use his Ethereal Hand to help himself across the branch, but Tonius and Robinson would notice from their perch on the other side. So he continued, bracing himself against the occasional gust of wind until he stepped back onto solid ground.

"I can't believe you did that," Tonius said, shaking his head. "You might have fallen." His lanky body lay plastered to the tree's knobby bark, and even his pale face was gaining color in the sun.

"Lighten up," Robinson said, holding his oversized belly. "He is the Airwalker, remember?" Cayden threw himself next to Leyna, who lounged in a shaded corner.

"You put the idea in his head Tonius," Leyna said, sitting. "I would know." Her red hair gleamed in the midday light as Cayden shot her a sly glance, smiling when he sensed her relaxed state of mind. The mental connection he'd formed with Leyna after Mogen's death had been strengthening daily as they grew accustomed to one another's thoughts. Sensing her emotions now came without conscious effort, and Cayden found he enjoyed the sensation.

"Without wings, it's foolish to follow the Perchidians out here," Tonius said, rolling onto his stomach to peer at the distant ground. Though the airship they now flew swayed under them, its wooden trunk—which stretched down below them in a wide ring—had a reassuring stability.

"I can fly," Cayden said. "At least, I did once."

"No, I wouldn't call that flying," Robinson said, recalling Cayden's fall from the tower in Stomatus' market. "Flopping around in the air like a beached fish isn't flying."

"Technically, he was adjusting the air's density..."

While Robinson and Tonius bickered, Cayden poked his head over the side of the tree ring. Below, he observed the bottom of the wood ring as it hung in the air like a giant bicycle wheel. On the ground beyond, a broad, flat river wound through the lower reaches of a mountain range, and while he noted green foliage near the river, most of the land was a uniform grey-brown. *Our world is dying,* he thought, but as he was about to look up, a glint caught his eye.

A brilliant light reflected off an enormous structure far below. Squinting his eyes, he decided it looked like the white crystal used to build the oldest towers in the Perianth Empire, those surrounding the great tree in Stomatus where he'd trained with Tonius and Robinson to become a Perianth soldier.

"I found a clue," Cayden said, leaning further to gain clarity.

"There's nothing there," Robinson said, joining him at the edge.

"I don't see anything," Tonius added.

"Really? It's right there, so big you can't miss it." Tonius offered Robinson a doubtful shrug but said nothing.

"Cayden," Leyna said, "you're using your Ethereal Hand to sense it."

"Was I?" More and more, Cayden used his Hand for even the most mundane tasks. Moving an object with his mind was more natural than grasping it with his fingers, which seemed like clumsy sausages in comparison. His thoughts drifted around him like a web, probing his surroundings before any of his traditional senses. "I suppose I was," he said to himself.

Cayden stretched his mind as far as it would reach, focusing his Ethereal Hand into a tendril that extended to the remote ground. The odd structure resisted his probe, for the moment his Hand grazed its unfamiliar surface, it pushed him away. Then it vanished, leaving no trace, no matter how he looked.

"What was that?" Leyna asked, for she had sensed its power through the connection they shared.

"Beats me," Cayden said. "But we should investigate since someone wielded affinity to defend itself against my vision." With that, he turned and strode through the tree's outer wall, which parted like a curtain before his Ethereal Hand.

Robinson looked at Tonius, saying, "I don't suppose I'll get used to him doing that."

* * *

***

Inside, Cayden sent his mind in search of Balint. Ever since he'd envisioned Astor torturing the Dumrolls inhabitants, Cayden had worked hard to develop his ability to sense people and objects from a distance. By forming an affinite bond with the flying tree under his feet, he felt the weight of Perchidians as they walked across the floors, while his bond with the air exposed their shapes. He hadn't recreated the clear picture he'd experienced that night, but locating Balint wouldn't take too much skill.

Already, he caught Balint's form in the steering room far overhead. The bulky man was hard to miss as he stood planted on the ground as firmly as a rooted tree. Most people shifted their weight, even standing still, but Balint never moved.

Cayden wound his way through the narrow passages, his memory of the great tree in Stomatus still fresh. The nine months he'd spent in the Perianth Academy filled him with a lifetime of experiences, and he struggled to accept the witches might have destroyed it all. When last he'd seen it, from his perch atop Jericho's airship, the witches had emerged from the forest and were pouring into the city through the breach in the wall he had created.

I can't dwell on that, Cayden decided as he nodded greetings to any Perchidian he passed. *I've got to push forward.* The man who called himself the Alchemist lay somewhere to the north and beyond that—a land called Earth.

Cayden continued onwards until he arrived at the steering room. At the apex of the tree wheel, the room offered a complete view of the surrounding area. Tree sap grew outwards in a clear, golden bubble, not unlike glass, so that only the howling of wind gave any sign of the unusual weather that tore at the tree.

"Cayden, my boy," Balint said with gruff pleasure. The Perchidian elder, though shorter than Jericho, stood even wider than the Perchidian leader. He stepped off the steering platform, which contained a series of paddles growing from the floor like a bunch of spring flowers, and another Perchidian took his place. "Not unlike playing an instrument," he said, nodding towards the paddles.

"And you're pretty good at it," Cayden said.

"Should be. I've been at it since I was a pup. But you didn't come to hear stories from an old warrior."

"No, I guess not. Actually, I came to tell you we should land." Cayden relayed what he'd seen on the ground.

"Hmm," Balint grunted after scratching his broad chin. "I've flown these lands my entire life, and I've never seen the structure you describe."

"They were shielding it with their Ethereal Hands," Cayden said, though that was a guess. "I don't understand how they managed it, but I got a brief glimpse before they pushed me away. It looked a lot like the diamond towers in Stomatus." The more he learned about affinity, the less he understood. Much of his understanding was inborn, emanating from the man Lysander now buried deep inside his mind, but he didn't dare reach inwards for answers. He shuddered at the memory of the pain Lysander had caused. *If only Mogen were still alive*, he thought.

"You said something pushed you away?" Balint asked. Not waiting for an answer, he continued, "Our search is open-ended, so every detail is important. Let's land." Then, to the other Perchidians, he shouted, "Open the vents! We're setting down the ship. Order the first troop patrol ready with spears. Come, Cayden."

While the other Perchidians erupted into a flurry of activity, Balint led Cayden towards the slide that would carry them down to the base of the tree ring. Over the past few weeks, Cayden had learned to appreciate Balint's decisiveness, a confidence born of experience that made him—in Cayden's estimation—a remarkable leader. But his style differed from that of Jericho, the aloof commander of the Perchidian Sky People. Cayden needed to choose his words around Jericho, but he'd never been so at ease with an adult as he was with Balint. *I wonder how Jericho came to lead the Perchidians.*

Cayden was just about to ask when Balint tripped, almost barreling over Dugal, who had slipped out from an unseen crevice. Despite Dugal's protests against Cayden's trip during at the Flying Council, the small man had insisted upon coming. He maintained that "someone with sense" must observe the Airwalker. Cayden, though, considered it more likely Dugal remained intent upon waking Airwalker Lysander, the corrupted personality lurking deep inside Cayden's mind.

"Why are we descending?" Dugal asked. He was smaller than his fellow Perchidians, and he often used his compact size to hide just out of sight. With a calculated narrowing of his beady eyes, he tried to bore holes in Cayden to reach Lysander's wicked presence behind Cayden's golden iris. Dugal's wish to awaken the Airwalker definitely hadn't subsided.

"Cayden has discovered something worth investigating," Balint answered, careful not to let slip their true purpose.

"We're in the middle of the dead lands. There is nothing to investigate besides dirt and dust."

"Nothing to see with your eyes, anyway," agreed Balint. "But Cayden sensed something on the ground."

Dugal grunted. "You'll be going out with him?"

"Why? Want to accompany my warriors?" Balint asked, letting out a snort. Dugal was unamused.

"You'll let me know what you discover, of course," Dugal said, allowing a stiff smile to touch the corners of his mouth before retreating into the corridor from which he'd emerged.

"I'll ensure you're at least the fifth or sixth person I tell!" Balint shouted after him, resuming his walk through the tree with such gusto that Cayden had to jog.

"What does he want, anyway?" Cayden asked. Besides the sinister man's interest in the Airwalker, he'd learned nothing about Dugal.

"I'm not sure," Balint said over his shoulder. "But you can bet he's shepherding a sour purpose in that wrinkled head of his."

Cayden didn't respond, for they arrived at the slide. The landing zone lay far below the bridge, and the slide was the fastest, if not most pleasant, way to descend. Without hesitation, Balint grabbed a sturdy branch overhead, using it to swing his wide body into the dark tunnel opening. He slid out of sight, and Cayden, after counting to five, followed suit.

If he wasn't so frightened of smashing his head, he might have enjoyed the ride. The polished surface of the slide offered little resistance, and Cayden plummeted at breakneck speed through the tree. Gradually, the incline lessened, and he popped out behind Balint, rising to his feet and moving out of the way—an instinct he'd developed since Robinson landed on his back a couple of weeks ago.

At the bottom of the tree ring, the rough soil approached with alarming rapidity through a gap in the floor. A dozen Perchidian troops had gathered around the opening, dressed in garb that resembled the witches' outfits. Interwoven branches and leaves covered most of their bodies, but while the witches' garments seemed alive, the Perchidians' clothing was long dead. They strapped broad shields of solid oak to their arms and slung spears of pine tipped with black obsidian across their backs.

A noise behind Cayden caused him to turn, and he saw Leyna and Tonius pop out of the slide as the tree fell the last few feet towards the ground. Balint looked at them without comment.

"Thought we'd tag along," Leyna said.

"Where's Robinson?" Cayden asked.

"He's still tired from practice yesterday," Tonius replied. Since they'd left the Academy in Stomatus, Cayden had insisted they keep up the combat training regime drilled into them by their combat master, Priven. The last time Cayden had seen the axe-wielding man, he'd been running towards Stomatus' outer wall, where the witch and gremmel attackers pounded into the city. *I wonder if he's still alive,* Cayden thought. *I wonder if any of them are.*

"Well, no use standing around," Balint said, motioning for them to follow. They stepped onto a platform, which had detached from the bark-like ceiling and lowered itself to their level. As soon as they were aboard, the platform sank to the ground.

Cayden looked around as he stepped from beneath the tree, waiting for his eyes to adjust to the bright light. As usual, his left golden eye took much longer to adjust than his right brown eye.

When his pupils finished contracting, he saw they stood in a barren field, empty as far as the eye could see. A uniform brown bled into the muddy gray horizon, and only the swaying and creaking of the tree ring against its moorings showed movement. Closing his eyes and bringing his total concentration into his Ethereal Hand, Cayden was dismayed that he could no longer sense the structure, even from a much shorter distance. Luckily, he remembered that it had to be somewhere just ahead.

"This way!" he shouted, waving his hand for the entourage to follow. The twelve Perchidian soldiers, along with Balint, Leyna, and Tonius, followed just behind him as he walked into the still plain. The complete silence brought him back to the dead forest on the border of his hometown, where he'd walked with the other children in a silent march towards an unknown future. So much had happened over the past year that it made his head hurt thinking about it. Best to focus on the task at hand, he decided.

By now, the tree ring had shrunk into the distance until it was the size of Cayden's clenched fist. He quickened his pace, but Leyna grabbed his shoulder and whispered, "Stop." He looked back at her with alarm as she knelt to the ground, fingers pressed hard against her pale temples. "There are other people here besides us," she said.

As if on cue, glittering figures of gold burst from the ground in a wide ring around them. Perianth soldiers, Cayden thought instinctively, until he noticed several women dressed in the golden leaves favored by the Perianths. *But the Perianth soldiers don't accept women,* he realized. He had no time to examine them further, though, because the ground shook and then sank, lowering them thirty feet. Above, the earth clapped shut like a trap door, casting them into darkness.

Pulling out the light crystal he still wore about his neck, Cayden poured energy into it, casting a warm glow into the cavern. "Look," Tonius said, pointing up with one thin arm. Cayden raised his head to see the ceiling sliding downwards. In seconds, its unforgiving mass would crush them.

"Stand back!" Cayden shouted, adrenaline pumping through his limbs. Leyna, seeing in Cayden's mind what he had planned, guided the soldiers and Tonius to the back wall. Relying on the instincts drilled into him over countless hours by Priven, Cayden sent his Ethereal Hand lashing out at the speed of a flying hammer, slamming it into the ceiling above in search of a grip. The rock trembled mightily as Cayden attempted to form an affinite bond, but the rock didn't break. Another force more potent than his Hand held it together.

Cayden knew he'd only have time for one more try, so he braced himself against the ground below, forming an affinite bond with the rock underfoot. To his relief, it seemed to be unaffected by the force pressing down from above, and with several feet of rock in his grasp, he thrust it against the ceiling with every bit of power he could muster.

"We can't hold him," a muffled voice from outside said as the rock above shattered with a loud crack. Once more, Cayden slammed the rock into the ceiling above like a sledgehammer, and the roof exploded outwards. A sharp thrust from the stone beneath his feet catapulted him free from the trap, and Cayden vaulted out with the flying debris to land in front of the golden figures. They scuttled away, unsure how to handle the fearsome child who stared them down with unforgiving ferocity.

"Who are you?" Cayden asked. His knees weakened, and for a moment, his stomach dropped as he detected Lysander's dark presence stirring inside his mind. For the first time since he'd formed the bond with Leyna, Cayden sensed traces of what had become a familiar sensation, but it soon faded, and he gave no outward sign of his fatigue.

The eldest of their group stepped forward and said, "We are the Forgotten." Cayden estimated that the sixty-year-old man was as strong as ever, but although he wore the traditional Perianth uniform —a shimmering coat of thousands of interlocking golden leaves—his limbs were all flesh and blood.

"Or we had hoped to be forgotten," said a young woman at his side, whose eyes now bore into Cayden's. She was only a few years older than Cayden himself, though he saw she wore the Perianth uniform like a second skin. *She's been training with that armor for years,* Cayden guessed.

"You're not with the Perianths," Cayden said.

"No," the young woman said. "We left them the day the Airwalker joined the great tree in Stomatus."

"That was a thousand years ago," Cayden whispered to himself. Leyna, who listened to his thoughts, pushed a sense of trust into Cayden's mind.

By now, the Perchidian soldiers had clambered from the hole behind Cayden. With Balint leading them, they formed ranks, pointing their glimmering spears at the would-be attackers. Three of the Forgotten retreated when Leyna joined Cayden's side and rested her hand on his shoulder.

"We might be allies if you're not Perianths," Cayden said. No one spoke, so he continued, "Look, I'm happy to continue fighting. You might have us outnumbered, but I promise many of you will not escape with your lives should you decide to attack." Then, in his most menacing voice, he asked, "How many of your warriors already attempted to restrain me?"

After another lengthy pause, the young woman said, "Very well."

"But my lady," the old man said, "these are strangers. You know the law. Your mother—"

"My mother is dead," snapped the young woman. Then her expression softened, and she said, "Trust me, Casheen." The man nodded, and the young woman turned towards Cayden, her long legs carrying her forward. "My name is Naya." Up close, Cayden examined her Perianth battle uniform, an outdated design Mogen had favored.

"I'm Cayden," he said, collapsing against the ground as exhaustion overcame his ruse.

Naya snorted, offering her hand. "You looked as though you were ready to fight us all—and win." She laughed. "And here you are, unable to stand."

Cayden smiled sheepishly, allowing her to pull him to his feet.

Naya nodded to Leyna, and they locked eyes. Then she shouted, "We're going home!"

The air shimmered like waves of heat over hot baking sand. A deafening crack sent a gust of wind racing past Cayden's ears, and a city exploded into view. As soon as he saw it, Cayden felt his knees go weak again, and he thought he might fall.

"What is it?" Leyna asked.

"That's… that's a piece of Stomatus," he whispered. "Before the Dumrolls were destroyed, it looked just like this city."

"The Dumrolls were never destroyed," Naya said. "We just… moved them."

Chapter Three

Henrik's thin fingers traced the rim of the glass he held in his left hand. "I don't like you," he said over the pounding music, raising his eyes to study the woman who danced inches from his face.

"Sure, I'll have another," she yelled back, trying to press her greasy cup into his empty hand and spilling the green liquid on his pressed shirt when he refused to take it. He estimated her to be about twenty-five, though smoking had introduced more than a few wrinkles onto her otherwise youthful face. Behind her, a smokey sea of bodies surged and moved to deep bass reverberations while prisms beamed down rainbow shots of light, transforming human flesh into something far more artificial.

"What am I doing here?" he asked himself. When no reason came to mind, he decided to leave, placing his drink on the wet, narrow bar. He'd ingested more alcohol in the past hour than in years, and the entire room spun around him. The girl tried to follow, but she fell against Henrik, and he let her slide to the ground. She laughed, reaching up to grasp his wrist, but Henrik stepped over her like any object blocking one's path, and he wove his way towards the door.

Outside, Henrik's shirt clung to his forty-year-old body in the humid air. Even though the sun had set, much of the day's heat remained trapped among the city's concrete towers. He gazed at the stars as he had often done as a child, but that had been on a farm, where only the porch light threatened to eclipse the night sky. In the city, the sky glowed yellow from light that bounced against the pollution hanging overhead in a permanent cloud.

Soon, though, Henrik's attention returned to the ground, for the street held as many drunks at night as it did scavenging pigeons during midday. Locomotion became an exercise in evasive maneuvers.

Desperate to escape the crowds, he wandered towards the city's edge, where black water splashed against the seawall. The thinning crowds let Henrick quicken his pace into a sprint to survey the open water.

At the river's edge, Henrik raised his hand against the glare of a street lamp and watched the smoke bellow from the electric plants across the river. The sight turned his stomach, and since he no longer had the strength to walk, he lay down on the sidewalk with his face pressed to the rough curb scant inches from the road. Every so often, passing trains channeled deep vibrations through the pavement, and he reflected on the energy powering these massive trains—energy that his power plants across the river provided. In this moment, however, he imagined the electricity flowing instead from his own body, draining down through his skin into the city's metal veins.

A jab in his back interrupted his thoughts. He ignored the prodding, but it came again and again, followed by a soft voice asking, "Are you dead?" Henrik rolled over and pulled himself up into a sitting position. A young boy, about nine or ten, peered down. The boy's dark irises blended with black pupils, and his face was as pale as moonlight.

"No, I'm still alive," Henrik whispered, finding he'd lost his voice from all the yelling he'd done in the club.

"Good." The boy sighed with relief. "I saw you were lying there, and I worried you might have died." The boy sat on the curb, and Henrick wondered at his immaculate enunciation of each word.

"You're homeless, huh?"

"For a long time," the boy said. Henrik didn't donate to charities, but he still reached for his wallet. Instead, his hand slipped into an empty pocket.

"My wallet's gone. Now there's irony for you."

"You're a wealthy man?" the boy asked.

"I am."

"Without your wallet, you're as poor as I am."

"I suppose so," Henrik said.

"Then we have something in common, at least until your chauffeur offers you a ride home." The boy pointed, and Henrik looked, seeing his personal assistant's familiar car. But the car stayed where it was, motionless.

"Look, kid, I'm not in the mood for conversation. Would you leave me alone?"

The boy nodded as if he understood, but he continued speaking anyway. "While it's impossible to inject new energy into our universe, artificial fusion is within your grasp—despite your recent doubts."

Henrik blinked. "What did you say?"

"You heard me."

"Who are you?" Henrik asked, forcing himself to think through his intoxication. Did one of his competitors send this boy on a mission to collect business intelligence? Was he a spy?

"I'm Dakota. You're Henrik Von Broder, right?" Henrik said nothing, so Dakota continued, "You're very close to solving the problem you've been working on all these years. Closer than anyone else on this planet, at least. You're missing a key element, though. Without it, the reaction will never stabilize."

"What are you talking about?"

"The fusion reaction you've been attempting to start in your private laboratory."

"Look, I don't know how you—"

"Relax, Henrik. I am trying to help you." Dakota stood, offering his hand to Henrik, who, to his surprise, accepted it.

"But how could you learn about my work? My assistants don't even know." Henrik allowed himself to be pulled to his feet, and though he towered over Dakota, the almost machinelike intelligence glinting from the boy's dark eyes and motionless face erased Henrik's perception of the height difference.

"It was a simple examination of the raw material influx into your lab, which I traced from your suppliers' databases. You should instigate proper network security, though it won't matter in a few hours."

"Oh? Why's that?" Without noticing, Henrik slipped into the loose, almost casual persona he'd adopt when discussing a research project with an intellectual peer.

"We won't be on Earth in a few hours."

"I see," Henrik said. As a child, he'd often made outrageous proclamations to his teachers. He remembered the mix of amusement and distaste in Ms. Kermingham's tone when she'd responded to Henrik's declaration that he'd be the first man to step on Mars. "Go join the other children," she'd said. "You can use this crayon to draw a picture of yourself standing on Mars." Henrik accepted the crayon from her open palm, though he drew nothing like the crude pictures of his third-grade peers. Instead, he designed a rocket capable of carrying a small ship to the Red Planet. Now, facing Dakota, he understood his teacher's frustration with a child who demonstrated an understanding exceeding her own.

In Dakota, he recognized his younger self. But perhaps that was his middle-aged mind trying in vain to reconnect with his youth. "Will you come with me to my lab?" Henrick asked, again surprising himself.

Dakota nodded as though he'd expected the invitation. "That is why I'm here."

"Then let's go." Henrik couldn't believe he allowed this homeless child to lead him to his private lab, a place he'd not dared share with his most trusted assistants. All his rational thoughts protested against it, but his intuition urged him more strongly than it had in years, and he'd learned long ago to trust his instincts. He led Dakota across the street to the car, where the rear door opened, and Dakota entered, followed by Henrik.

"Take us to the office, please, Benjamin," Henrik called up to his driver.

"Perhaps we should drive the boy home?"

"The boy is accompanying me to my office."

"Very well, sir," Benjamin said after a slight hesitation. He urged the car forward, accelerating into the city's heart. In the dim light of passing street lamps, Henrik eyed Dakota. Two holes pierced the chest of his unusual white jumpsuit, and the material was wrinkled as though it had recently dried.

"Where did you live before you were homeless?" Henrik asked, overcoming an odd reluctance to break the silence.

Dakota's head swiveled atop his neck like a rotating doll, and he bore into Henrick with his somber eyes. Henrik had to steel his neck to prevent his head from snapping away against his will. "I was born in the country you now call Egypt. From there, I traveled across the world."

"I traveled a lot when I was younger, too."

"You were born in Germany, but you left when you were my age to begin your studies in England. By the time you were fifteen, you had earned the highest degree in theoretical physics the country had offered. After moving to the United States, you founded what was to become the largest electricity provider in the country."

"You read the Times article from a few years ago," Henrik said, and Dakota nodded.

"A fascinating source of information."

"Especially for the environmentalists."

"Yes, leading activists accused your business of contributing more airborne pollutants than any other entity."

"Maybe so, but I only did it to fund my research into developing unlimited, clean energy." Dakota offered no judgment or emotion, but Henrick still wanted to defend himself. Feeling foolish, Henrik jerked his attention towards the window, and they rode in silence until the car pulled into the Broder Industries tower. The vehicle entered a large elevator, which rose to the heights of the building, stopping at Henrik's lab.

"Your office, sir," Benjamin said.

"What? Oh, yes. Right."

He got out, followed by Dakota, and they entered the lab. Henrik felt shy and protective of his lab against Dakota's searching eyes, almost like a painter inviting a critic into a studio of unfinished work.

"Do you want a drink?" Henrik asked, more to distract himself than for Dakota's comfort. "Water, or a coffee, maybe?" As soon as he'd asked, he bit his tongue for offering coffee to a child.

"We don't have time for refreshments." Dakota approached the center of the room, where the prototype lay beneath the floor in an ultra-secure steel vault. A panel flush with the floor required DNA, biometric readings, several layers of passwords, and a physical key Henrik kept strung around his ankle at all times to unlock. But Dakota paid no heed to the panel. He placed his hand against the cold tile over the hidden machinery.

The locks thudded open in perfect sequence, and the three-foot-thick steel plate slid back. Henrik believed his security to be impenetrable, as any unauthorized access would cause the entire reactor to be super-heated into a molten pile of its thousands of components. Dakota, though, had bypassed his security precautions in seconds.

Once the vault door retracted, the prototype rose. A ring of electromagnets, surrounded by another ring of high-powered lasers capable of generating enough heat to vaporize steel, nestled within a sphere of sensors. The sensors allowed the building's super-computer core to make billions of micro-second adjustments to stabilize a budding fusion reaction. So far, all they had done was record thousands of failed attempts.

"An efficient design," Dakota commented.

"But not functional." The boy ignored Henrik as he circled the machine, reaching out to touch various components and pressing his small hands against the chill metal for seconds. Henrick stood by like an ape with his arms hanging at his sides, watching the curious boy examine his most precious work.

"Do you have a toolbox?" Dakota asked.

"On the table over there."

"This will suffice." The boy worked around the machine for a quarter-hour. Several times, Henrik almost reached out to stop him, but Dakota seemed only to be repositioning the electromagnets. They could be re-calibrated if necessary.

"Alright, we're ready," Dakota said.

"Ready for what?"

"To create the second artificial fusion reaction on Earth."

"The second?" Henrik asked, his mind jumping to his competitors.

"My brother, Lysander, created the first two thousand years ago."

"Oh, of course he did. That was in Egypt, was it?"

"It was." With no fanfare, Dakota depressed the red lever to start the generator. Now that the boy had activated the prototype reactor, Henrik returned to reality. Any miscalculation might trigger an explosion that wouldn't only kill them; the blast would incinerate half of New York City before the artificial sun expanded and then collapsed.

Henrick leaped across the room to reach the safety shutoff, but before he covered half the distance, a blinding light ignited in the central chamber. Dakota's compact body disappeared into the blaze, and Henrick slid to a halt when Dakota plunged his arm into the burning center of the reaction. For a second, the light flickered, but then it stabilized and intensified as its color shifted to a uniform white.

"I can't... I can't believe it." The reactor glow remained steady. "How... how... how did..."

"I introduced an element of mental manipulation," Dakota said, stepping back from the miniature star. "Your computers are not quick enough to make the adjustments to stabilize the reaction before the natural instabilities push it beyond its breaking point."

"But your hand! Your entire arm should be dust."

"My Ethereal Hand shielded me," he said.

Henrik crumpled onto a stool. "Should I bother asking what an Ethereal Hand is?"

"I'll tell you on our way."

"Where?"

"To the super-cooled chamber in the basement. We will need it to transition to my brother's world."

Henrik gave one more look at the stable fusion reaction sitting in the center of his laboratory, and he said, "You'd better lead the way."

"Very well. We'll take your private elevator."

Henrik followed Dakota into the lift, pressing the button for B40, the lowest point in the structure. While they sank through the center of the building to the ground, Dakota spoke.

"You asked me what my Ethereal Hand is. May I borrow your ring?" Henrik slipped the ring he wore around his pinky and dropped it into Dakota's open palm. The boy lifted his arm, and the ring rose into the air, rattling around the enclosed space before falling to the floor. "I was never good at elements that aren't pure gold," he said. "My brother Lysander was by far the most talented."

"You just… moved that ring with your mind?" Dakota nodded, and Henrik fell back against the elevator wall. "I can't believe this. I just saw it, and still, I do not believe it."

"It's not magic."

"I don't believe in magic," Henrik said sharply. Dakota's statement ignited his reflexive scientific indignation.

"Of course not."

"So," Henrik said, standing and attempting to regain his composure. "What is it, then?"

"Two thousand years ago, my siblings and I were born on Earth, but we are not quite human. Our bodies contain an extra sense, an innate ability to manipulate energy to interface with foreign elements."

"So you are two thousand years old?"

"No, I just turned ten."

"But—"

Henrik didn't get to finish his sentence because the elevator jolted to a halt. The whirring motors fell silent as the elevator swung against the cables. He reached for the emergency phone, but it was dead.

"Don't bother calling for help," Dakota said. "They've arrived to stop us."

"Who?"

"Whomever was holding me captive. I didn't expect them to allow my escape after centuries of imprisonment."

"You're a prisoner?" Henrik asked, struggling to follow.

"Something like that. Now, we must exit this elevator. Is there another way out?"

"Via the shaft. I think we've stopped between floors."

"Let's go."

"What, climb up the elevator shaft? I don't think so. I've seen enough movies to know that's not a good idea."

"Listen to me," Dakota said. "The beings who have come are here to capture me. They don't care about you, though. They will kill you without hesitation if we do not leave this elevator." Henrik studied the severe boy. His face showed no emotion, unlike an average child's, and after all he'd seen already, Henrik didn't doubt Dakota for a moment.

Chapter Four

Cayden had first entered Stomatus, capital of the Perianth Empire, through the Dumrolls, a ruined part of the city where mindless drones toiled away in labor. Now, in the middle of a featureless desert, he stared at the Dumrolls as they once were before an unknown calamity had turned a glorious collection of palaces into a pile of mud. The glimmering city sat like a diamond upon the brown sands, as if a giant's hand scooped the buildings from beneath Stomatus' great tree and deposited them hundreds of miles into the wasteland.

"I remember those towers," Cayden muttered under his breath. "Lysander's recollection is clear, but I always figured the witches destroyed them."

"Follow along," Naya said, laughing with glee. "We rarely get to boast to visitors. I'll show you the city, and you will see how these mighty palaces came to rest here."

"Dugal will be upside down with anger for staying behind," Balint said as the troop moved towards the gleaming city. "He's probably peering through a telescope at us right now from a secret porthole." Smiling to himself, Balint put his heavy arm around Cayden's shoulder to lend support. Still weak from his brief fight with Naya's forces, Cayden accepted the help as they walked towards the gleaming towers.

The city's delicate spires rested upon a bed of thick crystal, three stories high, with rings the size of small houses protruding from the perimeter every two hundred feet. Considering the city's age, the decay of time didn't touch any buildings, and Cayden squinted against the overwhelming gleam of sun against white stone.

Upon approaching the edge of the crystal plateau, Cayden tensed as over one hundred Ethereal Hands swept out from the city, probing, touching, and prodding. He wrapped himself in his own Hand, creating a cloak-like barrier against the intruding presence, which faded as Cayden strengthened his shield. If any of the Perchidians were aware of the imposition, they hid it well.

Just ahead, a small, square part of the crystal barrier slid aside, and Cayden followed Naya into the glowing tunnel, where carved stairs carried them onto the platform upon which the city rested. *That climb would have exhausted me a year ago,* Cayden thought as strength returned to his limbs. The architecture was identical to the oldest buildings in Stomatus—with one exception.

Behind Naya, a smooth white tower stretched towards the heavens, its height rivaling the great tree of Stomatus. At its peak, two segments branched off at oblique angles, tapering to points so thin Cayden could not see them with his naked eye.

"Welcome," Naya said, turning around to face them, "to Afterlife." She raised her arm towards the tower, and a pendant around her wrist in the shape of a star glowed. A boom shook the air, and a blinding light flashed high between the tower's two forks, pulsing before settling into a steady glow.

"What was that?" Leyna asked, fingers in her ears.

"It's what has shielded us from the world outside for a thousand years," Naya answered. "We call it forced perception. If you come to the tower, I'll show you what I mean." Balint's troop made to follow, but Naya raised her hands and said, "My apologies. Only two may go with me to the tower."

"We shouldn't separate," Balint said, eying the tower with measured suspicion.

"It's fine," Cayden said. "I'll go with Leyna, and Tonius can explore the city. We can handle ourselves. Anyway, I don't think they mean us harm. Do they, Leyna?"

Leyna explored Naya's eyes before responding. "Naya intends no harm." If Naya wondered at Leyna's certainty, she kept her thoughts to herself.

"Come this way, then." Leyna took Cayden's hand and pulled him after Naya, whose long legs had already propelled her around a corner and out of sight. Cayden jogged to catch up, but a sea of people blocked his way. Adults, with friendly smiles on their faces, lined every street they passed while children peeked their heads from windows or behind their mothers' legs.

"Don't mind them," Naya said, referring to the growing crowd. "I doubt any of them have ever seen an outsider. Most never leave Afterlife."

"Are they prisoners here?" Cayden asked.

"Goodness, no. We live in paradise, free to do whatever we please."

"Except leave," Leyna said.

"Your Perianth Empire is not the idyllic utopia promised by your king. War ravages the land and its people. Inequality forces all but the most privileged to suffer. Hunger gnaws at the stomachs of children whose parents cannot afford your merchants' high prices. These troubles are absent from our lives since the tower of Afterlife allows us to live in peace for eternity."

Nothing lasts forever, Cayden thought, though he kept quiet and instead asked, "That massive spire is Afterlife's tower?"

"Yes. Like your great tree in Stomatus, Afterlife's tower sits at the center of our existence, literally and figuratively. Do you realize what your tree's true purpose is, Cayden?

"A group of Elders surrendered their bodies to the tree, and their collective consciousness allows the king to control anyone with a leaf in their neck."

"Your knowledge of the tree is deeper than most. What you describe is true. Tell me, how did you come upon this knowledge? My mother taught me that few in the Perianth Empire understand the tree's sinister role."

"It's a long story," Cayden said. "I lived in the tree for nine months, and because the leaf doesn't affect my thoughts, I discovered a few of the tree's secrets."

"I'd enjoy hearing about your explorations later, but for now, understand that Afterlife's tower is similar. The Alchemist built it a thousand years ago to absorb bodies, allowing the consciousness of our elders to continue. Unlike Stomatus' tree, our process leaves individuality intact. We have no collective consciousness that can impose its will upon the population."

"I'm beginning to understand why it's named Afterlife." They had come to the tower's base, and Naya motioned them inside. To Cayden's surprise, the tower was hollow, a solid, golden tube stretching up as far as he could see.

"Yes," said Naya. She lowered her voice to a whisper. "After the age of eighty-nine, citizens may choose to surrender their physical forms to live within the tower's mental paths and become Departed."

"And the Alchemist created this tower in Stomatus?" Leyna asked.

"I'll bet the Perianth king wasn't too happy about that."

"No, indeed, he was not. He considered Afterlife a threat to his control over the Empire, and he planned to destroy the tower. The Perianth soldiers, still loyal to the king, marched upon Afterlife, and the Alchemist put his plan into motion. For a year, he worked secretly to build the crystal bed upon which Afterlife rests, and when the Perianths attacked, the Sky People lifted us to safety. They affixed their floating tree ships to the crystal and lifted the entire tower and surrounding buildings into the sky. I imagine it was quite a sight."

"The Perchidians left the Dumrolls behind."

"Yes. After the Airwalker's death, only the Alchemist held the skill of building new crystal towers, so the Perianth king used the Dumrolls as a holding pen for his slaves."

"The Perianth Empire never came after you?"

"Oh, the king wished to destroy us! But how could he? Afterlife's tower protects against prying eyes and minds, giving us the gift of centuries of peace… until recent events disrupted our vigilance. But let's step outside to speak further." Cayden watched light play across the tower's walls in subtle waves of gold, but as soon as he stepped into daylight, the city's sounds and smells erased the tower's mysterious aura.

"Something disturbed your peace?" prompted Cayden, already having some idea of what he'd hear.

"One decade ago, an army of shadow assaulted our walls, and only the Alchemist could repel their attack. Since then, we've not seen them, though the Departed of Afterlife told me they sense a great darkness looming in the north. I don't perceive its exact nature, but its presence is like a growing shadow, stretching ever closer to our city."

"We've learned of the darkness," Cayden said. "It captured the founder of your city from the Perchidians. It has the Alchemist now."

"This is terrible news," Naya said, leaning against the nearest wall.

"Sharing our deepest secrets with strangers?" asked a man who stepped around the corner. His strikingly handsome and youthful face was ruined only by suspicious and beady eyes, which swiveled between Leyna and Cayden with ill intent. *Not unlike Dugal's eyes,* Cayden thought.

"These strangers are with the Perchidians, Doris. If the Perchidians trust them, then our trust should be automatic."

"You seem determined to prove your inexperience through foolish decisions."

"And you seem determined to incite anger."

"I act in my people's best interest," said Doris, which earned him an enraged glare. "Ahem. I mean *our* people, of course."

"Do you have anything else to say?" Naya asked. Her tone made it clear she'd heard quite enough from Doris.

"No, my leader. As you have everything completely under control, I'll take my leave." Doris inclined his head in a bow, then strolled down an alleyway, taking his time.

"Who was that?" Leyna asked after Doris had left.

"We have a council here," explained Naya. "Their wisdom balances my power as ruler of Afterlife, and a two-thirds majority may overrule my decisions. A unanimous vote can even strip me of my pendant, though no such vote has succeeded in our history. Doris is the youngest council member, and while I believe he does what he thinks is best for Afterlife, ambition often rules his judgment."

"Be wary of that man," Leyna warned. "He hides his true purpose with every word he speaks, though I can't guess what that purpose might be."

"What makes you say that?" asked Naya, though her knowing tone suggested the question was rhetorical. A blaring alarm cut off Leyna's reply, and Cayden slammed his hands over his ears before the piercing shriek tore through his eardrums.

"What's that?" Cayden asked, shouting over the alarm.

"Our perimeter alarm. Come, quickly: to the gate!"

Cayden and Leyna followed Naya, sprinting back towards the edge of the crystal platform. The crowd had dissipated, and the streets now stood abandoned. Near the city's edge, Tonius, Balint, and his troops had formed ranks above what appeared to be a small, dark patch of sand. As Cayden arrived at the edge of the platform, the dark sand pushed upwards, flowing over itself until it formed the loose, ever-changing form of a man.

"Come no further, dark one!" Naya yelled. "We have repelled your kind before, and we can do it again."

"I carry no threat," hissed the creature. Its voice was the steam boiling from a kettle shaped into words. The sound bubbled and whistled through the air, and though the figure hovered far below the wall, it was as if the bone-chilling sound originated mere inches from Cayden's ear.

"What are you?" Cayden asked. The creature gurgled in what almost sounded like a laugh.

"I was a boy once, like you." Seeing the look of doubt on Cayden's face, the creature whistled, "You don't believe me? Well, I was a boy. I grew into manhood before I died, as all men must."

"You're no man," Balint said. "Your kind slaughtered almost three hundred of my brothers."

"I remember you," the creature said, and its nebulous body stretched until its head drew level to Balint's. "You brought the Alchemist to us. We destroyed all who would protect the man our master bade us retrieve."

"Your words are poison, monster."

"I'm no monster," the creature said, undisturbed by Balint's outburst. "I am… a soul without a body. When I died, everyone on Earth believed sailing far enough would lead to the world's edge. That was long ago." At the mention of Earth, Cayden's ears pricked up. "After a sickness lasting many weeks, I passed as my wife stood over me in tearful sorrow. My voice caught in my throat, and I sank from my body like a stone into the deepest ocean. Where would I have gone had a monster not pulled me from the depths? Its sour stench filled my nostrils, and I wondered whether my sins lured the devil's servants to carry me to hell. Yet I landed not in hell or heaven but on the mortal plane. A dark power, more devious than the most unscrupulous pirate, dragged me into its wicked service."

"This is at least the third time I've heard of the darkness," Cayden said. "What is its nature?"

"Nature? No. It is unnatural, born on another world. But my position as its lowly servant does not allow me insight into its heart. My purpose is to enact its foul plans."

"But why?" Balint asked. "Why obey this villain? Are you so afraid of death that you would be in endless torment and servitude to evil?"

"Service brings pleasure beyond your imagination, a euphoria not found in life. Even if I summoned the will to abandon this bliss, another power binds us to our mortal forms and controls our thoughts — not unlike your Perianth Empire."

"If what you're saying is true, why are you here now?"

"The one you call the Alchemist severed the bond that tied me to my master. He sent me to find you, Cayden, so that you might come to his rescue as he once did yours. But now my time is almost gone. My master calls again."

"Then go, foul creature," Balint said.

"Wait," Cayden said. "Tell us where the Alchemist is."

"Yes, that is my purpose. Continue north. Before I leave, I will arrange this sand that gives shape to my spirit into a map of the stars, and you would do well to remember it. Follow the path I lay out, but beware: my master plans a trap for you even as we speak."

"Then join us as we journey and redeem yourself by battling that which you once called master."

"I cannot, for I must return. Heed my warning and prepare yourself for the most devious trap. My master is wicked and cruel, and he desires enslavement."

"Enslavement of humankind?" Tonius asked.

"No, humanity is nothing, a speck of sand in this desert. I speak of the enslavement of all consciousness in all places." With that, the gentle morning breeze blew the creature into the sky.

For a long time, no one spoke. Cayden and Balint stared down at the sand where the creature had stood. True to his word, he'd left a map of the stars, which Balint scribbled onto a scrap of paper he pulled from a pocket. Leyna's eyes met the northern horizon, and Cayden felt more worry emanating from her than ever. Tonius was the first to speak.

"There's no use delaying. Nothing this creature said changed our mission, so we should leave at once."

Balint looked at him, then down at his feet before raising his eyes again. "More of his kind will guard the Alchemist, and we have no defense against their attacks."

"We either keep going, or we turn back now," Cayden said. "The Alchemist saved me once, and I intend to return the favor. And perhaps he will know something about Dakota on Earth." Then he turned to Naya and asked, "Do you recall how the Alchemist defended Afterlife?"

"No. He would not give us the knowledge to defend ourselves, insisting that the power was not meant for our people."

"Then we'll just have to improvise."

"I wish you luck," Naya said. "Though I can offer little more than hollow words."

"Thank you," Leyna said, smiling.

"You are most welcome. Before you leave, I would speak to you in private." Leyna nodded, and Naya led her into the city. Though Cayden still didn't understand Leyna's thoughts, he sensed a powerful wave of excitement pouring forth from her mind.

Chapter Five

Henrik and Dakota crouched behind a lead curtain in an empty laboratory. Beyond the frosted glass doors of the lab, two figures stalked the halls, their boldness a claim to ownership of Henrik's building. They were intruders, invaders of Henrik's castle, his sacred keep, the tower he'd built as a statement to his detractors. Now, these men prowled the corridors with impunity, bypassing all his careful security measures and violating his space. Clenching his teeth, Henrik stood up and stepped to a nearby workbench. His hand found a wrench, fingers grasping the cool metal. Time seemed to slow as his pulse throbbed against the steel tool.

Thirty years ago, his mother kept a rusty pipe leaning next to the door, a last-ditch defense against any intruder who broke the four deadbolts securing their apartment. Henrik would hold the pipe with such tense fear that his fingers lost all sensation while gunshots echoed against the shabby brick tenements. Powerless and afraid, he'd hide for hours, unable to sleep, certain a hoodlum would burst through the door at any moment.

"Don't leave the room," Dakota said, pulling Henrick's wandering mind back to their current danger.

"They're in my building, damn it," Henrik said, thinking only of his childhood helplessness. After attending college at fourteen, he had vowed never to allow his situation to force him into playing a victim. Twenty-six years later, with the reassuring solidity of the wrench in his fist, he believed himself capable of facing any threat.

"You must calm down," whispered Dakota, seeing the veins pulsing along Henrik's temple.

Henrik ignored the boy, and he shouted at the figures beyond the door: "Hey, come and face me!" Before he'd finished his taunt, the door slid open, revealing two hulking men. They looked to Henrik like the generic bad guys from the direct-to-tape movies he'd collected growing up, their cheap black suits framing wide, meaty heads.

"Get out of my building, thugs," Henrik said, raising the wrench. In unison, the two men reached into their black jackets and pulled out thin, golden sticks with glass protrusions along the sides. Wires extended from the sticks, snaking into their jackets' breast pockets.

"Are those… wands?" Henrik asked, almost laughing.

"Get down," Dakota said, kicking the back of Henrik's legs. As Henrik's knees hit the granite floor, he felt something like the heat from a hairdryer pass where his head had been, singing his scalp.

"What was that?" Henrik asked, rolling back behind the curtain with Dakota.

"Those devices generate intense, directional heat quite capable of incinerating flesh. We must reach the super-cooled chamber below your office tower at once."

The anger had boiled off with Henrik's burnt hair, and reality descended upon him. Fear slid in where rage had been moments ago. The clack of the men's hard shoes against the tile signaled their approach; in moments, they would reach the curtain. Henrik cursed himself for being so foolish, for losing control.

"Are those beakers made of gold?" Dakota asked, pointing at the lab apparatus across from them.

"Yes."

Dakota raised his arm, and Henrik watched as a hundred gold beakers resting against glass supports melted and spun out alongside Dakota, who pivoted rather clumsily from behind the curtain. The intruders raised their wands and fired, but the heat rays struck a golden barrier that Dakota held before Henrik. The gold softened in the heat, which raised the room's temperature by twenty degrees, but it solidified into a dull shield once the attackers paused.

"Well, well," said one of the intruders in a whisper that seemed to originate beside Henrick's ear. "We are at an impasse." Henrick peeked from behind Dakota's shield to examine the man's unusual face. His skin glistened in the laboratory's harsh overhead lights, like a salamander that had just emerged from a pond.

"For the moment," Dakota said. "Since we might be here for a while, I may as well confirm what I suspect—you're one of his agents, yes?"

"I'm more than that. I am Sevron's Seer here on Earth." The man's body melted into the ground and reformed into a grotesque black orb resting on three legs. Slick oil dripped from the globe to stain the scuffed tiles, and a terrible sulfur odor wafted down the hall and into Henrick's nostrils. He coughed, gagging on the dreadful scent. "Consider yourself privileged, for you may bask in my presence before my master consumes your souls."

"Your master calls himself Sevron?"

"Don't feign ignorance, child. You know him well."

"And he promised you immortality for your service, did he?"

"He has done more than promise. He pulled me from a reality of darkness so I may bask in the light of his universe."

"Yes," Dakota said. "I imagine he has." Then, turning to Henrik, he held out his hand. "We're ready to leave now."

Henrik took Dakota's hand and allowed himself to be pulled close. The gold shield spun around them and sank, boring a hole straight through the floor. Henrik's stomach dropped as they fell into the open space below, floor after floor, as the golden chainsaw spun and cut through steel and concrete just ahead of their dangling feet. Seconds later, they landed in a pile of rubble, and though Dakota attempted to cushion the fall by forming the golden material into a spring, Henrik's right arm took the brunt of the force. Bone snapped, and he screamed. Dakota's left hand hung backward from his wrist, but he stood, apparently oblivious to the pain.

"Your arm broke," Dakota said. "You'll have to ignore it and follow me at once."

Henrik used his good arm to push himself to his feet, grunting from the pain that radiated across his entire body. He didn't dare look at his arm for fear of fainting, so he limped behind Dakota until they reached the supercooled room.

"Come inside." Dakota beckoned. Henrik looked down the hall one last time as one of their attackers dropped from the ceiling where he and Dakota had landed moments ago. The man's knees didn't flex from the several-story fall; he just hit the floor like a stone. The sight drove Henrik scrambling into the spherical space with Dakota, where the door sealed with a hiss.

"What now?"

"Now, you stay silent while I draw power from the fusion reaction above through your building's energy matrix."

Henrik groaned, allowing his legs to give out beneath him. His arm throbbed with a blinding pain, and his vision closed in until he blacked out.

* * *

***

Henrik opened his eyes to complete darkness. He lay on his back, and below him, damp soil chilled his aching bones. Water dripped onto his chest from somewhere far above, but the darkness hid all sensations besides his breathing and the pounding pulse radiating from his injured arm.

"Am I blind?" he asked, waving his hand in front of his eyes.

"There is no source of light." It was Dakota's voice, though it came from a short distance away. "Here, this will help." An object glowed in Dakota's working hand, radiating a cool light that grew in intensity until it filled the cavern in which they lay.

"Where are we?"

"A nameless world that houses my brother's Perianth Empire. Specifically, we're in Stomatus, the capital city. Someone will have heard our arrival, I imagine. In the meantime, I will dress your wound." Dakota had ripped off part of his left sleeve and wrapped it around his injured wrist. Using his right arm, Dakota tore off the rest of the sleeve and walked towards Henrik, who flinched.

"Do not behave like a child; if I do not set the bone, infection will claim your life."

"Ok, just do it." Before Henrik had time to prepare, Dakota grasped his forearm and slid the bone into place. Henrik cried out and almost fainted, but he clung to wakefulness. To distract himself from the fading pain, he asked, "Who are the men who attacked?"

"They were agents of the... entity... that imprisoned me."

"Sevron?"

"Yes," Dakota said as he wrapped his torn-off sleeve around Henrik's arm. "The Seers serve their master, Sevron, a being older than any other and whose power stretches across galaxies."

"Across galaxies," muttered Henrik. "Who has that much power?"

"My father."

Henrick let Dakota's statement sit. The unusual boy transported him from a grimy bar in New York City to another world, an outrageous journey that boggled his mind. Yet the notion of an intergalactic tyrant proved too absurd, and he laughed.

"I've long considered myself well educated, but there's much beyond my understanding," Henrik said, attempting to control his raging emotions through logic. "Not that I'm ungrateful, but why did you bring me with you here? You didn't need my help to access the fusion reactor, and I can't fathom what use I might offer another world."

"My every action is defined by reason," Dakota said, and though Henrik eagerly awaited an explanation, the boy remained silent.

Before either spoke again, the ceiling cracked open, and sunlight flooded the space. The cave walls peeled back like flower petals, and Henrik looked towards the sky. Only there wasn't any sky, for a tree trunk so large its branches shot higher than the tallest New York skyscrapers loomed overhead. A dizzying array of golden leaves fluttered in the breeze, but Henrik's eyes refocused on a young man who appeared over the edge of the hole.

The young man leaped into the pit and raised an artificial limb of gray stone to command a boulder to lift from the rubble and pin Henrick to the soil. Looking over at Dakota, Henrik saw that he, too, lay trapped beneath a stone, though his stoic expression remained unchanged.

"How did you break through our defenses?" asked the young man.

"We arrived via the tree," Dakota answered. "It connects our two worlds."

"Spoken like a witch spy," he said, raising his stone arm. Rocks coiled into the air and writhed like a python, ready to strike, but an older man dropped into the pit and placed his oversized hand on the young man's shoulder.

Henrik blinked, for the newcomer was the largest human he had seen, a frightening tower of rippling muscle packed onto an eight-foot frame. A massive axe hung from the man's broad back, lending the impression that he might kill any who dared defy his will.

"Astor, what's happening?" the man asked in a booming voice that rattled Henrik's chest.

"I don't know, Priven, sir. They just appeared in the cavern that's used for the Ceremony."

"Did the witches send you?" Priven asked, turning his attention to Henrik and Dakota.

"No," Dakota replied. "Jaffa is not my master, nor did I come from her den. When your Ceremony didn't seal the rift between our two worlds, I understood the Perianth Empire's fate hung over a knife's edge — so I transitioned from my world to yours so that I might help restore your faltering Empire to its former glory. Where is your king? I must speak with him at once."

"Don't you know? The king fell when the witches first struck. Perhaps he plummeted to his death, or maybe the witches captured him, as our scouts never recovered his body."

"That is unfortunate," Dakota said. "But it does not change my task. If you are to defeat your enemies, the Perianth Empire must unite all humans on your planet."

"While I appreciate your apparent patriotism, I don't trust your words, not after the dangers threatening our kingdom… not after Mogen's betrayal." Priven pulled the axe from his back and swung its gleaming edge at Dakota. With the pointed weapon inches from Dakota's nose, he asked, "Who are you? Do not lie, for though you may be a young boy, I won't hesitate to separate your head from your shoulders."

"Your eyes see a boy, but time has passed differently for me. Your Perianth king is my brother, and if he is truly gone, then I must succeed where he has failed."

"Even if you are the king's brother, our great king could not defeat the foul witches."

"Jaffa is a worthy opponent, and I do not believe I can defeat her — not yet. However, I promise to secure Stomatus against further assault."

Priven snorted. "How? Astor defeated you in seconds, and decades of teaching tells me your Ethereal Hand is weak and unpracticed."

"My skills are hidden from your vision, Priven, just as the ground beneath your feet hides magnificent machinery capable of protecting Stomatus from almost any danger. Your city is the key to your salvation." Priven lowered his axe to his side, but he didn't release his iron grip on its worn handle. "Think of it this way," Dakota continued, "you yourself observed my weak Hand. Even your least capable trainee is strong enough to incapacitate me in a moment should my words prove untrue. From my perspective, you have little to lose."

"And what of the man with you? Is he mute, or does he prefer a child to speak for him?"

"I'm a stranger here," Henrik said. "But I'll help Dakota however I can."

"Hrmph. In truth, we do have little to lose. The witches attack in waves, sending their gremmels to beat against our outer defenses. Before the week expires, their forces will breach our walls and overrun our depleted army, so perhaps a slight risk is worth the chance of a great gain… Very well. Astor, release them. But follow and keep a close watch. This is your new task."

"Yes, sir. They won't step out of line." Henrik didn't enjoy the wicked smile that spread across Astor's smug face.

"See that they behave," Priven said. With the decision made, he jumped from the hole and jogged to rejoin his troops at the wall.

Chapter Six

The Perchidian tree ring flew over vast expanses of ground so dry the slightest breeze would kick up billows of fine grey dust, which hung below the airship like dirty clouds. Cayden paced with nervous energy across the sunny surface of the tree ring, oddly claustrophobic with nothing blocking his view of the horizon. The confinement originated from his inhuman origins, not his physical surroundings. Lysander's revelations transformed his body into a foreign vessel, as unfamiliar as the branch protruding from the tree near his foot. *Where can I run when I want to escape from myself?* he wondered.

"If you keep pacing like that," Leyna said, "you're going to wear a hole in the deck." She sensed the nervous edge of his thoughts, and her eyes exposed to him the worry her smile hid from others.

"Surely, we should be there by now," Robinson said.

"Where?" Tonius asked. "That creature did not indicate distance, only bade us follow the star map he laid out."

"And we've been flying north for seven days."

"To the north, as we go, to the north, the winds will show," spoke a voice from behind. Cayden spun around to see Dugal standing in the dark doorway, his small, pear-shaped body lost in a frame built for much larger men. "You appear agitated, Airwalker."

"Please don't call me that," Cayden said. On Dugal's tongue, the word became a taunt.

"My mistake, boy. You are quite right. You may carry the Airwalker's power, but you are certainly not the man of legend."

"No. I am not." But he wasn't sure of his identity. He'd spent countless hours poring over the pages of Lysander's journal, reading each page dozens of times to glean more meaning from every word. His desperate need to understand the journal was so great he'd even tried to form an affinite bond with the pages. To his dismay, the book resisted all bonds. Despite his constant failures, Cayden believed that the book held more substance than mere words.

"Do you sometimes wonder why we're here?" Dugal asked.

"Huh," Cayden muttered, bewildered by Dugal's sudden shift in topic.

"Why we're all here," Dugal repeated, raising his voice and spreading his stubby arms. "Why do we live in this world?"

"You're asking how life began," said Tonius, rising to his feet.

"Perhaps." Dugal retreated into the doorframe and away from Tonius.

"No one can answer that question," Tonius said, advancing in step with Dugal's retreat. "But since the animals died while humans live on, life's origin and meaning are of more immediate concern."

"You're certain that humans are alive?"

"I trust what my eyes tell me, and I see five live humans right now, including myself."

"Yes, yes." Dugal waved his arm in dismissal. "Humans still exist, but they're dying just as the animals died a decade ago. They're killing one another right now, a mile beneath our feet. Just as the animals slaughtered one another until none remained, so too will humans find their extinction through endless war."

"The animals didn't kill each other," Robinson said, squinting as he dug up memories of his childhood education. "Institution taught us that a mysterious illness swept across the Perianth Empire, and a few short years later, all the animals were dead."

"How interesting. Then I guess you've never heard about the Blood Caves." Cayden looked to Tonius for a reply since his mind was an encyclopedic vault of history, but Tonius shrugged. After a period of uncomfortable silence, Dugal's nostrils flared as though sniffing at something in the air, and he turned on his heel, scurrying back into the tree as quickly as he'd appeared.

"What's wrong with him?" Robinson asked, rolling onto his back to stare at the sky.

"I wonder…" Tonius trailed off, pressing the back of his hand to his brow in the same pose Cayden had seen him adopt countless times since the first day they'd met.

"What is it, Tonius?"

"It's nothing. Not yet, anyway." Now it was Cayden's turn to shrug, for experience taught him that no amount of prodding would unseal

Tonius' lips until he was ready to talk.

"Let's go inside," Cayden suggested, changing the subject. "It's getting chilly, and my stomach's rumbling."

"Now there's a suggestion I can stand behind," Robinson said.

Cayden turned towards the entrance into which Dugal had vanished, but he'd not taken a step when the tree flexed beneath him. His feet left the ground, and he flew, landing on his elbow and narrowly avoiding a sharp branch that protruded from the tree. When the witches attacked the great tree in Stomatus, he'd been thrown off his feet, but this lurch made that one feel like a gentle swaying.

Robinson rolled to his feet and caught Tonius, who almost toppled into the open sky. *That's the thing about Robinson,* thought Cayden in a daze. *Despite being overweight, he moves with effortless grace when the situation demands it.* Cayden struggled to brace himself against the violent wind that swept across the bark as the wood released a series of ominous creaks and snaps. Cayden recalled Balint's proud declaration that his airship's flexible hull had weathered many storms, but he wondered how far the tree would bend before splitting.

"That'll get your heart pumping!" Tonius shouted over the wind with his usual detachment. He'd righted himself with Robinson's help, his thin arms clinging to a small branch while the ship continued to rock and twist underfoot. Robinson and Leyna both crouched close to the ground while Cayden dug his fingers into a deep crevice in the bark. The wind redoubled its efforts, concentrating its force under Cayden's fingernails to pry them from the deck.

"We've got to get inside," Cayden said, but the wind tore away his words. Instead, he motioned with his head towards the door. They nodded, but none dared release their grip on the tree for fear of being blown away.

Balint appeared in the doorway, struggling against the pummeling force of the gale, and he shouted, "The entire ship will splinter apart, Cayden! This is no natural storm." Even his booming voice arrived as a faint whisper against the gale's incredible power.

Cayden inched across the tree on his belly and squinted over the side. The entire wheel, which bent down hundreds of feet below, warped and buckled, and the cracking wood resounded over the storm's roar. But it was no ordinary storm, for the sky was still clear of clouds. Thousands of feet below, the air shimmered like a desert mirage, parting to unveil an obsidian castle. Its steeples dripped with slick oil, which flowed into a moat surrounding its towering walls.

Cayden reached out with his Ethereal Hand, probing down into this fortress, which seemed to welcome his affinite touch. The city guided his Hand, pushing and pulling it between towers and over buildings until it came to rest on an amber pod. Within lay the Alchemist, either unconscious or dead.

Don't, Leyna said into Cayden's mind. She'd sensed his plan before it had even bubbled up to the conscious part of his brain.

But Cayden looked at his friends, who struggled to cling to the imperiled airship like barnacles, and he shook his head at Leyna. A ferocious gust of wind slammed into the ship, tearing a hundred-foot hole in the outer hull with a horrible rending snap and sucking five unlucky Perchidians to their deaths.

Cayden, please don't, Leyna said, but her warning fell on deaf ears. Releasing his grip on the deck, Cayden allowed the wind to blow him upright, using his Ethereal Hand to shape two makeshift wooden boots. On each downward step, he bonded the wood around his feet to the airship's structure, preventing himself from being smashed against a wayward branch.

He walked with an unpracticed rhythm, stumbling and limping towards the edge of the airship. A branch whipped past his cheek, tearing a small, bloody line from the corner of his mouth to his ear. The pain was nothing, though, and in moments, he'd reached a part of the ship clear of any debris. *No time to hesitate*. So he jumped.

The airship shrunk overhead, and he flipped over to face the ground. The winds pulled and tugged his falling body, but he formed his limbs into a hard rod as he shot downwards, slicing through the atmosphere. Maintaining his position was exhausting, and he hoped he'd have enough energy to manage a landing.

The last few hundred feet passed in an instant as the fortress grew until it filled his entire vision. Cayden spotted an opening near where the Alchemist lay, and, using his Ethereal Hand to form a bond with the turbulent air around him, he asserted control. With one massive effort, he righted himself, using the air as a cushion to pad his landing. He hit the ground with a thud, falling forward onto his arms. The moment he touched the ground, the wind faded. The fortress melted, too, disappearing into the sand. Only the Alchemist remained, along with a man who loomed above the amber pod.

Sun colored the stranger's ruddy flesh a deep olive, but his narrow face held no wrinkles. Cayden shuddered at his unnatural expression, which more reminded Cayden of an inanimate object than a human.

"You expected a castle," the man said. "So I showed you one." His voice gushed like the oil between his black lips, bubbling and echoing their juicy syllables right next to Cayden's ear. "Well, your human structures disgust me." The word "human" spat from his mouth like a curse. He wore his clothing tight across his body, with black pants and a jacket covering a buttoned white shirt with a skinny strip of red fabric hanging from his neck.

"You look human enough to me," Cayden said, struggling to his feet. His ears still rang from the wind, and his limbs shook from the energy he'd spent upon landing.

"Do I?" The man's body melted into the sand, and his disembodied voice said, "The sad truth is that I don't have a true form, so I adopt the bodies of those who do." He materialized from the sand behind Cayden, who spun around.

"What are you?" Cayden wanted to keep the man talking while he regained his strength. The tree sap encasing the Alchemist would resist any affinite bond, so Cayden considered dragging the cage if he could incapacitate the stranger.

"Like your unconscious friend, I am a scientist — but instead of awaiting results, I demand them. Since my experiment here has failed, I'll erase your planet from the universe."

"Did you lure me into helping you destroy the Perianth Empire?"

"Goodness, no, boy. I destroyed THAT years ago. I'm here to destroy YOU."

Cayden couldn't help but take a step back, but he quickly gathered himself into one of Priven's fighting stances.

"You hope to defy me? The energy at your command is nothing. You are a candle attempting to overpower the burning furnace of a thousand suns."

"You'd prefer I lay down and surrender?"

"Of course, that's what I expect from a boy who's not real. You are an empty shell that contains the sliver of a once-great man."

"You know nothing about me."

"Oh, but I know EVERYTHING about you, Cayden. And you know nothing of yourself."

"I know who I am."

"Do you? What's your favorite color, then?"

"I..." Cayden didn't have a favorite color.

"Nothing comes to mind? How about your favorite activity? What do you do for fun?" Cayden remained silent. "Still nothing, I see.

These are questions any boy your age should be able to answer, no? You think you're a real boy, but you can't answer the simplest questions. Perhaps you have no soul."

"I don't..."

"That's right. You are nothing. You are an object."

Cayden's anger boiled up, and he welcomed it.

"The darkness in your eyes doesn't frighten me, child. Mine are darker." The man's entire eye sockets filled with black oil, which soaked his cheeks like burned tears.

Cayden mustered his Ethereal Hand to form an affinite bond with the sand at his feet. He propelled the sand like a million tiny projectiles at the man with enough speed to tear an animal's flesh from its bones, but the stranger stepped through the pelting hail with a grin on his shadowed lips. A pang of anxious energy rattled Cayden's spine as he understood his Ethereal Hand had as much a chance of breaking the man's defenses as did a feather boring through twenty feet of solid rock.

"Let's end our discussion," the man said. "While toying with my prey is a joy, further delay invites more problems... so I'll kill you now." The man swung his fist at Cayden in a wide arc, and Cayden pulled away, relieved the attack would be so easy to dodge. But mid-swing, the man's arm transformed into a wicked golden blade, which drew a deep gash across Cayden's chest. Blood spurted into the dry sand, and Cayden collapsed to his knees.

Leyna's voice spoke in his mind, *"Release Lysander. Let him control your body, but don't worry — I will find you and bring you back to the surface."*

"Leyna," he muttered to himself. "I hope you're right."

"What?!" shouted the apparition.

Every rational thought screamed against letting Lysander out, but if he couldn't trust Leyna, he couldn't trust himself, so he dove into his mind. With alarm, he located Lysander's hovering consciousness just below the surface.

Do what you want with me, Cayden thought, relaxing his grip on Lysander.

With pleasure. Lysander's latent personality surged, and Cayden slipped beneath the surface to observe Lysander like a submerged fish gazing up at an eagle soaring across the sky. As he sank, his perspective swung into Leyna's mind, and he watched his body from her position atop the airship, where she stood beside Tonius and

Robinson. A string linked Leyna's consciousness to Cayden's, and he gripped their connection with all his might to prevent Lysander's complete takeover.

Lysander commanded Cayden's body to rise, and it obeyed like a puppet as the man struck again with his golden sword. Cayden's hand transformed into a silver blade, which met the gold in a mighty clash that echoed across the empty lands for miles.

Cayden's voice shouted, "NOT ONE MORE STEP, FATHER!" The stranger paused with a look of shock etched into his unnatural features.

"You left us behind," Lysander said with Cayden's voice.

"I'd hoped to forget my mistakes on Earth."

"You ran like a coward."

"Do not speak to me of cowardice, son, for you and your half-breed siblings run from death, too. How does my mission differ from yours, except in its scope? But you need not fear that which lays beyond this universe for much longer, Lysander. My return marks the end of free will on this world and, with it, an end to several mistakes I made two thousand years ago."

"Your mistakes have only grown in the two thousand years you've been gone. They've grown large indeed." Lysander growled and threw himself at Sevron, who stumbled backward. Cayden's body melted and reformed into a weapon; feet turned into knives, shoulders into spikes. His flesh hardened into a war machine, which spun across the sand like a wild top, striking Sevron faster than a boxer's swiftest punches. The blows landed, but they cut into nothing more than sand blowing in the desert wind. Cayden's body followed Sevron, turning into sand and flowing after Lysander's fleeing father.

Particles of sand tore against one another, individual molecules attacking their neighbors, yet Cayden remained aware of his own consciousness, tied to Lysander and his ever-shifting form. Cayden lost all sense of time, but eventually, Sevron's energy ebbed, and his atoms condensed into a mound of black sludge. Cayden's body shifted back to its original state, and he stood over the bubbling substance.

"You're not my father," Lysander said.

"No," gurgled the false Sevron. "The true Sevron, your father, is still far away—though he will return. He left me behind as a nanny to watch over his malcontent children, and though I've worked without rest in his stead, my manipulations can match neither the subtlety nor the grace of Sevron. Still, your world is ripe for domination. Ten thousand souls linger in the north like a virulent fog, fed by the malice that festers between your warring nations. Every battle between the Perianths and the witches grows the hatred in your hearts and weakens your wills, making your consciousnesses ripe for Sevron's control. Soon, my army will march south to consume the fields of ripe souls, fields that I have sowed through long and careful labor."

Lysander's surge of hatred was so pure it seared Cayden's thoughts as he smashed his heel into the creature's vulnerable flesh.

Cayden, said Leyna, *you must help me push Lysander back under.*

Leyna's consciousness swam towards Cayden, pushing at Lysander's thoughts. He joined with her, imagining Lysander as a ball he needed to force under the water, driving him with the full strength of his Ethereal Hand.

You cannot do this, Lysander wailed, but his will splintered against the conviction of his twin foes, and sensation returned to Cayden's limbs. Lysander fell silent as Cayden stretched his arm out in front of him, seeing the veins and subtle pigmentation shift in the fading light. Of the war machine he'd been minutes ago, there was no sign. Only flesh and blood remained, though the experience shook him to his core.

The Alchemist's prison melted beside the fallen creature, and Cayden wished the ancient man would offer insight.

***

"I don't know what I'm doing," Cayden said, sobbing as he smashed his fist into the stone table. It cracked under pressure from his Ethereal Hand, splitting down its center. The airship had landed nearby, having come through the treacherous windstorm mostly intact, and Cayden rejoined his friends, allowing Leyna to tell them what had transpired on the surface.

"Not even Mogen could have prepared you for such a strange confrontation," Tonius said. The Alchemist rested in the neighboring room, and only Leyna's warning prevented Cayden from shaking the old man awake and demanding answers.

"For what?" Cayden asked. "The truth? That I have no soul? That I'm not a person?"

"We know you're a person," Tonius said.

"I don't know who I am anymore. Lysander rattles inside my head, a man so ancient I am a newborn compared to him. Or is this his head, and I stole it? Every time I clench my fist, I wonder whether Lysander's will guides my flesh. Do I have a will of my own? He changed my body into metal and sand, transforming the substance that gives me form. If I'm not conscious, and my body isn't real, then I'm not a person. How can I be human?"

"Cayden, I—"

"Think about it," he demanded. "After my hunt for Lysander's journal, I swore no one would manipulate me again. I promised myself that I'd always follow the path I chose. But what if there's no such person as Cayden? What if I don't exist?" Cayden pulverized the nearest half of the table with a single blow.

Robinson and Tonius stood up, backing away, but they bumped into the Alchemist, who stood in the doorway.

"You're awake already," Leyna said, surprised to see him.

"Sleep doesn't last for long at my advanced age. Plus," he said, eying Cayden, "you were making a great deal of noise." The anger faded from Cayden's mind, replaced by an overwhelming sense of hopelessness. The ancient man leaned on his staff, and, smiling down at Cayden, said, "So now that you've met my father's reflection, what do you think of Sevron?"

Chapter Seven

"There's no other way?" asked Henrik. It had taken Dakota four hours to locate the access tube amidst the rubble from one of the witch attacks, a narrow, wet passage that cut straight down, perpendicular to the ground. Henrik looked with dread at the ladder rungs, which were more rust than metal. All his forty years weighed upon him; his knees throbbed with pain, his back was so tight he could barely bend, and his broken arm throbbed, despite the poultice an old healer had applied. A vertical descent into a never-ending chute promised more suffering.

"All other access points will be in similar disrepair," Dakota said.

"And you insist I can help you repair whatever's down there?"

"In all probability."

"Then that settles it. Lead the way."

"Hang on," Astor said. "I'll go first. I might have to catch one of you clumsy fools if you slip." Astor appeared irritated by Priven's order to watch over Henrik and Dakota, and his apparent malice showed he had better ways to spend his time. Still, he stuck to them like glue since their suspicious arrival, which gave Henrik a chance to eavesdrop on his conversation with the other Perianth soldiers; Astor hid a foul plan separate from Priven's instructions.

Henrik shrugged. "Suit yourself."

Astor swung himself into the chute and climbed, followed by Dakota and Henrik. Every rung, Henrik had to release the ladder with his left hand, leaving his upper body unsupported, an uneven motion that further increased the stress on his weary limbs. The climb continued until all of Henrik's body ached so that pain radiated from every direction.

"Are we nearly there?" he asked.

"Almost," Astor shouted. But several minutes later, they still hadn't reached the bottom.

"I'm too old for this," Henrik muttered, but he kept pace, and eventually, his feet landed on solid ground. The crystal around Dakota's neck brightened, and Henrik saw they stood in a corridor lined with metal panels, most of which were eaten away by rust and age so that the soil poured in along the walkway. The basic structure, though, appeared intact, with much of the thick plating above stable. Henrik walked over to a metal strut and ran his hand along its smooth surface.

"There's advanced technology down here," Henrik said, blowing dust from a corroded circuit board embedded in the strut. His practiced gaze detected wires weaving around the rusted panels to form complex circuitry. "So different from the city above our heads."

Dakota made no reply, only turning to walk down an offshoot tunnel, and Astor and Henrik followed him through a maze of twists and turns. Dakota chose a precise path without hesitation, but it still took them half an hour to reach their destination: a vast open space lined with towering machinery. To Henrik, the control panels that dotted the room in a semicircle around them seemed pulled straight from a 1970s nuclear bunker. One panel stood out from the rest in the room's center, and Dakota approached the obelisk. He pressed a large, red button in the center of the panel, and Henrik winced, half expecting an explosion or light show. Seconds passed, then a minute, and nothing happened.

"The power reserve shouldn't be depleted," Dakota said. "We must reconnect the city's reactors before activating the machinery here."

"Lead on," Henrik said. Again, they followed Dakota through the dark labyrinth. While they walked, Henrik constructed a mental map of the place, imagining their turns on a flat surface to get a sense of the overall structure. As he built a map, a strange thought caught his attention, a notion too unlikely to be possible.

"No," he said to himself, "it can't be."

"What did you say?" Astor asked, turning to look at Henrik.

"It's nothing. I was talking to myself." He wanted to ask Dakota a question, but not in front of Astor.

"Repeat what you whispered."

"I was thinking there's something familiar about this place."

"Astor, seal off this tunnel," interrupted Dakota. The whites of his eyes surrounding his dark pupils shone in the dim light, and while his expression hadn't changed, Henrik could sense the urgency emanating from the small boy.

"You don't tell me what to do," Astor said, pressing one rock finger into Dakota's tiny chest. "Remember, I give the orders around here."

"If you don't seal this tunnel now, gremmels will attack us within a minute. Now, seal this tunnel or die."

Astor's cheeks reddened, and for a moment, Henrick worried the proud boy would strike Dakota. Instead, he let out a scream of rage while swinging his rock arm, collapsing the tunnel several meters ahead. When the dust cleared, he put his finger back on Dakota's chest and said, "No one speaks to me that way. If Priven didn't think we needed you, I would kill you where you stand."

Dakota stared back, with perhaps a hint of curiosity, before he asked Henrik, "Can you rewire that transformer to accept power from the conduit in the ceiling there?" Henrik squeezed his eyes shut, picturing the map he'd drawn in his mind, for the structure's layout was more familiar than it should have been. When he looked back over the panel, a wave of déjà vu washed over him, but the sound of scratching from the collapsed tunnel distracted him. Several high-pitched cries penetrated the stone, like the squeals from a whining dog. Something about the noise wasn't quite human, he decided. "Do as I say," Dakota said, pulling Henrik's sleeve.

"I can try," Henrik said, forcing his attention back to the panel. "But I'm not familiar with the technology here."

Dakota nodded with satisfaction as if Henrik had promised a successful outcome. "Astor, block the other corridors leading to our location while Henrik works. The gremmels will no doubt try to circumvent that rubble."

"Fine," Astor said, jogging into the darkness.

Henrik wandered towards the power transformer, pried off the protective cover, and examined the wires. To his immense surprise, he found the configuration matched that of his power plants on Earth.

"If this machinery is thousands of years old, why does the transformer conform to the design specifications of 21st-century Earth?"

"Coincidence," Dakota said in his usual monotone. Henrik examined Dakota with rising suspicion, but Dakota was hard at work over an adjacent transformer. Now the sense of familiarity with his surroundings itched at the edge of Henrik's conscious thoughts, and he realized the sensation had only grown since they'd arrived in

Stomatus. Underground, though, the feeling intensified. Corridors were familiar, he recognized the circuitry, and Henrick thought he may as well have designed the city's power systems himself. Untangling ancient wires and connecting them to the electronics above, he struggled to organize his thoughts, to justify why it felt as though he'd walked through this space many times.

"Are you done?" Dakota asked, stepping back from his panel.

"Just one more cable here… and… yep, that should do the trick."

Dakota checked Henrik's work before nodding his satisfaction and flipping a switch behind a support pillar. The reassuring hum of electricity filled the narrow corridor, followed by several distant rumbles. A breathless Astor came into view.

"We'd better go. This place is a maze, and the gremmels will discover another was soon."

"We'll return to the control room."

"I blocked the way," Astor said. "Is there another path?"

"Yes, of course."

The creatures behind the wall worked with incredible speed, and from their scratches, Henrik thought they'd soon break through the barrier. Dakota led them to the central control room, where he hit the red button. The machinery whirred to life, and a disembodied voice said, "Activation sequence complete. Diagnostic sequence commencing." Henrik had learned Latin as a kid in school, so he understood the foreign words, but Astor grew angry at the jumbled sounds.

"Silence this evil tongue," he said, raising his fist to smash the machine.

"Cancel diagnostic," Dakota ordered, stepping in front of Astor's arm and forcing the violent boy to lower his hand. "Begin hostile climate lockdown procedure," continued Dakota. "Secure perimeter."

"Diagnostic canceled. The outer dome will activate in T-Minus ten minutes. All active duty officers report to station omega."

"Why is that machine speaking Latin?" Henrik asked.

"What did it say?" Astor asked.

"No time. We must return to the surface unless you'd like to be attacked by the gremmels."

Henrik noticed Astor's jawline flex, but he relented. "Fine. But you will explain when we reach the surface."

Dakota nodded and returned his attention to the console. "We'll ride one of the working elevators to the surface."

A few steps away, a door slid open to allow them entrance to a circular room. Dakota jabbed a button, and with a complaining screech, the elevator rose. Henrik had never ridden in an elevator without a roof, so he looked at his feet to avoid growing queasy from the endless shaft that stretched towards Stomatus' streets. Soon, a slice of gold opened above, growing larger and larger until they emerged into daylight. Priven stood at the ready with his axe poised to strike. When he saw Astor, he lowered his blade, and the accompanying soldiers relaxed their fighting stances.

"You're just in time," Priven said.

"In time for what?" Henrik asked.

"To die. Look." Priven pointed his axe out towards the edge of the city. They stood much nearer to the city's outer wall than before, and in the distance—beyond the city's crumbling wall—he could just make out a sea of beings pouring from the forest. Thousands of small creatures and hundreds of witches rode thick trees whose roots scampered across the ground like tiny feet in a mad rush for Stomatus.

"I reckon they've run out of patience," Priven said, "so they're sending all they've got. We're not organized, but we'll protect Stomatus as best we can."

"Order your soldiers to stay," Dakota said. "Stomatus will protect us by the time they reach the wall."

As though commanded by the sound of his voice, nine spikes rose from the ground at equal distances around the city's perimeter, groaning as they struggled through layers of stone and dirt. Henrik watched as they soared up towards the sky, soon realizing that they weren't spikes but the tips of a segmented dome. The segments widened while speeding towards a single point far overhead until they clapped together to form a black, opaque dome.

Darkness descended, but as his eyes adjusted, Henrik realized the tree had cast a warm glow across the city. Everything took on a golden hue, and he'd have thought it quite beautiful if he wasn't on the verge of total physical exhaustion.

"What is this?" Priven asked, eying the dome.

"Protection from the witches, as requested," Dakota said. "If you dispatch a regiment to clear the gremmels who already entered underground, we'll be safe. The dome is actually a sphere that extends beneath the streets.

"A few gremmels won't be a problem. Are you certain your bubble will protect us from the witches? Their cleverness has overcome all other obstacles."

"I'm sure. This city's original designer built it to withstand much greater force than almost anyone on this planet can muster." As if to prove Dakota's point, distant thuds reverberated across the city, continuing for several minutes. At no point did the dome show any visible signs of stress, and soon enough, the noise ceased. Dakota looked at Henrik, then pointed between his feet. "Our true job is down there."

Chapter Eight

"Determination is less important than relaxation right now," said the Alchemist. He stood, unaffected by the wind, atop the airship as it sailed south towards Stomatus. Cayden sat several feet away on a plush cushion, trying to let the tension out of his body. Though the two were alone on the platform, Cayden appreciated how Leyna's thoughts helped soothe his mind.

"How can I possibly relax? Lysander's always there, ready to take control of me at the slightest sign of weakness."

"Can you have a logical mind while you're breathing?"

"Huh?"

"While your lungs pull air into your body and release it—can you relax?" The Alchemist leaned forward.

"Of course. I'm always breathing."

"To keep my brother Lysander from gaining control over your mind, you must dedicate the same part of your consciousness that regulates your breathing to maintaining the Ethereal barrier that divides your two minds. With this protection, you may separate your consciousness from your body."

"Hang on. Why would I want to leave my body?" While Cayden had let his consciousness wander before, a part of him always remained grounded in the physical sensation of his beating heart. Disconnecting from his body seemed too unnatural even to contemplate. *Lysander would take over your body if you left it,* said Leyna in his mind.

"You must learn to detach your consciousness from your physical form," the Alchemist repeated.

"But why?"

"Because you need to master this skill." The corners of his ancient lips pulled down into a frown. "Of all the life forms in our great universe, few own Ethereal Hands capable of controlling any element. Your soul's almost unique ability to exist without flesh and blood gifts you this incredible power."

"Look," Cayden said, fighting to keep his frustration hidden. "When I asked for your help to examine Lysander's journal, I didn't expect a lesson on souls."

"After the lesson ends, perhaps I will help you decipher the book. For now, set it aside. Its pages hold no meaning for your tasks ahead."

"Why not tell me first? I'm sure there's more to the book than mere words," Cayden said, and the Alchemist's frown deepened. "You yourself told me I had to get the book a year ago. Why did you ask me to get it if not to read it?"

"Don't question me."

Cayden shook his head, struggling and failing to quell the frustration that swelled in his chest. "Your advice pushed me into Stomatus and months of torture at the Perianth Academy. Now, after risking my life to save you, you owe me answers. I won't listen to any more lessons or 'wisdom' until you tell me everything about Lysander's journal."

"I… I can't." The Alchemist turned his back on Cayden, his bony knees bending until he stooped in a crouch.

"Can't or won't?"

"You don't understand, boy," the Alchemist said, falling forward onto his knees and spinning to face Cayden. "When I say, 'I can't,' I mean it. I don't remember why I asked you to retrieve the book, let alone the hidden meaning behind its pages."

"What? You lost your memory while in prison?"

"Yes. And no. All my memories are fleeting because my consciousness exists in a single moment, neither reaching back nor stretching forward. Memories are constructs of my distant past, trivial and irrelevant to my ongoing work. I don't even recall my name." The Alchemist's silver eyes glistened, and tears ran down his creased cheeks. Cayden recoiled, stunned by the pleading expression one might expect on the face of a lost child more than from a wizened man.

"Your name is Damek," Cayden said, struggling to understand the meaning behind the ancient man's words.

"Is it? Well, that's a good, powerful name. What else did you learn about me?" For a moment, his eyes opened wide, but they narrowed once more. "No, it doesn't matter. I won't remember even if you tell me."

"So let me get this straight," Cayden said through gritted teeth. "You commanded me to retrieve Lysander's journal because it held the key to saving our world. Unlike you, I remember that day very well, and you weren't at all uncertain when you turned my life upside down."

"If you heard certainty in my tone, then I still believe my advice was correct."

"Is every adult on this planet insane?"

"Insane? Perhaps, perhaps not. Logic often leads to decisions that might appear deranged to those who do not follow the connective thread. Over a thousand years ago, centuries of memories clouded my mind with a permanent fog. Though I devised clever means to maintain my body's functions, I failed to increase my brain's capacity. So… I altered my brain's function. Instead of basing decisions upon wisdom from stored memories, my Ethereal Hand absorbs information from my surroundings, uses that data to conduct an analysis, then discards the material once it has served its limited purpose. Rather than look back, I march forever into the future, using my unbiased decision-making abilities to guide our world to a brighter future."

"If that's true, you wouldn't recall your goal."

"Some directives are permanent, such as my mission to protect this reality. Others, like the reason I asked you to retrieve the book, are fleeting—yet they still serve my overriding objective. They must."

"Alright, Damek. You're asking me to trust a version of you from a thousand years ago, when you first programmed your mind."

"I'm pleased you understand. Now that we've dispensed with explanations, shall we continue? You must learn to release your physical form and transform your flesh at will, much as Lysander did when he fought a copy of my father, Sevron."

Cayden examined the Alchemist for almost a minute before he responded. "Your siblings mutilated themselves. One became a machine, another a plant. But you've distorted yourself with more drastic changes than anyone I've met. How can I trust someone who cannot even trust himself? I don't trust you, Damek."

"Who is Damek?" the Alchemist asked, confused. "No matter. I trust myself. That's the beauty of it! I gear my every action towards ensuring humanity's betterment without bias or hidden agenda." Cayden harbored nothing but disgust for the creature before him, a shadow of a once-proud leader whose wish for immortality twisted his spirit into something unrecognizable.

"Selfish desires drive everyone to make the decisions they deem right," Cayden said with a bitterness beyond his years.

***

Cayden arrived at the mess hall with anger in his heart. *I rescued Damek for answers, and I got nothing but more confusion. He's just as bad as Lysander, the Perianth King Adam, or the witch queen Jaffa.* Cayden sat next to Leyna, who was eating with Tonius and Robinson.

"He'd just be a flat, bloody pancake in the desert sand if I hadn't saved him," Robinson was saying to her.

"You're exaggerating," replied Tonius. "As usual."

"Your skinny body would have sailed off the airship if I missed you. There's a reason I maintain a healthy weight."

"Oh? You eat three dinners each night so you don't get blown off the side of a floating tree? Sounds unlikely."

"Guys," Cayden said, raising his voice. Usually, their antics entertained him, but after his discussion with the Alchemist, he found no enjoyment in the company of his friends. "We have to talk."

"So talk," Robinson said. "No one's stopping you."

"Not here. In private."

"We're eating, Cayden. Let's talk later."

"No. Now."

Robinson opened his mouth to argue, but he closed it after looking at Cayden. Trembling, Cayden could barely keep his hands at his sides; they itched to fight, to claw at his enemy, or to rip apart whatever lay before him. Lysander stirred below his mental barrier, ready to take control, and Leyna grabbed Cayden's wrist. Closing his eyes, Cayden strengthened the barrier, pushing Lysander even deeper.

"Okay," Robinson said, shrugging. "Lead the way." Cayden stomped into the tree without bothering to see if his friends followed. He descended to the landing bay, which housed a dozen pods that swung from the tree's bark like acorns on a branch. The larger pods could seat a dozen adults, so he picked a medium one with room for six.

"We're not leaving the tree, are we?" Robinson asked. Each pod's mechanism allowed it to detach from the tree and shoot towards a chosen patch of ground.

"No," Cayden said, picking a seat and motioning his friends to follow suit. "I just wanted somewhere private. The Alchemist's powerful Ethereal Hand is always probing for information, and who knows where Dugal's spies might be hiding." Once they settled, Cayden swung the pod's door closed, blocking any sound from escaping.

"Well, we're here now. What did you drag us away from our meal to say?"

"There's no use dancing around the issue, so I'll come right out and say it: we need to change our approach. Our whole lives, adults have told us what to do by feeding us information that we can't trust. It's time to stop allowing forces with agendas to sway our decisions. From now on, only we decide. Here and now."

"You feel manipulated?" Tonius asked.

"Don't you?"

"If you choose to frame it as you've stated, yes. External forces with independent agendas always push their own plans. Now that we're free of the leaf, though, it's up to us to decide what plan to follow. Mogen gave his life for that gift."

"Exactly," Cayden said. "We're free to choose our own paths. But how do we make an informed decision when our sources of information are all unreliable monsters?"

"One can never master every variable. A few unknowns always persist."

"There's more than a few unknowns," Cayden said, lowering his eyes. Just hours ago, Lysander had transformed one of his hands into a deadly silver blade. Cayden flexed the hand now, watching the bones move under flesh and tendons stretch as the muscle contracted. The violent anger that had overtaken him moments before changed, morphing into something else. I *have no idea what I'm dealing with,* he realized, and the aggression peeled away to show its true nature: a crushing hopelessness pervading his thoughts. "I'm lost. We wanted to rescue the Alchemist for his help with finding Dakota on Earth, because it seemed right. I figured Damek would have answers, but he's worse than useless." Cayden explained the man's lack of memory, the strange way he'd approached immortality. "Now I'm unsure how to proceed. Talk of Sevron and his army of souls is so completely beyond any of our experiences that we can't make a rational choice. My only decision is that I'm done taking orders."

"Wisdom is gathering more information before acting. You're suggesting we explore our options, no?"

"I suppose so."

"Then our path is clear," Leyna said. Cayden, Tonius, and Robinson all looked at her, confused. "Naya said that Afterlife's memory stretches back over a thousand years. Those who choose to transfer their consciousness into the tower hold memories from hundreds of years ago… just like the Elders in Stomatus' great tree. I bet the Elders can tell us what happened to the Perianth Empire."

"But Sevron corrupted the tree," Robinson objected. "Cayden read about it in Lysander's journal, remember? When Lysander's consciousness passed through the corrupted part of the tree, it turned him into that evil thing that lives in Cayden now. No offense, Cayden."

"None taken."

"Anyway, we can't very well venture in there ourselves. What if Sevron contaminates us, too? And that's assuming the tree still stands, since the witches were tearing through the Perianth soldiers when we left."

"We might not have to pass through the tree to explore its memories," Cayden said, remembering the caretaker's chamber nestled between the tree's roots. "Several Elders lay within golden contraptions near the tree's roots as the tree absorbs their bodies are and transfers their minds. A couple were intact. Leyna, when I first arrived in Stomatus, you went inside my head. You played back memories of my life like a tape. Can you read the memories of an Elder who's not yet absorbed?"

"There's no simple answer. Exploring your memories was difficult, and I risked losing myself in your subconscious. A more powerful mind would have an even greater chance of consuming my personality."

"Then it's too risky."

"It might be worth the risk," Tonius said, earning him a stern look from Cayden. "I don't want harm to come to Leyna, but as you've already pointed out, we're at somewhat of an impasse. We cannot act because we don't have enough information. We can't rely upon the Alchemist, and we don't have anywhere else to turn."

"I can do it," Leyna said softly, looking at Cayden. He sensed her uncertainty, but he also felt her resolve. *We are desperate for more information,* he thought.

"Alright. I suppose it's decided, then. We'll return to Stomatus and try to enter the tree."

Chapter Nine

"What's that?" Cayden asked. With Balint at his side, he peered out the airship's window at Stomatus. Instead of the great tree surrounded by a ring of crystal-white towers, a pitch-black dome stood alone, large enough to fit the whole city underneath. Hundreds of craters pocked the surrounding ground, transforming the open plains into a lifeless tundra of shredded vegetation and upturned soil.

"Listen to omens when they tell you to flee," said Dugal, who, per his custom, snuck onto the bridge without notice.

"Do not voice your fantasies," Balint said, scolding Dugal. "Our spotters say the soil is too unstable to anchor the airship, and our scouts have relayed that gremmels lurk in shadow beyond the edge of the forest."

"It is no fantasy to suggest the witches have conquered the Perianth Empire," Dugal said, undeterred. "We should support their campaign, for it is folly to side with a fallen kingdom over our kind."

"Your kind?" Cayden asked, puzzled.

"Before we took to the skies, our relationship with those women was different," Balint said.

"You're usually so direct, Balint," Dugal said. "Why speak of our wives in such vague terms?"

"They are hardly our wives. It's been hundreds of years since we've had relations."

"Let us put an end to our isolation. Land the airship," urged Dugal. "Let us talk to our lost family. Too long have we pretended we're human when our wives could elevate us to a superior race."

"Is that what you want? All your plots and schemes end with this absurd proposal?" Balint asked. Dugal made no reply. "In your excitement, you've exposed your motive. No wonder you are so eager to wake the Airwalker. He was once the head of our order, bringing our two peoples together. You imagine the original Airwalker can redo history."

"And why not? While you worry about events beyond your comprehension or control, you get more of us killed every year until we dwindle to nothing. You throw aside our future with such casual dismissal, and for that, history will remember you and Jericho as fools."

"Our place is in the sky. We are the one neutral force in this world. The Alchemist taught our people this. You would abandon our noble task for your selfish need?"

"Peace will descend only when we conquer the Perianth Empire once and for all—with our forgotten family. With Jaffa. How is delivering glory to our people selfish?"

"Fighting begets more fighting. You'd have us kill and destroy to achieve our end when we swore to prevent bloodshed. No, Dugal. Your ambition misleads you."

"And you lead us down a path that ends in war and our destruction. Our numbers are too few to police the world, yet our formidable army can fight alongside Jaffa to tip the balance of the conflict in her favor. Let me help you find the peace for which you yearn. War invites death either way, so do not let our people suffer without need."

"It is a betrayal!" Balint shouted, slamming his fist into the wall inches from Dugal's round head.

"I see your mind is inflexible," Dugal replied, bowing beneath Balint's massive arm. "This is where we part paths." The short man reached into an inner pocket, and a siren gave three short bursts throughout the ship. A thud rocked the airship, then three thuds, then seven more before all fell silent.

"What did you do?" Balint asked.

"Those with me have landed near the forest using the escape pods. More will join us soon as the time for negotiation has passed."

Balint growled, grasping Dugal's neck and lifting the man off his feet.

"Do it," Dugal squeaked. "Kill me."

"There's no point," Cayden said, placing his hand on Balint's quivering shoulder. Balint's wide eyes latched onto Cayden, and he wondered whether Balint might strike him down. But the moment passed, and Balint lowered Dugal, who lay coughing on the ground.

"Go," Balint said. "Join those who would wage war on our brothers in the Empire. But the Airwalker taught us that war is never the true path. It will not lead you to an honorable end."

Dugal dragged himself to his feet and turned to leave, saying nothing. Before he rounded the corner, though, he looked back at Cayden one more time, and Cayden saw an unquenched hunger burning in Dugal's eyes. *He considers the Airwalker as the key to his goal,* Cayden thought. Then Dugal was gone, and a minute later, another dull thud shook the ship, marking the departure of Dugal's escape pod.

Balint, meanwhile, shouted to a bridge officer, "I want a full list of everyone who departed, including their recent whereabouts and activities. We'll return north to find Jericho and report what has transpired."

"What about us?" Cayden asked.

"Eh? You may return with us, or we will drop you where you please. I'm sorry, boy, but the Perchidians have lost unity, and without unity, we have little strength. Jericho must root out this weakness before it spreads."

Cayden had never seen Balint so worried, not even when he'd recounted the battle that had cost him most of his previous crew. No words would convince Balint to stay, so Cayden said, "Lower us atop the dome before you leave."

Balint nodded curtly to two crew members, and five minutes later, Cayden, Leyna, Tonius, Robinson, and the Alchemist stood at the dome's apex amidst the ruins of a shattered escape pod. The airship slipped back into the sky, disappearing behind a gray, low-hanging cloud. It had been their home for weeks, and Cayden felt abandoned after Balint's sudden departure. *I can't rely on anyone,* he thought.

"You can rely on me," Leyna said. "And Tonius and Robinson."

"Sure, bud," Robinson chimed in. "We're with you for the long haul."

"Thanks," Cayden said, finding his throat tight and his eyes flush with tears. He turned towards the forest to hide his face, only to see the tree line alive with bizarre structures.

"Uh, guys…" Cayden trailed off, pointing at the tree-like machines crawling towards the dome.

"Those appear to be weapons," Tonius said. "See, that one holds rocks in a trebuchet sling while that one resembles a straightforward slingshot. But they appear to be grown from the earth rather than constructed."

"When I tried to rescue my friend Charlie from the witch camp, the entire structure was grown in a complex pattern of walls and tunnels."

"The witches have an uncanny talent for guiding natural growth, turning vines into walls and, evidently, trees into massive weapons."

The dome below Cayden's feet must have resisted all their attacks, or they would have breached it long ago. He reached out with his Ethereal Hand, finding the material impervious to inspection. Several feet away, the Alchemist crouched with his wrinkled hand pressed against the dome.

"Do you recognize the material?" Cayden asked.

"I don't remember," the Alchemist snapped, but Cayden just looked at him, nonplussed.

"I'll figure it out myself, as usual…"

"Ahem," Leyna said. "That won't be necessary." A circular section of the dome irised open, and a boy rose on a golden platform.

"And who might you be?" Cayden asked, readying himself for a fight. Though the boy appeared to be nine or ten, he might wield a powerful Ethereal Hand. He stepped forward with no expression on his thin, pale face, and his black eyes shifted among them before resting on Cayden.

"I am Dakota."

"Dakota," Cayden repeated, stunned. "Dakota from Earth?"

"Yes, how did you hear of me?"

"I—"

"Cayden!" Leyna shouted.

The alarm she projected from her mind coursed through him, almost like a shot of his own adrenaline, and out of the corner of his eye, he sensed the danger. Faster than he could turn his body, his Ethereal Hand spun out from the dome, locating what Leyna had already spotted. A barbed spear, as large as a house, soared towards them from the tree, guided by the Ethereal Hands of several witches.

Priven's training kicked in, and Cayden, having nothing at hand with which to form a shield, slid into the second combat option: direct confrontation of the enemy's Ethereal Hand. Cayden's mind found the bonds guiding the deadly weapon to its target. There were three of them—the Hands and the resulting affinite bonds. Breaking the bonds would require a projection of his own will to overpower the witches.

Careful to maintain the barrier holding Lysander in check, Cayden let his Ethereal Hand grow in strength. It seeped into the wooden projectile and explored every atom of the interwoven branches, examining the twisted tangle of wood as though it were his flesh and blood. Then, he forced himself to pretend that the branches extended from his arm like a third appendage.

Three screams echoed across the dome from a great distance as Cayden broke the witches' affinite bonds. From their perspective, Cayden had severed one of their limbs, and losing such a powerful bond would cripple them for days. Cayden only had a moment to spare—not enough to halt the projectile—so he blasted it to sawdust, ripping it apart at the molecular level. A shower of soft pulp rained down upon the six of them.

"Your Ethereal Hand is almost as powerful as my brother Lysander's," Dakota said. "I didn't predict that such a formidable force occupied this world."

"Uh, yeah. I'll tell you about it as soon as we get inside this dome." Cayden nodded meaningfully towards the ground, where gremmels prepared several more projectiles for launch.

"That would be advisable. Follow me, please, and stay very close together."

The six of them crowded around Dakota, where he'd first emerged from the dome, and a part of the dark surface around them sank into the structure.

"Oh. Oh, my." Tonius gasped in an uncharacteristic display of emotion. They stood on a sinking platform just beside the great tree with the full splendor of Stomatus splayed out below them. Cayden could even see the Dumrolls, a bruised patch of muddy earth, where he'd first entered the city with Leyna over a year ago. They sank through the tree's branches, past the marvelous towers near the city's center, landing in a makeshift encampment near the tree's base.

A dozen hastily-erected tents surrounded the tree, and Cayden spotted some familiar faces. Besides three commissioned Perianth soldiers, all the other fighters were trainees, boys with whom Cayden had shared the Perianth academy for months while searching for Lysander's journal.

"You are in Stomatus now," said Dakota, and Cayden wondered whether the boy ever broke the even cadence of his monotone speech.

"Home, sweet home," Robinson said, rolling his eyes.

"Glad you remember us," said a deep, booming voice. Swinging around, Cayden blinked at Priven's unexpected appearance. The imposing man's clothing lay in bloody rags atop his broad shoulders, and his axe's edge bore multiple chips—but he seemed unharmed. "I can't decide whether to flee in fear or have you arrested for desertion, Cayden."

"I, uh…" Cayden was at a loss for words. Priven's last encounter with him had been during Lysander's possession, when Cayden tore a path of destruction through Stomatus' outer wall. Robinson and Tonius both took noticeable steps back.

"I'd have killed you on sight if you'd arrived a few weeks earlier. But much has changed. Before I sentence you to death, I'll hear what you have to say." Cayden searched for signs of humor in Priven's grim expression but found none.

"We've returned…" Cayden said, ashamed of his wavering tone. While training with Priven to become a Perianth soldier, he'd seen the man as unimpeachable, but Cayden now had to remind himself of his decision to choose his path. He couldn't let memories or fear control his actions, so he cleared his throat and spoke again. "We've come back to learn the history of the Empire inside the great tree so we can plan our next move. I promise we do not bring harm to the Perianth Empire. In fact, I intend to save it." *Even if that means destroying parts of it,* he thought, and Leyna shot him a knowing look.

"I recently trusted two strangers, and we would all be dead, or prisoners of the witch queen, were it not for them. Tonius," Priven said, turning to him. "Does Cayden intend to save the Empire?"

"Cayden did not lie," Tonius replied, holding Priven's gaze.

"Then I'll make another decision with unknown consequences. Very well. You may enter the tree. I have little time for you, though, as other matters demand my attention." He walked away, muttering, "Save me, I'm taking liberties almost as great as the traitor Mogen himself."

Cayden released a deep sigh of relief, then said, "Let's go."

"I must speak with you first," Dakota said.

"No. I won't put our mission off for another second."

Dakota stared at him in silent debate. "Very well. I will await your return." The boy sat where he'd been standing a moment before, cross-legged on the ground. Cayden shrugged, motioning for his friends to follow him. The Alchemist wandered off by himself, and Cayden thought, *Good riddance.*

With Leyna, Tonius, and Robinson by his side, Cayden entered the arena within the tree. The memory of severing Astor's arm during the tournament came rushing back to him, and for a moment, Cayden felt sick. He'd abhorred violence then, vowing never to use his Ethereal Hand to break another's affinite bond again. He'd broken that promise not a few minutes ago when he'd injured the witches controlling the missile. *What am I becoming?*

"You are becoming your own person," Leyna said, placing her hand on his shoulder.

"I'm never going to get used to them carrying on this creepy psychic conversation," said Robinson.

"It is somewhat unnerving," Tonius agreed, smiling at Leyna.

"Cayden's worried that he's becoming more violent," Leyna said.

"Have you not acted in self-defense?" Tonius asked. "You dove off a moving airship hundreds of feet in the air to save us, and you again rescued us from the witches minutes ago. You know how much I hate violence, don't you?"

"Yes," Cayden said.

"Circumstances sometimes call for defense. I don't view any of your actions as uninvited, but if you'd like, I promise to tell you when you step out of line."

"Thanks. I've just been so shaken these past few days that I'm not feeling like myself, almost like when Lysander was gaining control over my mind. Your friendship means everything to me, though—all of you."

"We know," Robinson said. "You need us."

"I do. Will you wait for us while Leyna and I enter the underground chamber? Crowding the Elders isn't a wise idea."

"Sure, we'll pretend we're back in school and run laps," Robinson said.

"We'll be here when you return," Tonius stated, ignoring Robinson.

Leyna took Cayden's hand as they walked to the hidden passageway leading into the depths of the tree. Cayden opened the doorway with his Ethereal Hand, and they descended to the golden corridor where Astor had attacked him with a group of his friends during Jaffa's attack. They found the stairs to the Elders, and to Cayden's relief, their bodies were still linked to their elaborate golden cages.

"Who goes there?" asked the Caretaker, who hobbled from the side chamber. Then, spotting Cayden, he said, "Oh, it's you again. Are you running another errand for the king?"

"I'm on an important mission to help save the Empire," Cayden said. "Which Elder did you most recently attach to the tree?"

"It is Faulk, this noble fellow," said the Caretaker. "Why must you know?"

"Trouble festers within the tree, and we're here to diagnose its illness. My friend, Leyna, can explore Faulk's mind to discover the issue."

"Trouble, yes. Big trouble. For years, I've aided the Elders' transitions, but I am the last caretaker. I failed. The tree no longer accepts the chosen minds…"

"Let us help," urged Cayden. "We might return the tree to its former glory."

"I won't stop you," the Caretaker said, raising his canes into the air. "My skills are insufficient to save the Elders. These brave men are dying under my care, so I have nothing to lose."

"Thank you," Cayden said. "Are you ready, Leyna? Are you sure you want to risk it?"

"We've already decided: it's the only way to figure out what to do next."

Chapter Ten

Henrik stared in disbelief at the map he'd created of the structure under Stomatus. Over the past four weeks, he'd painstakingly mapped every corridor, room, and machine throughout the vast complex. Dakota helped occasionally, but he devoted most of his time to organizing repairs in portions of the city that the witches damaged during their weeklong assault. So, the job fell to Henrik, who pursued his work with methodical precision and a growing sense of unease. His scientific sensibilities tingled at his discovery that the apparatus was a vast terraforming machine capable of planet-wide atmospheric transformation given a long enough time frame. Further, the city seemed space-worthy, with vast fusion engines and chemical thrusters.

Now that he'd finished his map of Stomatus' underbelly, he knew with certainty why the space had felt familiar. With his eyes squeezed shut, he saw another set of diagrams from thirty years ago: drawings he'd made as a child of a colony ship designed to populate Mars. While the schematics weren't exact copies, they bore more than a passing resemblance to Stomatus. Someone had used his designs to build an actual vessel, which now sat upon a planet far from Earth—unless the similarity was a bizarre coincidence. But Henrik didn't believe in coincidence.

On the one hand, completing the repairs would be easier now that he'd uncovered Stomatus' true purpose. On the other hand, the implications of his discovery and its sheer impossibility raised countless questions he didn't dare guess. He decided to speak with Dakota at once.

***

* * *

Cayden stood beside Leyna in a murky, ever-changing space. Landscapes blended with indoor structures, which meshed with people and faces. Every attempt to focus melted his surroundings into a muddy pile of brown sludge. Only Leyna, a white figure amidst an oozing world, grounded him to reality.

"I take it we're inside this man's memories," he said, and she nodded.

"The Elders are flooding Faulk's mind with experiences from a hundred lifetimes, but without his cooperation, we may never bring order to this chaos."

"Then how do we find Faulk?"

"I'm not sure." Leyna frowned. "I've only ever done this before when the person was asleep. It's a lot easier to guide an unconscious mind than an active one."

"You did this to me," Cayden said. "The night we first met, I had the strangest dream. It was my whole life, but it felt like I was watching everything happen from an outsider's perspective."

"Mogen tasked me with discovering why the leaf didn't affect your mind."

"Did you learn about my unnatural birth? How the tree produced me?"

"No. Your memories only stretched back to your adoption by Mr. Reynolds. A potent force blocked me from seeing further."

"Lysander."

"Yes, probably. We face a similar problem here. Faulk isn't yet integrated with the tree, but he does share its memories. His mind is like a library after a hurricane, with pages torn from a thousand books and strewn across the floor. It's disorganized, and as long as Faulk is confused, we'll share his confusion."

"We'll have to try another... wait... did you hear that?" Cayden tipped his head as if the gesture would improve his hearing in Faulk's mind. A faint wailing, which faded in and out of perception, pierced the static. "It sounds like someone's crying."

"I can hear it, too. You're right: it's a crying child."

Distance was impossible to judge, but as Cayden and Leyna walked, the sound became stronger and more defined until a small boy appeared. He was only four or five years old with ginger hair and bony knees clutched by stick-thin arms. He wore no clothing, and Leyna pulled off Cayden's coat, draping it over the boy. She kneeled to comfort him.

"It's okay."

"I'm scared," the boy said between gulps. "Where's my home?"

"You're not lost anymore," Leyna said, running her hand across the boy's back. "We'll help you find your way."

"I expected it'd be fun, but I wouldn't have come if I'd known it would be like this." Gradually, the boy's sobs slowed. The tears dried on his cheeks, and he hiccuped twice before asking, "Who are you?"

"We're citizens of Stomatus," Cayden replied. "Do you remember Stomatus?"

"Yeah, of course I do."

"Tell me about it. Did you grow up in Stomatus?" Leyna asked. She looked at Cayden, and he nodded, seeing what she was trying to do. By forcing the boy to remember his life, she hoped to force order upon the chaos.

"I don't remember."

"What about your parents?" Cayden asked. "Do you remember them?"

"My mom loves me. She has rosy cheeks and always smells like the freshest tulips."

***

After asking a Perianth soldier where Dakota was working, Henrik located the boy by the great tree. Though his eyes were closed in obvious meditation, Henrik didn't have the patience to wait for him to rouse.

"I've gotta talk to you," Henrik said, stopping before Dakota's feet. Dakota opened his eyes, examining Henrik with a look that would usually make Henrik's skin crawl. But not this time.

"It is unwise to interrupt my thoughts," Dakota said, rising. "The thread I was following just now is likely to help you."

"To hell with your thoughts. You lied to me."

"No, I haven't."

"Then you've been keeping things from me."

"I keep things from everyone. All humans do."

"Quit playing word games. To be clear, you've been withholding facts about my childhood."

"Oh? Your certainty implies you've already discovered these alleged facts for yourself."

"Damn right. The moment we stepped into that underground labyrinth, my surroundings held a familiarity I couldn't explain. Now that I've finished mapping the structure, look what I've discovered!" Henrik brandished his blueprint like a sword, wagging it before Dakota's nose.

"It looks like a terraforming craft."

"Oh, does it? And how would I recognize a terraforming machine? Me. A little human who's never seen a rocket larger than the shuttle, an ignorant peon who emerged between a giant tree's roots into a world that happens to hold a spaceship matching my childhood designs. I created Stomatus' blueprints when I was eleven years old!"

"And you don't believe it's a coincidence."

"Impossible."

"Unlikely. Not impossible. But I'll respond to the intent behind your words since my projection is vindicated."

"Your what?"

"My projection. That is what I call the branches of my probability trees, which I create to guide me through time and space. They're not actual trees, of course, like the one that 'birthed' you into this world. My trees are complex maps of the future, built in my mind with data I use to inform my every decision."

"We'd better sit," Henrik said, his anger cooling. He'd run through half of Stomatus to reach Dakota, and now that his adrenaline was subsiding, he just wanted answers.

"I don't like being manipulated," he said.

"Yes, I am aware. Allow me a few minutes to explain myself."

***

Faulk guided Cayden and Leyna, and as he walked, the ground solidified. Warped shapes turned into metal walls, while six chairs and a table sprang up from the floor.

"Here's the tree's oldest memory. Look," the boy said, pointing to three figures seated at the table. Cayden recognized the Perianth king, the witch queen Jaffa, and the young Lysander as he'd appeared to Cayden in the golden mirror.

"Stomatus is failing," said Adam, king of the Perianth Empire. While still ancient beyond reckoning, his face was less wrinkled than when Cayden had last seen him, falling from the tree during the witches' attack on Stomatus.

"Then good riddance," said the witch queen, spitting at her feet. She, too, appeared younger—though nowhere near youthful.

"Stop it, both of you," Lysander said. "How long will our world thrive if my brother's Empire falls? We've learned that unity is strength against the tendrils our father seeks to weave into this world. Do you want our paradise to decay into a second Earth, filled with warring factions held by invisible borders? Do you want our greatest strength to become our most brittle weakness?" Adam and Jaffa said nothing, so Lysander continued. "You declared your plans to live forever. Eternity is endless, and time has already exacted a heavy toll. Adam—after a thousand years, your body is more metal than flesh, and Jaffa—I'd be surprised if your stomach could still absorb the nutrients most mammals require. Your body is more plant than flesh. Damek, who has taken to calling himself the Alchemist, is, by any definition, mad."

"What has he done to himself?" asked Jaffa. "We have not spoken for many years."

"He has fundamentally altered his mind and body so that his cells are constantly replacing themselves. As a result, his long-term memory is absent, and he is more animal than human, reacting to situations as they arise in a way his short-term memory sees fit." Adam shuddered at this, and Lysander continued, a slight edge to his voice, "You should not judge him, for the paths you two chose are no more flattering to your humanity."

"And what of you?" asked Adam. "Isn't that why you've called us here? You are dying, are you not?"

"I'll get to myself in a moment after I've finished our little family overview. You forget two members of the family."

"Dakota rejected our plan and remained on Earth," Adam said. "He has been dead for a thousand years. Our father left after our mother's death. That covers everyone. Now let's move on to you."

"In a moment. You dismiss our father as absent, yes, but his agents inhabit Earth while his influence continues to spread. And he may return unless you imagine he died as well." Adam and Jaffa remained silent. "No? Well, as for Dakota, neither you nor I can say what became of him for certain."

"Dakota must be dead," insisted Adam. "He rejected our ideas long ago. I doubt he's made use of them to prolong his life."

"You're likely correct," Lysander said.

"And our father doesn't revisit planets upon which he has planted his seeds for conversion."

"He never has before, but he also never had children before he visited Earth, so he may break his pattern. Besides, what I am about to suggest may attract his attention."

"So we come to it at last," said Jaffa, sitting back in her chair and sighing. "Always an agenda, eh, brother?"

"You shouldn't judge. Have you heard what they're calling you, a passel of ladies mucking about in the forest? Witches. And you remember what they did to witches back on Earth…" Jaffa frowned. "Perhaps you should consider adding fire resistance to your altered plants."

"Are you threatening us?" Jaffa asked.

"Of course not. I seek to highlight the importance of unity, of presenting a united front to our father. War threatens our lands, yet you don't seek to understand the true root of this brewing conflict."

"Human nature," Adam said dismissively.

"No. It is our father's nature that looms. Adam, you ritualized the process that shuts our conduit to Earth with a ceremony, but the conduit is nevertheless opening. It's leaking with a drip so small that only I detect the crack."

"You claim to possess skill beyond mine?"

"My Ethereal Hand is more powerful than all of yours combined. Perhaps our father's genetics feature more strongly in my blood, or perhaps a chance mutation gifted me superior strength. Whatever the case, I see that which is invisible to all others."

"A leak means we're doomed," Adam said.

"Not necessarily. Keeping our little haven shut off from the rest of existence demands massive power and a towering consciousness to wield it."

"You offer yourself?"

"In a way. My current form lacks the required concentration to wield my Ethereal Hand in this manner for any extended length of time."

"No," said Adam, realizing with horrible certainty what Lysander intended. "That would be suicide."

"It would indeed be suicide. You said earlier that I was dying. You are right. Our father's curse of long life has reached its limit, and as I am unwilling to take drastic measures to preserve my consciousness, I intend to die. Why not allow my passing to save our world? I urge you to use my death to preserve life."

"You speak in riddles," said Jaffa.

"He's talking about transferring his consciousness to the tree, sister. The tree's neural network could support it, of course, but it would mean an end to his thoughts. All that makes our brother Lysander would vanish. Forever."

"But you would gain control over my Ethereal Hand and use its power to prevent any leakage from Earth."

"The ethical implications of assisted suicide are not easily overcome," Jaffa said. "Besides, it's too late. If your claim proves true —if Earth contaminated our world—then sealing the conduit will do nothing."

"Not necessarily. Adam may also wield my consciousness to remove the contamination. Given enough power, of course."

"A comprehensive removal would require absolute control over every single…" Jaffa trailed off with a hushed gasp. "No. That path is madness. You're suggesting mind control, aren't you? Only erasing free will can banish our father's presence."

Lysander remained silent, his head down, but Adam said, "It would be but a temporary measure."

"We left Earth a thousand years ago to avoid just this kind of distortion of power. I won't play a part in your wicked plan."

Jaffa rose to leave, and Cayden watched Lysander's face as he said, "Adam, will you help me? We'll need Damek's expertise, as well…"

***

"My father, who calls himself Sevron, is not human," Dakota said.

"You told me that already. He's an alien who invaded Earth, had a few kids with a local woman, and jetted back into space. Oldest story in the book."

"While colorful, your description is inaccurate. My father is not 'an alien.' He is the sole non-alien, as his consciousness is older than any other in existence. His birth predates everything you know, and he has no end. Since the universe's origin, he has sought to control all other life. But the process of dominating another species is subtle. Even his infinite lifespan is insufficient to complete his mission, so he commands an army of agents who spread hatred and war across inhabited planets. Violent, base emotions weaken our natural barriers to mind control, allowing him to dominate entire species in one fell swoop."

"It sounds as if you're describing an all-knowing creature. A god."

"Sevron is far from all-knowing. His singular purpose to control blinds him to many avenues of thought and space."

"Why does he seek to control?"

"I have no hypothesis."

"He's a species whose primary purpose is not to reproduce," Henrik said. "I believed reproduction must drive every species, but your father's supposed immortality makes that irrelevant."

"Until around two thousand years ago, my father never reproduced. Then he arrived at Earth. I do not know why, but he shaped himself into a creature compatible with human physiology, and he produced five children with my mother: myself, Adam, Damek, Jaffa, and Lysander. But as I suspected long ago, he produced one more child."

"You're suggesting this child is me, but I don't remember this."

"His agents captured you during the same timeframe they took me. However, you were younger, too young to remember. Your parents adopted you at the age of four?"

"Yes, but—"

"And though human parents raised you, your intellect far outstripped any of those around you. You are too smart to be human, Henrik. Before Sevron's agents froze and then awoke you, you designed the craft that carried my siblings to this world. The reason the design is familiar is because you designed it—over two thousand years ago."

Henrik felt his head spin, and he stood up, leaning against the wall. Dakota sat in silence, his dark eyes unreadable.

***

"Did I do good?" Faulk asked with a look of hopeful expectation.

"Yes," Leyna said. "Our little history lesson explains much."

"Relations between the Perianths and witches must have deteriorated," muttered Cayden. "The Perianth king, Adam, never released the citizens of Stomatus from the mind control Lysander and Damek developed. And we already know what happened to Lysander—conscious but stuck in the tree until he wrote his journal and created me."

"And Jaffa turned her back on her brothers, whom she deemed evil," Leyna said. "Lysander hoped his sacrifice would usher peace, but Jaffa's refusal to cooperate may have doomed us all. Still, I may have made a similar decision in her shoes."

"What of the Perchidians?" Cayden asked.

The boy squeezed his eyes shut, and Cayden opened his eyes to the underground chamber with the Caretaker and Leyna.

"What happened?" Cayden asked.

"The darkness entered Faulk's mind, so I pulled us out. You may have a headache for a few hours—I know I will."

"We learned more than I had hoped. I think it's pretty clear what we have to do."

Chapter Eleven

Cayden and Leyna emerged hand-in-hand. Tonius nudged Robinson, who'd fallen asleep on the stone floor of the training grounds. He grunted but didn't open his eyes, so Tonius stood and joined Cayden and Leyna by the stairs.

"Back so soon?"

"How long were we down there?" Cayden asked, realizing he'd lost all notion of time while inside the Elder's mind.

"Perhaps an hour. Did you learn anything?"

"We learned about the darkness in the north…"

"That seems like a lot," Tonius said, raising an eyebrow.

"I imagine it's all bad news," Robinson said from where he lay.

"If you are awake," Tonius yelled, "why don't you come and join the rest of us?"

"Because I'm waking up. Respect the process, man."

Tonius rolled his eyes, but Cayden noticed the corners of his mouth twitch into a smile. "Anyway, Cayden, is it bad news?"

"Depends on your perspective. An evil entity born alongside the universe is eating our planet alive. Lysander and his siblings fled from Earth to escape, but they failed."

"We won't fail," Leyna said.

Robinson stood and stretched with a loud groan before joining them. "If you're so sure we'll succeed, you must have a plan."

"Sort of," Leyna replied. "We learned how to wipe Sevron's darkness from the planet, but it requires everyone to stop fighting. The evil feeds on conflict, giving power to the dead souls in the north, so the witches and the Empire must abandon all animosity. There's no point in trying to eliminate Sevron's presence unless everyone agrees. If even one person is not cleansed, the darkness will spread anew."

"We should speak with Dakota," Cayden said, halting further questions. "He wanted to talk to us, anyway."

The four of them walked in silence through the empty tree. Cayden recalled a time, not too long ago, when the corridors were full of Perianth trainees, pupils of Priven and Mogen destined to become soldiers of the Empire. In a month, everything had changed. Now, the burden of unwelcome leadership weighed on Cayden's shoulders. *Is this even my battle to fight?*

No, it isn't, Leyna said in his mind. *Not really.*

But I see what's wrong. I learned how to fix it. If I do exist apart from Lysander, my inaction will betray humanity.

I agree, though we're like a speck of dust trying to knock a grown man to his knees. I don't see how an ant can topple a mountain.

We first have to aim for a single target. The next goal will seem more attainable when we achieve the one before, finished Cayden, repeating Mr. Reynolds' lesson. Cayden understood the wisdom in his former guardian's words. Planning too far ahead could paralyze you, while focusing on one step at a time would open unseen paths in an impossible endeavor. Even with so many powerful forces at work, Cayden suspected he might make a positive difference. He smiled to himself as the memory of Mr. Reynolds warmed his heart. *Whatever we do, we can't make the situation much worse.*

They passed through the tree's main entrance, a gap wide enough to allow Perianth soldiers to march ten abreast. Grand wooden archways stood abandoned and dark. Missing were the ornate Perianth guards, either dead or tending to more urgent matters. Indeed, all who'd survived the witch attacks had scattered throughout Stomatus under Priven's command to help repair efforts and watch for gremmels, though no gremmel had wormed its way into the city since Henrik and Dakota had erected the black dome.

Henrick crouched near the crater's edge, and Cayden reached out with his Ethereal Hand to spy Dakota standing behind a nearby boulder.

"Dakota," Cayden called, cupping his hands around his mouth. Henrik turned towards Cayden and waved. Cayden, Leyna, Tonius, and Robinson jogged over to join them in the shadow cast by the crater wall.

"Turns out I'm Dakota's stepbrother," Henrik said with feigned cheer. Cayden had been prepared to shock both of them with what he'd discovered. Instead, his mouth opened in surprised silence.

"Yeah," Henrik continued, "this alien father of Dakota's had another baby, and I'm it. It also turns out I designed the spaceship we're standing on—did I already mention the city of Stomatus is a spaceship? I guess I'm two thousand years old, though I don't look a day over forty."

Leyna reached out to touch Henrik's shoulder, and the man recoiled. She persisted, placing her hand on his arm and saying, "To have absorbed all this new information about yourself must be very troubling."

"What do you know?" He sat in the dirt, frowning, and Leyna sat beside him. Cayden shrugged at Tonius and Robinson, who both kneeled. Only Dakota remained on his feet.

"I share all the memories of a man named Mogen, who lived over a hundred years. Do I look a day over twelve?" Henrik's expression softened. He'd become so absorbed with the absurdity of his personal situation that he'd forgotten the fantastical world around him.

"I'm sorry. Clearly, you've had your slice of rotten pie. It's just that… after decades in my body, I fancied myself an expert until… poof! One conversation shoots my understanding out the window in a heartbeat." Now it was Cayden's turn to laugh. *That is too true,* he thought ruefully, recalling when he'd slung water balloons at Mr. Reynolds with his childhood friend, Charlie, just before the Perianth soldiers came to his village.

"It's fine," Leyna said. "It's more than fine. We learned a great deal from the tree. If we combine our knowledge, perhaps we'll formulate a plan." She recounted to Dakota and Henrik all that they'd learned, and Dakota spoke as soon as she'd finished.

"You intend to unite this world and cleanse it of my father's influence. First, I must point out that you lack the knowledge to succeed. Second, enacting a forced peace is unnecessary."

"You prefer to submit to your father's will?"

"Not at all. I intend to repair Stomatus and leave. This world is a failed experiment. It's time to abandon it."

"You can't be serious."

"I am always serious. The chances of uniting the peoples of this world and ridding it of all traces of my father's influence are infinitesimal. I was going to ask you earlier to leave with me. Operating Stomatus requires capable humans, though I now see from your reaction that you are unwilling to accept my offer."

Cayden stared at Dakota in stunned silence. This cold, hard boy would permit the deaths of tens of thousands so he could escape. In that moment, Cayden's mind realigned as if a spinning gear caught after months of ineffectual rotations. He considered the good people he'd met over the past year. Mr. Reynolds, despite his severe punishments, had raised Cayden with valuable lessons on logic and humanity. Mogen, a trained soldier of the Perianth Empire, invented a tool capable of enabling free will. Balint's position in the clouds didn't prevent him from undertaking any sacrifice—even if it meant threatening the safety of his own people—to keep the peace. Tonius and Robinson, two older boys who had no obligation to be kind, helped him through one of the most challenging periods of his life. And Leyna, the closest friend he'd ever known, offered a fierce kindness that humbled him every day.

I forged relationships with each of them. They are mine as I am theirs, and Lysander had no part in it. For every person who is special in my life, countless others have similar relationships across the Perianth Empire. I can't abandon them to save myself.

Leyna, who'd been following the path of his thoughts, asked, "And why can't you just abandon them?"

"Because that's not who I am. Me. Cayden."

"So you see now what I have always seen: you are a real person. Despite the origin or composition of your flesh, the events of your life have shaped you into an individual."

Tonius and Robinson shot one another knowing looks, but Henrik raised a puzzled brow. Dakota, who held his eyes shut in thought, opened them and examined Leyna with renewed interest.

"I hadn't considered you before," Dakota said. "You can read minds."

"Under the right circumstances."

"And Cayden anchors your sanity."

"Yes."

"Ah, well." Dakota paused, closing his eyes again.

"There's no use talking to him now," Henrik said. When Tonius raised an eyebrow, he continued, "The boy can stay like that for hours."

"I don't need hours," Dakota said. "This information alters my timeline."

"Does that mean you've changed your mind?" Cayden asked.

"No. I intend to proceed with the ship repairs and leave as soon as they are complete. However, if you unite the people of this planet, then the certainty variable upon which I have been basing my plan will shift enough to warrant a similar shift in my projected timeline."

"You're saying that if we can unite this planet, you will stay to help us defeat the agents of the creature that threatens us," Tonius said.

Dakota nodded.

"How long do we have?"

"Henrik may have an answer if he remains and lends his expertise."

"This is a lot to process," Henrik said, shaking his head. "I'll stay to help with the repairs, but I can't promise to finish them. I need time to think."

"Estimate an end date for your repairs, assuming you stay," Dakota insisted.

"If the Perianths lend me people and materials, we'll have Stomatus flying in six months."

"Then you have six months," Dakota said with finality.

***

Cayden strode through Stomatus' empty streets with purpose, trailed by Tonius, Robinson, and Leyna. Dakota's emotionless, calculated attitude frustrated Cayden. Dakota's behavior made his actions easier to predict, but it also meant he was impervious to persuasion. The boy would do whatever it took to elude his father's grasp, even if it meant abandoning every other human on the planet. *At least I have a deadline,* Cayden thought with grim determination.

"Why are we rushing?" Robinson asked, puffing to keep up.

"We're running just far enough away to make sure we're not overheard," Cayden said, stopping in an alley about halfway between the tree and the city's outer wall. "Dakota's Ethereal Hand isn't powerful, but I want to put distance between us, just in case."

"I'm unsure distance will help," Tonius said. "He has an uncanny ability to guess what's happening, even if it's not stated."

"Still, I'd rather enjoy privacy when I ask if you and Robinson will wait in the city."

"Stay?" asked Robinson, motioning towards the Dumrolls.

"You want us to rally the citizens of Stomatus," said Tonius.

"Exactly. Though I hate to suggest splitting up, it's the right move. Any chance we have of uniting everyone will depend on the Perchidians' airships, so Leyna and I will find Jericho and Balint. While we're away, you two must stabilize Stomatus because without a stable capital, the Perianth Empire will crumble."

"But we're just a couple of kids," Robinson said. "No one's going to listen to us."

"Perianth citizens are afraid," Leyna said. "The king controlled their minds for decades, but his fall gifted them a newfound freedom—despite the leaves in their necks. Besides, Tonius is the son of one of the richest merchant families in the city, and unless I'm mistaken, they have filled the power gap left by the king."

"Astor's family has, that's for sure."

"I know how much you dislike your family," Cayden said, catching Tonius' eyes. "I met them, too, so I know how despicable they are. But it's time to return to the life you've been avoiding. Without the king, everyone's looking to the merchant families for guidance. Why not give them a positive direction to follow?"

"We'll stay behind," Tonius said, and Robinson nodded. "But I cannot promise to accomplish anything while you are away."

"Just do whatever you can. Leyna and I will return with help," he promised, walking towards the outer dome with Leyna.

Cayden didn't look back, though he maintained contact with Tonius via his Ethereal Hand for as long as possible. Despite the confidence he tried to exude in front of his friends, Cayden was uncertain and sad. Leyna was right, after all. The size of the task they'd taken on made it impossible to understand the effort required, let alone plan how to carry out their goal. *The world has simmered in war for a thousand years, so what makes me believe I can stop it?*

His thoughts turned to Tonius and Robinson, two friends who'd become family over the course of the year, supporting him in more ways than he could count. Leaving them in Stomatus might be the worst mistake he could make. *Maybe the only reason I've scraped by so far is because of them. Without them, perhaps I'll fail.* He frowned, but it wouldn't do to turn back now. There'd be little point. The search for Balint and the other Perchidians lay before him. Failure would bring death or something worse at the hands of Sevron's dead souls, and if that happened, nothing else would matter anyway. Leyna heard his troubled thoughts, though she kept silent while struggling with similar concerns.

At the city's edge, Cayden paused, looking back at Stomatus. The dome blocked out daylight, and much of the city's illumination came from the great tree, turning white stone to glittering gold. He couldn't see the Dumrolls from where he stood, so the entire city shone with glorious brilliance. Still, he felt no attachment to the place. It wasn't home.

"Neither of us has a home," Leyna said.

"No. The training camp where I grew up never felt like home, and I don't think I ever grew used to Stomatus."

"During my years with Mogen, I called the Dumrolls home, but now..."

"Now we're both displaced. Come on. We should get moving if we want to slip past the witch encampment while it's still dark."

Chapter Twelve

"Who imagined I'd miss the little guy so much?" Robinson asked, sitting against the stone base of a nearby tower.

"He's barely been gone three hours," Tonius said. His eyes were closed, and the back of his hand rested upon his dark brow. After Cayden's abrupt departure with Leyna, he and Robinson had wandered Stomatus aimlessly in silence, eventually coming to rest outside the Western Market, where they'd gone on their first patrols with Cayden.

"Yeah, but we've been following him for a while now. You get used to someone else doing all the hard work, right?"

"Perhaps you shut off your brain upon Cayden's introduction to our lives, but I did not."

"I'm trying to lighten the mood a bit. He's our friend. Don't pretend you're not sad to see him go."

"I am sad; you're right. But right now, I'm processing what we learned. We have a task, and I'm unsure how we should approach it. Leyna was correct when she said the Merchant Circle holds much influence over Stomatus' citizens, but it's for a reason: those who run the Circle are ruthless, selfish, and power-hungry. I'm not sure how to persuade them to relinquish control. With them in power, Stomatus can never unite because they thrive on division."

"It's their survival, man. Surely they'll behave themselves if it's a choice between giving up power and death."

"I agree. Still, how do we convince them that doom is at their doorsteps? If there's one thing I've learned from my parents, they'll accept whatever is convenient. I'm not sure truth holds any weight in their calculations."

"Okay, we'll have to find something to shove into their fat faces. A danger even they can't twist to their advantage. But first, shouldn't we talk to them? See what we're up against?"

"As much as the notion repels me, yes. We should gather as much information as possible. Although we're certain that the power structure has shifted towards the merchant class, we need to understand how that shift has played out."

"Well, we'll go see your parents straightaway," Robinson said, tugging Tonius to his feet. "Are they still living in their mansion?"

"I have little doubt." As they began the hike to his father's palace, Tonius' gut churned with an uneasy nausea. Most of Stomatus' twenty thousand residents labored near the outer walls, which had absorbed the brunt of the attack, but that didn't explain why the streets were practically abandoned. Aside from a single child kicking loose debris about the road, Stomatus was bereft of life. Tonius narrowed his eyes suspiciously. There were signs of activity if one looked hard enough. A shadowed head might shift behind a window shade, or a dark figure would dart behind a slatted fence just in time to avoid Tonius' roving eyes.

"We are being watched," he whispered to Robinson.

"Yeah, I'm getting creeped out. Where did all the people go? The witches can't have killed them all."

Tonius shook his head, continuing under the great tree's looming branches. The impenetrable crystal towers surrounding the tree remained as pristine as ever, though witch projectiles had blasted rubble clear through the tree itself. By the time they neared the towers, whose peaks stopped just short of the tree's lowest branches, a heavy silence had fallen.

"Did Priven order a curfew?" Robinson asked. "I can't hear a sound."

"Another force is at work, a power we've yet to uncover."

"Should we turn back?" Ahead, the surface of Tonius' childhood home glittered a golden hue, an effect caused by the millions of golden leaves overhead and amplified by the dome.

"No. Cayden asked us to make everyone aware of the common threat."

Tonius stepped onto the shallow stairs leading to his family's palace. The door was ajar, its silver and gold surface glowing bright against a dark interior. Now he knew something was wrong. His parents valued appearance over all else, and their home reflected their obsession. A single transgression, such as a servant failing to close the door, would invite their neighbors to gossip for days.

Robinson tiptoed across the threshold and entered the grand foyer, a cavernous room whose gaudy decorations faded to a muddy gray in the gloom. The grand staircase to the second floor had partially collapsed, leaving only one banister intact. Tonius surveyed the room, eying several scratches along the wall by the stairs and a dark stain on the floor near his feet. Blood? It was too dark to tell.

Robinson shot Tonius a questioning look, and Tonius nodded towards the stairs. "If anyone's home," he whispered, "they'll be up there."

They half walked, half climbed up the sturdy railing to the second floor, where they found the hallway filled with a barricade of paintings and furniture. Tonius touched the corner of a framed picture, which protruded from the wall like a stuck arrow.

"Only an Ethereal Hand can cause this level of destruction."

"Look," Robinson said, poking Tonius' shoulder. Ahead, a dim light shone from the dining room, and muffled voices bounced down the hall, audible in the eerie silence. Tonius crept to the door, both he and Robinson craning their heads around the doorframe like two children spying on their parents.

The room was much as Tonius remembered. A single, large table dominated the ornate dining area below glass chandeliers hanging overhead. Months ago, when his parents summoned him, a grand feast covered the broad table. Now, only Tonius' father, Tevin, sat in his chair, and he was no longer the obese tyrant Tonius recognized. Indeed, Tonius struggled to identify the gaunt, wrinkled man whose thin hands trembled against the table.

"Father," Tonius said, stepping from behind the door. Love never figured into their relationship, but one glance at his father's cloudy eyes introduced an unexpected stab of sorrow. "What has happened to you?"

"No, no, nothing, you mustn't ask. Mustn't be here. Leave now. Get out of my sight, you filthy street rat."

"It's me," Tonius said, edging closer. "It's your son."

"My son, my son, my son," Tevin repeated, scratching one of his long nails into his arm so hard he drew blood. "Yes, I know my son, but he's just a small child. You can't be my son."

"Where's Miranda?" asked Tonius. "Where's your wife?"

"They took her." Tevin sobbed. "Oh, they came in the night and took her. Those filth. Those disgusting, rotten peasants." His lips twisted into a snarl, and Tonius recoiled from his outstretched claw. Then the anger drained, replaced by a slack jaw and pleading, wide eyes. "Believe me. I did everything to stop them." His thin arm whipped out to grab Tonius by the wrist. Tonius tugged his hand away, but his father held on, and the chair, along with Tevin and Tonius, toppled over sideways.

"Tonius!" Robinson shouted, rushing to grab his friend. As they turned, Robinson and Tonius screamed in horror. Tevin lay cackling on his back with stumps where his legs should be. The bandaged appendages waggled above him, only a few inches from his hips.

Tonius felt his stomach churn, and he turned away just in time to vomit while Robinson rubbed his back, whispering, "It's okay. It's going to be okay."

"No," came a voice from the shadows. "Your luck has run out." Astor emerged from a dark corner with a wicked smile across his handsome face.

"What did you do?" Robinson asked.

"Oh, this?" Astor asked, continuing his march and waving his hand at Tevin. "Just a little warm-up. Nothing serious."

"But… why?" Tonius sat on the ground, his head between his knees, struggling to breathe. Robinson, though, waited for Astor to move closer.

"The road to power is blocked by others who seek authority themselves. My father taught me this basic truth, bless his soul… which is all of him that remains."

"You killed your own father?" Robinson asked in disbelief.

"I did, though I admit it was an accident, an argument that spun out of hand. Still, his death opened up fascinating possibilities after our dear king's fall."

Astor reached Tevin, and Robinson leaped at the grinning teen. But before he'd covered half the distance, two stones dropped on his shoulders, forcing him to the ground and pinning him. Ten more figures stepped into the room, and through his pain, Robinson noticed that they, too, had rock arms matching Astor's artificial appendage. Tonius tried to stand, but two newcomers raised their arms, forming affinite bonds with stones on the floor. They flung the rocks at Tonius, and he fell beside Robinson, clutching his chest in pain.

"It's too bad I missed your friend, the Airwalker, but I'm sure he'll be back before too long."

"And when he gets back, he'll put you in your place!" Robinson shouted, trying to pull himself free from the restraint.

"I've changed since we last met. War erased the weakness that stayed my Hand. Though I was furious with Cayden when he cut off my arm, I now see it was a sign."

"Yeah, a sign that you've lost what little brains you had."

"Quite the opposite. I've learned more than I'd ever hoped, more than Priven taught me at the Perianth Academy—though, of course, he still thinks I'm the loyal soldier following all his absurd orders. You see, after you and your friend Cayden left us here to be destroyed by the witches, the city fell into chaos. Without the king, the leaves no longer held power over the population. It was every man for himself. The soldiers, led by Priven, mounted a defense against the witches, but my father, fat as he was, scrambled into the heights of the tree, searching for the chamber from which the king commanded the population. I got there first."

"You interfaced with the tree," Tonius said, rolling onto his back with great effort.

"Oh, yes. My father was about to plug his fat fist into the golden pillar at the center of the tree, but I pushed him aside—a bit too hard—and he fell from the room, knocking his head against a wall. I'm afraid that was the end of him. But I connected with the tree. I felt its power course through my body, and then—"

"Then it spit you out like a sour grape," Tonius guessed. "It takes equal strength to command power like that."

"I admit, the connection rejected my touch. But oh, what I learned! Mogen trained us Perianth soldiers to control the leaf if we came into physical contact with a person. A finger pressed to the neck may control a single mind. When I connected with the tree, I saw a way to control anyone from any distance."

"If that were true, you would already have the entire population under your control."

"So I faced a few setbacks. The door into the tree's center shut itself after I left, but I'll break its seal. While Priven occupies his time with pointless repairs, I'll build my army." He waved at the rock-fisted men, who circled closer. Robinson recognized their faces from training, though mixed in with the teenagers were several older men he'd never seen. They each stared straight ahead with cloudy eyes, unseeing and unthinking.

"It corrupted you, Astor," Tonius said. "The tree holds an immense evil, and anyone who touches this disease risks contamination. You've never been the nicest person, but think of what you've done. You killed your father, tortured my parents, and enslaved these people. That's not cruel. That's evil. You're not yourself."

"Oh, it's me, alright. It's my time to grab control of the actual source of power in Stomatus, its people. With enough of them under my thumb, I will become the next Perianth king. I will rule the Perianth Empire, and all will bow to my will."

Tonius shook his head. "And what of us? We're immune from the control of the leaf. Do you intend to kill us?"

"Someday. But I'll take little pleasure in the act unless Cayden bears witness to your deaths, powerless to stop me. When he returns—if he returns—I will command the whole of Stomatus. My servants will pin him down while I crush the life out of you, one by one." He stopped for a moment, closing his eyes. "Yes. That moment will be worth the effort of keeping you around."

Chapter Thirteen

A blast roared near Cayden and Leyna, splintering dozens of brittle trees around them. Leyna tackled Cayden to the ground as a broken trunk flew by and landed with a thud scant inches from his head. Cayden struggled to make sense of the sudden commotion, but he barely had the strength to stand.

For a month, they'd hiked north through the dead forest without even a breeze to break the utter silence. Leyna had stopped speaking after exhausting the last of the rations from Stomatus a couple of days ago, a decision that both conserved energy and prevented them from arguing—an all too easy outlet for their frayed nerves. Though Perianth settlements littered the forest, they were bereft of people. Even Cayden, with his Ethereal Hand extended, never sensed another living being. He contemplated returning the way they'd come, but starvation would kill them long before they reached Stomatus. At least water trickled through clear stream beds every few miles, giving them another week of life.

"Thanks," he said, sitting.

"You awake now?" she asked, and Cayden's smile was his answer. She smiled, too, helping him to his feet and commenting, "At least we found people at last."

"Stumbling into a battle wasn't what I wanted, but I'll take any human contact at this point. Let's go see what's happening—but quietly."

Together, Cayden and Leyna crept between trees and around thorny bushes, covering their ears as more thunderous crashes and shouts echoed around them. The forest ended at a final line of trees standing between them and a training village laid out like the town in which Cayden had lived. A familiar schoolhouse sat at one end, while several dozen houses rose in a circle before the Institution hall opposite the schoolhouse.

One of the Perchidian's great airships lay smoldering in a crater along the outskirts of the town, brought down with such force that splinters of wood as large as doors had embedded themselves across the landscape. Several Perchidians stumbled from the wreckage while a handful of witches, followed by a hundred gremmels, stalked the town. Cayden realized the impact must have caused the first shockwave.

"Cayden, look," Leyna said, turning him to face the Institution building. Even from a distance, Cayden made out at least a dozen children watching the attack unfold. Several grim-faced men guarded the building, one of whom wore a distinctive, bushy mustache…

"It can't be," Cayden muttered in disbelief. But it was. Mr. Reynolds stood with ten guardians, their golden hands glittering in the midday sun. The witches would reach the building in seconds, and once they did, they would dispatch the guards, Mr. Reynolds included. *I have to save him*, Cayden thought desperately, but he didn't see a way to make it in time, especially given his weakened state. Leyna shook her head and sank to her knees, too tired to move further. Cayden willed himself to run, but his legs, deprived of nutrients for weeks, refused to cooperate. The best he managed was a limping, breathless jog.

He estimated it would take him five minutes to reach Mr. Reynolds, far too long to be of any help. The witches had already moved into combat range, and he watched with helpless anger as three witches, in unison, commanded a tangle of vines to leap at the town's protectors. Most of them jumped aside, but the vines grabbed one man and flung him halfway across the road, where he hit the ground hard. A plume of dust rose around his mangled body.

The remaining men formed affinite bonds with tiny metal pellets, which they flung at the witches. Though Cayden admitted they used their limited tools with skill, the protectors weren't trained Perianth soldiers. The witches outmatched them, deflecting their attacks with a wall of living vines while pushing forward.

I must move faster, Cayden thought, looking down at his legs to will the useless muscles to quicken their pace. All but two men had fallen before the devious witches and their gremmel companions, who hung back near the houses. Only moments remained for Cayden to mount a rescue, but his body refused to obey his mind's commands.

The Alchemist had insisted that Cayden didn't need his flesh to survive, a talent that might just save Mr. Reynolds. *It's funny how desperation can change one's perspective,* spoke Leyna in his mind. The Alchemist's words frustrated Cayden, who resented the notion of his body as a puppet under others' control. But now he understood.

Before Cayden learned of Lysander's true nature, he'd spent hours training with the mysterious man on the other side of the golden mirror, and though Lysander's purpose—to soften Cayden's mind—was sinister, he'd taught Cayden about the human body. Understanding its molecular structure contributed to strong affinite bonds, and Cayden studied his body down to its cells.

The Alchemist had insisted that Cayden could detach his awareness, leaving his flesh behind or changing it at will, much as Lysander had reshaped Cayden's arm into a silver blade. Cayden wasn't ready to leave his body. The darkest part of Lysander still lay trapped behind Cayden's consciousness, and there was no telling what would happen if Cayden left the evil presence unattended. Still, nothing stopped him from reshaping his own body or at least strengthening it.

Channeling his consciousness inwards, Cayden examined his weakened muscles. He focused all his attention on his thigh muscles, imposing an image of what the muscles should look like over their present, weakened form, and he willed the muscles to reshape themselves just as he would shape a rock with which he'd formed an affinite bond. Instantly, strength flowed through his upper thighs. Encouraged by the minor success, he expanded his focus to the rest of his legs, followed by his torso and arms. New vitality surged through him, days of weariness wiped out in an instant by the fresh muscle tissue he'd carved into existence with his Ethereal Hand. Satisfied, he directed his awareness back to his traditional senses.

Mr. Reynolds hadn't yet given way, though he had fallen to one knee. Blood darkened his shirt, and his arms trembled. Lifting his head, his eyes widened, for he spotted Cayden racing through the town behind the witches. To hold the witches' attention, Mr. Reynolds said, "You won't get these children today."

"You and your fellow protectors fell to us in minutes," said the closest witch. Though her back was turned, Cayden recognized her high-pitched voice, filled with a haughty superiority and an edge of danger. Her generous figure confirmed her identity to Cayden. She was the witch Neflina, an altogether repugnant woman who had twice bested him—once just after the soldiers took him from his village and once the day he'd earned the name "Airwalker." *It's time I repay her,*

Cayden thought, relishing the chance to teach the vile woman a lesson.

Neflina threw back her hood, releasing a tangle of dark hair interwoven with living vines. The vines moved sinuously in the hot air as she stepped forward, writhing like tempting fingers in rhythm with her swaying, ample hips. Mr. Reynolds could do nothing while the vines wrapped around his throat, lifting him to his feet so he stood face-to-face with Neflina, who kissed the corner of his mouth. He bared his teeth.

"Time to die," she said casually. But she never had the chance to tighten the vines around his throat. Cayden had arrived.

The gremmels noticed him first, and they turned in a wave towards him, leaping while Cayden remained ten paces away. A year ago, the creatures would have overwhelmed him, but without Ethereal Hands, they posed no threat. Cayden formed an affinite bond with the soil in a wide arc, using his Hand to lift several feet of dirt into the air and then releasing it to bury the gremmels. They'd dig themselves free, but their immobilization gave him a few minutes.

With an outraged cry, the two witches behind Neflina sent their vines to meet Cayden. Without slowing down, Cayden hardened the dirt before him into a gentle slope, which ended at a sharp cliff a dozen feet away. The vines thudded into the newly formed ridge, and Cayden threw himself from the top of his makeshift ramp, astonished at the power his strengthened legs offered. He sailed over the two witches' heads, clapping the compacted soil down upon them in one smooth motion, but leaving their heads free to breathe.

Neflina, distracted by the motion behind her, released her grip on Mr. Reynolds, who tore himself free of her vines and kicked her square in the side. She stumbled towards Cayden, an odd mixture of surprise and wicked pleasure coloring her face a bright red. Mr. Reynolds fell over, clutching his wounds, but Cayden didn't have time to help him.

"Surprised?" Cayden asked, pleased that the effort hadn't winded him. For a second, Neflina seemed at a loss for words, but then she laughed.

She squealed, clapping her pudgy hands. "I'm surprised and also happy, yes, thrilled indeed, little boy."

"You should watch your words. I am not the boy you once faced."

"But you are. Isn't that what you said when last we met? That you had grown into a powerful man, that you'd destroy poor, helpless Neflina? And then you toppled from a tower like a tiny, helpless toy."

"We'll soon discover if events play the same way again."

"You missed our dances, my plaything? Last time, I was under orders to leave you unharmed, for my queen Jaffa needed you to retrieve the book. Now that you have it, I'll enjoy killing you. I assume your pale, red-headed friend has it nearby? I wonder how the poor girl will live without you? Well, she won't have long to find out since I will destroy her soon after your death. This day has delivered more joy than I had hoped!"

Months ago, her words would have sent Cayden into a rage, but now he lowered his head and said, "Let's have at it, then."

Faster than her girth would seem to allow, Neflina jumped high into the air, thrusting a tangle of vines straight into the ground. Cayden barely had time to move aside when the vines flew up from beneath his feet, almost catching hold of his ankle. He flipped sideways, using his backward momentum to propel himself to his feet in a smooth roll. Neflina, seeing her first attack had missed its mark, now brought the vines in a wide circle around Cayden, wrapping them inwards.

Cayden softened the soil beneath his feet with a quick affinite bond, and he dropped as the vines snapped together. Neflina's effort threw her off balance, giving Cayden an opening to strike. He widened his bond with the ground, churning the soil into a whirlpool of dirt and dragging Neflina's feet from beneath her.

As she fell, she brought a thorny vine down upon Cayden's outstretched arms, drawing deep slices through his skin. He released his bond, and Neflina scrambled to her feet, vines already whipping the ground where Cayden had stood. Now several yards to her left, Cayden probed the soil for a weapon, gripping a large stone just below the surface with his Ethereal Hand, tugging it into the air and hurtling it towards Neflina.

Cayden watched the tensing of Neflina's right thigh as she prepared to throw herself to the left, and, anticipating her motion, he sliced a third of the stone from the larger whole and redirected its momentum. Neflina moved, but the rock flew faster, and it slapped into her body with a loud crunch, halting her in midair. She fell to the ground, unconscious, and Cayden shifted several heavy stones to pin her in place.

Then Cayden fell, too, as Leyna rushed to his side. Neflina's vines must have nicked the brachial artery in his upper arm, for blood pooled on the dry ground. He felt his vision fading as shock set in, but he also sensed Leyna reaching out.

You can fix this, she said. *Just as you did with your legs.* Before darkness took him, Cayden brought his entire focus to the artery in his arm, cradling it within his Ethereal Hand. *Heal,* he thought desperately, and the vein sealed itself, stemming the flow of blood. His outer skin mended as well, with Cayden directing the process. When he finished, he flexed his arm, grimacing in pain.

"Somehow, I don't think I put my arm back together quite right."

"An impressive first attempt," Leyna said, joining him. "Plus, you'll have time later to fix it after you've taken care of your friend."

Leyna bent over Mr. Reynolds, who lay facing the sky, caked in a mixture of dirt and blood. Neflina's thorns ripped part of his mustache from his lip, leaving an angry red patch of exposed skin where the hair had once grown. Cayden was relieved to detect no life-threatening injuries. He bent over his old caretaker's face, placing a cool hand on Mr. Reynolds' forehead. He tried to send his Ethereal Hand inside Mr. Reynolds' body as he had done his own to repair the damage, but he failed. Another person's body was too foreign to be affected by Cayden's Hand, so he instead helped Mr. Reynolds into a sitting position.

"I couldn't believe it when I saw you were running towards me," Mr. Reynolds said, squinting at Cayden through bruised eyes. "How did you know when to come? How did you even find me?"

Cayden looked at Leyna, but she just shrugged. "It was luck," Cayden replied. "Or coincidence if you don't believe in luck."

"Well, your arrival was timely. The witches appeared an hour ago to capture the children we've been protecting, kids from settlements across the Perianth Empire." Cayden noted the fearful faces of a dozen children behind the Institution building's warped glass. He pictured himself among them, as puzzled and afraid as he was the day the soldiers first came.

"Have the witches taken many children?"

"Yes," Mr. Reynolds said, trying to stand. Cayden helped pull him up to lean against the solid door he'd been guarding. Though his knees shook, his voice had steadied now that the adrenaline was draining from his system. "The witches visited a hundred Perianth settlements, capturing their entire child populations and murdering the adults. They hunt young Perianths to turn into gremmels for their assault on Stomatus. We protectors have taken as many children as we can under our care, though the witches are relentless adversaries."

"The leaf no longer controls you," Leyna said. "Yet you choose to fulfill your assigned role?"

"The leaf controlled our actions, my young friend, but beneath the external influence, many of us cared for the children in our domains."

"And the Perchidians are helping," Cayden said, eyeing the nearby wreckage of a Perchidian airship. The wooden ring had broken into three large sections, which stuck from the ground at sharp angles. Cayden closed his eyes, strengthening his Ethereal Hand to see if he could detect any survivors. "Several of their soldiers are alive and uninjured. We should speak with them."

"Hold on. I don't know what caused the ship to crash, though I hope it was a witch attack. When we see one of their airships, we never know whether they come to aid the witches or us. It seems the Sky People, too, fight amongst themselves."

"Dugal must have turned more Perchidians than Balint feared," Cayden said. "We need to reach their leader, Jericho, now more than ever."

"Is that what brought you here?"

"Yes, we have traveled many weeks in search of an airship. It's never been more critical for the Perianth Empire to unite, yet we're at our most divided. I'd hoped to enlist the Perchidians' help, though now I'm expecting you can help, too.

"I don't see how. Our ranks are few, and I can't promise any settlements are safe from further witch attacks. The Empire supported three hundred training camps, plus a dozen cities beside Stomatus. The witches besiege every stronghold in which our people shelter."

"Things are uncertain, but you should continue what you've been doing. Rescue children from the witches and lead them to Stomatus. We'll try to send an airship to aid you if we ever find Jericho. You might need it to get past the witch blockade of the city."

Mr. Reynolds looked at Cayden with curiosity and awe. Though covered in dirt and weary from his fight, Cayden stood straight, having shed the hesitation and fear that had ruled his childhood. Even his face had changed, shedding its childhood roundness for the high cheekbones and sharp nose of a young man. His voice, though still high, was steady and confident, inspiring trust. Mr. Reynolds felt both closer and farther from the boy he'd raised, a child who had transformed into a powerful and perhaps even dangerous leader.

"Very well," Mr. Reynolds said. "I will do as you ask."

Cayden shook the hand of his former guardian, a man who had once beaten him for misbehaving. He'd despised Mr. Reynolds, but their chance meeting changed his perspective, and Cayden now considered him the closest father figure he'd likely ever meet.

A surviving Perchidian limped towards Leyna, and she asked, "Will you take us to meet with Jericho?"

"He'll want to speak with you at once, Leyna of Stomatus."

"Good," Cayden said. "When can we leave?"

"Another of our airships lies to the east. We must gather the wounded and march before night falls."

"There are also several witches still alive, including a powerful one named Neflina, not to mention many gremmels."

"We will imprison them and take them as well. Do not worry. We know how to hold the witches in check."

"Very well. Please tell us when you are ready to leave. I want more time to talk with my old… friend," Cayden said, turning to Mr. Reynolds, who managed a partial smile.

Chapter Fourteen

Soaring through the clear air on a floating tree ring brought a sense of freedom Cayden never quite experienced on the ground, though, if he'd care to consider it, he was much more restricted in the air. A single step separated solid wood from the open sky, so he and Leyna tread with care.

"We should discuss what we'll tell Balint and Jericho," Leyna said. The surviving Perchidians had, as promised, guided Cayden and Leyna to a nearby ship, and they now sailed east toward the group of Perchidians led by Jericho and Balint.

"I don't want to talk about it yet," Cayden said, rolling onto his stomach and covering his eyes. "Let me nap."

"You've been resting for six days, and now we're almost there. Maybe if you'd come and eat with me, you'd be less cranky." But Cayden hadn't eaten since leaving Mr. Reynolds, and he wasn't hungry. In fact, he didn't have a proper digestive system any longer. The modifications he'd made to his muscles while running to save Mr. Reynolds had sparked his curiosity; how much could he improve his body? If other energy sources provided strength, did he need food? In the end, he decided he didn't, so he re-sculpted the inside of his body with his Ethereal Hand, eliminating many of his organs over two days. Only his cardiovascular system remained unchanged, though he took the time to strengthen his heart muscles.

"I don't need to eat anymore."

"This is a dangerous path," Leyna warned. "Alterations to your body will lead to a dark future."

"I'm being careful!"

"Oh, I'm sure you are—and that's not my meaning. I'm saying that the more you lose what makes you human, the less you'll care about what happens to other humans. Our entire goal revolves around saving other humans, remember? Imagine if you became like Dakota or his siblings. They're not truly human, and look at how little they care about other people."

"The Perianth king, Dakota, and the others lack friends. As long as we're connected, I'll always be human. Don't worry, Leyna."

"I'm uncertain," she said, unconvinced.

"We'll talk about this later since we've nearly arrived." Ahead, the sky darkened with a thick gray fog that rose from the ground, plateauing below their altitude.

"I don't see anything," Leyna said, peering into the fog. A series of blasts from the air jets near the center of the tree ring slowed their forward momentum until they came to a complete halt above the fog bank. The ship dipped into the fog like a diving submarine, and the air grew heavy with moisture, drenching both Cayden and Leyna instantly.

"We'd better go inside," Cayden said. Leyna nodded, shivering, as they made their way to the bridge, which bustled with activity. Various officers shouted orders into speaker tubes, which relayed information to crew members across the ship. Through the windows, Cayden saw what he'd sensed earlier: three other airships floated in tight formation, emerging from the fog as they grew closer. Several hooks shot from the nearest tree ring, grabbing their own airship and drawing it in until, with a gentle thud, they were touching.

"Get the fog generators working at once," the captain ordered. "We disturbed the cover with our hasty entrance." Several crewmen scurried to carry out his orders, and the captain turned to Cayden, saying, "Follow me if you would. I'm going aboard the other ship to give my report to Jericho, and I'm certain he'll want words with you."

"Lead the way," Cayden replied. With a curt nod, the captain led them through a docking port and into the adjacent ship. All Perchidian airships were designed from the same pattern, though Cayden noted a distinct change in odor as they crossed into the neighboring ship. It wasn't unpleasant, exactly, but it was foreign—a result of a different crew working long hours in a confined space.

Two Perchidian guards stood on either side of a large doorway, which Cayden recognized as the entrance to the conference room where he'd met the Perchidian Flying Council members. His last visit marked the Council's vote to adopt an active role in the events below. *I doubt anything turned out as they'd planned,* Cayden thought.

Jericho sat at the head of the table with Balint to his right, but Cayden noted that almost a third of the chairs were unoccupied.

"Cayden and Leyna," Jericho said, his deep voice rolling like thunder. "You returned to us. Please take a seat, and the council's ear will soon be yours. But first: Balint, you were saying?"

"We've confirmed that Dugal and his followers fled to the witch encampment near Stomatus. We cannot reach them, for the witches set up formidable defenses."

"And their intentions?" asked an old lady.

"Dugal hopes to add his strength to the witch queen Jaffa's army and overtake the Perianth Empire. They already captured many children from unprotected Perianth settlements."

"Much of the Empire's territory is already in dispute," Jericho said. "We halted the witch advances where we could, though our numbers are few. Gremmels overrun the training camps, absconding with hundreds of children for processing."

"Have the cities also fallen?" asked a man to Cayden's left. Cayden had never been to any Perianth city aside from Stomatus, though he supposed several must exist to accommodate a few hundred thousand Perianth citizens. Stomatus itself only held around thirty thousand people, after all.

"The three major Perianth cities outside Stomatus are better defended, so the witches have not attempted to take them—though they will, for we estimate that ten thousand children lay within their walls."

"Stomatus, too, holds strong," Balint reported. "An impenetrable dome covers the entire city. However, they are besieged."

"What are we to do?" asked another council member. "We decided to play our part in keeping the peace, but now Dugal's treachery leaves our people broken and divided. How can we fight against our brothers and sisters? Then again, how can we allow the witches to continue to consume Stomatus' children? The war poses an impossible question."

Throughout the conversation, Cayden kept his eyes closed. He formed a plan, though he kept it bottled behind the Ethereal barrier where he held Lysander. *I dare not let Leyna sense my thoughts.* Lysander, though, released a gleeful cackle and said, *Oh yes, I like it. Truly devious. A plan worthy of the great Airwalker.* Shaking his head, Cayden said, "Unity."

"What?" asked Jericho.

"An ancient evil named Sevron seeks to control all life in the universe, and he sends the souls of the dead to spread his ill will. These souls are the mysterious creatures that slaughtered Balint's soldiers. They feed off hatred and conflict, so Sevron's most important goal is to seed war and spread hostility. Lysander, before he became the monster who lives in my golden eye, planned to banish Sevron's evil from our world with unity. If we unite all the factions across the planet in a moment of utter peace, our harmony will blast Sevron into space. Unity must start with a strong Perianth Empire."

"You have a plan," Balint said.

"Yes. A wise man taught me that the unachievable becomes attainable if I take one step at a time. That man now collects children from Stomatus' outlying towns and leads them to Stomatus. While he completes this task, we will rebuild another fallen pillar of the Empire."

"Afterlife," Balint guessed, and Cayden nodded. "Their pride is based in independence, so I doubt they will agree to a partnership with Stomatus. As Perchidians, we understand their drive for freedom."

"When they face a choice between death and reabsorption into the Perianth Empire, their pride won't overpower their will to survive," Cayden said. Leyna shot him an odd look, but he tightened his Ethereal Hand and ignored her unspoken question. "The Perchidians once transported the city of Afterlife from the Dumrolls. You can return them now."

"A bold proposal," Jericho said. "Balint, what is your opinion?"

"Cayden's instinct is true. Stomatus will be stronger with the Dumrolls repaired. Unfortunately, I can't foresee any scenario in which Afterlife's leader, Naya, will allow our ships to move their city even an inch."

"You must try," Cayden urged. "Fly to them with a dozen airships. Help them understand the danger of isolating themselves. They are not stupid. When they understand how the impending danger threatens their families and friends, they'll see reason, just like your people did."

"You are persuasive," Jericho said. "But this requires further debate. Leave us, and we will call for you once we have reached a decision."

***

Later, in a quiet corner of the airship, Cayden lay on the knotted wood floor, attempting to relax. His shoulders were clenched throughout the meeting, and the tension refused to leave his body. Leyna crouched nearby, examining Cayden. Her eyes scanned him from toe to head, examining every detail of his compact frame.

"You are hiding something from me," she said. Cayden opened his eyes and looked at her. Her bright red hair flowed behind her back and over her shoulders, and her face brought him comfort through its familiarity. *She's beautiful,* Cayden realized. Leyna heard the thought, of course, and blushed a deep red.

"I *am* hiding something," Cayden said to cover up their shared embarrassment. "Balint was right. There is no way Naya or anyone else in Afterlife would voluntarily rejoin the Perianth Empire."

"You're not suggesting the Perchidians lift them against their will, are you?"

"Not exactly, no. I'm sure Afterlife's defenses are more than capable of fending off a few airships."

"What, then?"

"I'm going to talk to the witch queen Jaffa and tell her about Afterlife and where to locate it."

"You can't!"

"Yes, I can. And I will. Naya will only choose Stomatus if the only other option is death. If we time our movements carefully, the Perchidians will arrive right before the siege begins... and Afterlife will welcome the Sky People's help."

"But that's cruel and deceitful."

"Don't imagine I delude myself. Consider what's at stake. We're fighting to save an entire world from the darkest evil imaginable, and we've got a deadline. After Dakota leaves, we'll have nothing. We need Stomatus."

"I guess."

"Can you come up with a better way?"

"No..."

"Then our plan is set." Cayden softened his tone, saying, "We've taken on an enormous task, Leyna. We'd be fooling ourselves if we assumed we could unite the Perianth Empire just by asking everyone nicely. To get this done before Dakota leaves a big Stomatus-sized hole in the middle of the Empire, we'll have to get our hands dirty. Speaking of which, Jericho and the others have just decided to fly to Afterlife."

"How do you know?"

"I can hear them from here. Since I started altering my body, it's gotten a lot easier to reach much further with my Ethereal Hand."

Leyna touched Cayden's knee. She said nothing, but waves of concern emanated from her as clearly as rays of sunlight on a bright day.

If only she knew the full extent of my plan, Cayden thought under the protection of his Ethereal Hand.

She wouldn't understand, Lysander said. For once, he didn't struggle against the barrier Cayden had erected. His dark presence felt at peace.

No, Cayden thought, *she would not.* Leyna removed her hand and stood, exiting the small room without a word. Cayden almost followed, but he forced himself to remain sitting. He had hours of planning ahead.

Chapter Fifteen

"Naya said something to me just before we left Afterlife," Leyna whispered. She and Cayden crouched behind a pile of dead branches outside the witch encampment. The last time Cayden had been there, the witch queen Jaffa had drawn him against his will, using his childhood friend Charlie as bait. *It'll be different this time,* Cayden promised himself.

"What's that? Oh yeah, I remember she pulled you aside to talk. I was going to ask what you talked about, but I forgot."

"Well, I haven't forgotten. Remember when Dugal said all the animals killed themselves? He mentioned a place called the Blood Caves."

"Yeah, it was just before the windstorm."

"Naya also spoke of the Blood Caves, but not as a place where the animals slaughtered one another. She claimed the caves held great spiritual importance to her people as a place of pure thought and energy, where someone like me might find rest."

"Someone like you? Did you tell her about your abilities?"

"No, of course not. The Departed in their tower told her. They've always sensed a power emanating from the Blood Caves. They even discovered its location, though they've yet to mount an exploratory expedition. And they sensed the same power in me."

"Interesting, but why mention this now?"

"Because confronting Jaffa is a terrible idea. Promise me, if we make it out of here alive, that we'll visit the Blood Caves next."

"That's not what we talked about," Cayden said. "We agreed we should help Mr. Reynolds secure children from the outlying towns."

"I remember, but the Blood Caves are more important. Ever since Naya mentioned the place, I noticed it, too. I figured I imagined it at first, but it's been growing in my mind, like a pocket of silence in a cacophony of sounds."

"Okay, okay, we'll check it out," Cayden reluctantly agreed, though most of his attention was focused on how he'd get to Jaffa without detection.

"Thanks. Now, what's the plan?"

"You're waiting here. I'm finding Jaffa."

"That's not much of a plan. I don't have any of Mogen's fire rocks this time, so I can't save you if you get into trouble. Let me go with you. I can help."

"No, you'll be safer staying in the forest."

"You're not protecting me by asking me to stay here. If anything happens to you, our connection will be severed, and I'll lose touch with reality… meaning I'll be as good as dead."

"Leyna, as much as I'd like you to keep safe, I'm more interested in preventing Jaffa from taking Lysander's journal." Cayden pulled his satchel over his head and handed it to her. He hadn't let the book leave his side since taking it from the underground chamber in the great tree. Even giving it to Leyna for safekeeping made him somewhat uncomfortable.

"Okay, your point about the journal is good. I'll keep it safe. But don't take any unnecessary chances in there," she said, eying Jaffa's lair with suspicion.

Cayden nodded, then turned his head bravely forwards. The witch encampment hadn't changed since his last visit. A maze of tangled vines grew over the hill, at the top of which stood the entrance to Jaffa's underground lair. *It won't be like last time,* Cayden promised himself again. *She doesn't know I'm coming. She won't catch me by surprise.* He sent his Ethereal Hand ahead, probing for the swiftest route to the center of the structure. Several gremmels wandered the maze, but he sensed no witches. With luck, they would have committed almost all their forces to battle the Perianth Empire.

Stepping from the cover of the forest, Cayden sprinted across the open space, throwing himself headfirst into the outer, thorny wall of the maze. The vines parted before him with a bit of prodding from his Ethereal Hand, opening just enough to swallow his body before twisting shut. A shiver ran down his spine as he recalled the chill of Jaffa's control, of moving his limbs against his will. *Keep it together. Focus on the present.* Cayden didn't bother to follow the pathways since he could push the vines aside with a quick affinite bond.

It only took him two minutes to reach the hill's apex, where he stopped near a large, golden boulder blocking the entrance to the underground tunnels. *No matter. I'll drop in through the ground from above.* As he'd done so many times in Stomatus, he formed an affinite bond with the soil, commanding the ground to allow his body passage. He slipped through, propelling himself downwards, until, far below the surface, several witches loomed large in his senses. He slowed his descent, coming to rest just outside a hollow chamber.

With his head pressed against the wall, he spied on their conversation. I need to hear what they're saying. Ever so gently, he pushed his Ethereal Hand through the stone, sensing three figures. One sat atop a throne of vines while the other two kneeled. *That one could be Jaffa,* Cayden thought.

"We used the hardest stones we could find, my queen," said one woman. *Yes, it's Jaffa.*

"Did you try our stockpiled diamonds?"

"Of course. But even they grew dull against the dome. Stomatus is impenetrable."

"And what of the outlying towns? What of Neflina? Has she returned with the next group of children?"

"Ah… my queen. We have word from our scouts. There was a problem."

"What problem?" Jaffa asked.

"It seems several Perchidians interfered with the operation."

"Neflina can handle a few Perchidians."

"Someone else was there. The boy."

"The Airwalker," said a deeper voice, and Cayden scolded himself for missing the man's presence. Dugal stepped from behind Jaffa's throne, coming into view of Cayden's Ethereal Hand. He'd been so preoccupied with keeping track of the gremmels pacing above that he'd overlooked the devious Perchidian.

"Well, not the Airwalker, but the one who holds the Airwalker within," Dugal corrected himself. "He aided a contingent of Perchidians who are not loyal to our cause. They escaped along with the children while also capturing your sisters."

"That is but one camp," said Jaffa. "Surely our other expeditions have been more successful?"

"The remaining camps were abandoned," a witch said.

"Impossible!"

"We are searching for more children, my queen, for immediate processing."

"More soldiers are needed for victory," Dugal said, eyes narrowing. "The breeding programs will present a solution, but incompatibilities have developed over the years we've been apart. Our two peoples cannot yet conceive naturally, though our scientists will solve the problem, of course. For now, though, we need more children."

"I can help with that," Cayden said, pushing the wall aside with his Ethereal Hand so that he popped into the room. He almost laughed at their reactions. Dugal tripped over a root, tipping his pear-shaped body onto the floor while the two witches shrieked. Only Jaffa remained motionless, outwardly nonplussed.

"I was wondering when you'd join us," she said without surprise. "I don't suppose you've brought the book with you?"

"Last time we met, I promised you'd never get your hands on it." Cayden didn't let himself show any surprise at her non-reaction, keeping his senses on full alert. "You two, stay put," he ordered, pointing at the two witches edging towards him. They looked at their queen, and Jaffa motioned them still. "I came with an offer. You need children, and I know where you can find all the children your twisted heart desires."

"Why would I trust, even for a second, that you're telling the truth?"

"Because you took my friend, Charlie. Now it's time you pay."

"He's dead," Jaffa said. "You killed him yourself. Or don't you remember bashing in his head with a rock?"

"He was dead long before I killed that creature. And no, I'm not asking for him. I'm asking for a different payment."

"Very well. I'll play your game. What is your demand, and where is this alleged stockpile of children? You can't be offering Stomatus' children."

"No, of course not. My demand is simple, and granting it will also award you access to more children than you could process in a year."

"You have my attention," Jaffa said, leaning back. A few vines slipped off her shoulders, revealing her hideous skeletal form. She'd been thin before, Cayden recalled, but now her skin seemed to cling to the bone without muscle. *This is the moment of truth,* thought Cayden, trying to hide his anger at having to face Mogen's murderer.

"My friend—the redheaded girl you've seen—is being held captive in an extraordinary city that I'm prepared to reveal. A place with thousands of children and far fewer defenses than Stomatus." Cayden kept his breathing even and his eyes locked on Jaffa.

"We know your friend."

"Well, my condition for telling you about this city is that you rescue her. I don't care what happens to the other children as long as Leyna is free."

"This city exists," Dugal said. "I have seen it from a distance. It is called Afterlife."

Jaffa squinted, examining Cayden. For his part, Cayden started comprehending the absolute ruthlessness required to deal with those who held power. He was no longer an innocent child, and his golden eye burned ever brighter with a dangerous light.

"You've changed," Jaffa said finally. "And not all for the better." Cayden held his tongue, keeping his face a mask of impassivity. "Very well. You have my word. I'll deliver your friend if this city is all you say."

"Deliver her unharmed," Cayden corrected.

"Of course."

"Promise it."

"I promise. And you know I always keep my promises," she said. *You evil witch,* he thought, recalling the glee on Jaffa's face after fulfilling her promise to take Mogen's life.

"Yes. I trust your word." Cayden pulled a map from his pocket, on which were detailed directions to Afterlife with instructions about counteracting their primary defense. One witch reached for the paper, but Cayden let it slip through his fingers. While the woman bent over to grab it, he backed into the wall, commanding the ground with his Ethereal Hand to propel him to the surface. He'd only risen a few inches, though, when he sensed several vines shooting towards him from the chamber he'd just left. He rushed to extend his affinite bond to the vines, but his Ethereal Hand was already weakened by its bond with the soil. Most of the vines shot wide, but one found its mark just over his belly button. Cayden's scream caught in his throat as he momentarily lost his affinite bond with the soil. The surrounding dirt, now out of his control, pushed inwards, crushing his body and snapping a rib.

I have to cut the vine before they dig me out, Cayden thought desperately. If he'd still had a stomach, the pain might have been enough to knock him out, but he'd eliminated his digestive system a week ago. With considerable effort, he focused through the pain, re-extending his Ethereal Hand in a bubble around him. After strengthening his affinite bond with the soil, he twisted in place, winding the vine around himself several times. He clenched his whole body in preparation, jerking the vine, and it snapped, cruelly tearing a piece of his abdominal muscle as it went. When he was free, he rose to the surface as quickly as possible, emerging from the ground near where he'd entered.

For a few seconds, he lay on the ground with his hand pressed against the abdominal wound. Blood flowed past his fingers, soaking into the soil. If Leyna didn't await his return, he might have let himself die rather than endure another moment of agony. *My death would kill her*, he thought, willing himself to sit up before shock sent him into an unconscious stupor. He sensed Jaffa and the other witches racing through secret tunnels towards the surface while gremmels circled his position from their posts around the hill. With seconds to spare, a crazy idea popped into Cayden's head, and he thought, *If there's ever a time to try something like this…*

Grasping several of the thickest vines with his Ethereal Hand, he bent them towards the ground so that they flexed back from their vertical orientations, groaning as their ends touched dirt. Cayden rolled onto the vines, laying back against them. *Here goes nothing.* He released the vines from his affinite bond, and they snapped back into their natural positions, catapulting Cayden high into the air. He tumbled, head over feet, clear across the witch compound. The sharp branches of dead trees loomed below, and he tried to slow his fall by bonding with the surrounding air—but his strength failed him. He crashed violently into the forest, and while he didn't hit any tree trunks, his damaged body slammed into several thinner branches before he hit the hard ground.

He crumpled onto his stomach, pain overwhelming his every sense. *I'm going to die anyway*, he realized, horror erasing all rational thoughts. Then Leyna ran from behind a tree and kneeled over him. He would have shouted for joy if he hadn't broken his jaw.

"Cayden, you must heal yourself right now, just as you did after your fight to save Mr. Reynolds. The witches will be here soon."

I can't.

"Yes, you can. Draw strength from my mind. Use it to steady your Ethereal Hand. You can do this. You have to do this."

Cayden let his consciousness drift up the invisible string connecting him to Leyna, and a razor-sharp focus overlay his panic. He used her calm, clear state of mind to examine the inside of his body, probing with his Ethereal Hand to study his injuries. Cayden knew how his body should look, and he forced the image of his healthy frame over the damage he now observed. *Change*, he thought, demanding that his body match the image he projected from his mind.

It took every ounce of energy both he and Leyna possessed, but Cayden pushed through his body, wielding his Ethereal Hand like a scalpel to repair as he went. Bones fused together, joints slid into place, and organs sealed themselves. A minute later, Cayden sat up and ran his hands over his torso. The hasty repair job was far from perfect. One leg was shorter than the other, and a dreadful ache raged through his limbs—but at least he could move. *I can fix myself up after we're far away from here.*

"Come," he said to Leyna. "Jaffa is nearly upon us."

"You can walk?"

"I think so, though we need to run if we want to lose them in the forest. We can't let any of Jaffa's forces spot you, or it'll ruin everything."

"Then let's go," she said, grabbing his hand and pulling him after her.

Chapter Sixteen

Henrik twisted the final two wires together, soldering the connection before shoving the entire tangle back into the panel and slamming the door shut.

"Messy, but it'll do the trick," he said, smiling. Dakota didn't raise his head from where he worked nearby, and Henrik grumbled. "Why bother speaking at all?" The small boy only talked when he required information or instruction; conversation wasn't a part of his skill set. It was almost like working alone. Henrik was downright lonely, slaving away in the dark for a solid month. He rarely came to the surface since Dakota brought him food and water. At this point, Henrik would welcome that foul-mouthed youth Astor, but Priven had decided they no longer required a guard.

Only the thrill of solving problems kept Henrik sane. Each time he restored functionality to another section of the ship, Henrik would take a stroll, examining with pleasure the instrumentation panels that now displayed data and the comforting glow of lights that bathed the once-dark corridors in a cool, electric glow. For a two-thousand-year-old ship, repairs were progressing faster than Henrik had hoped. Two additional months of diligent work would enable the ship's primary functions, and another month of inspections would confirm Stomatus' spaceworthiness.

Henrik touched the warm metal and pondered his life on Earth. To his surprise, he didn't care what had become of his corporation or other enterprises. He'd developed no close friendships, and his romances were all short-lived and devoid of satisfaction. In essence, he had little to miss, especially considering the technological wonder now under his care. Loneliness, he decided, was a fair trade for Dakota's adventure.

"Be careful," said an unfamiliar voice, and Henrik turned to see an ancient man leaning against a bulkhead. "Thoughts are the most dangerous place in which a man can become lost."

"You're the one they call the Alchemist, right?" Henrik asked.

"I am, yes. The boy Cayden told me not too long ago about my birth name, though I'm afraid it's slipped my mind."

"How did you get down here? I thought Priven had sealed all the passageways." Henrik reviewed the entry points in his mind, trying to recall one he may have left unbarred.

"I needed to speak with you, so I found a way," the Alchemist said. "Now come along. Quickly."

Henrik crossed his arms and called for Dakota. A moment later, the boy rounded the corner, his pale skin darkened with smudges of grease and his expression as placid as ever. "Do you know this guy, the Alchemist? He says I need to come with him."

"Yes. He is one of my brothers. Damek, why are you asking us to leave this place?"

"Ah, yes. Damek. That is my name! I ask because you must come. I'm certain our escape from Stomatus is of the utmost importance."

"That's not an explanation," Henrik said.

"My brother is unusual," Dakota said. "He is likely aware of a danger above, in Stomatus, though the structure of his mind prohibits that information from being accessed. Since I've directed my attention towards repairs, I believe we should follow my brother's instruction."

"I doubt I'll ever understand any of this," Henrik said, shaking his head. "But alright. I've fallen down the rabbit hole this far. Why try to catch myself now? Off we go!"

"Great," the Alchemist said. "Which path to the surface will take us closest to the outer wall? Oh, and you'd better disable your repairs."

Henrik led Dakota and the Alchemist to the control room, where he locked down the central processing unit with a passcode. He doubted anyone in Stomatus would have the technical expertise to activate the machinery, let alone crack a security protocol. After he finished, they jogged towards the lift closest to the outer dome.

Now that power ran throughout the substructure, the emergency access chutes no longer had to be used—much to Henrik's relief. The lift ran on a simple crank and pulley system, carrying the three of them to the surface.

The Alchemist crouched low, his head sweeping back and forth in wide arcs while Dakota remained on the elevator platform, eyes blank.

Since the dome blocked all natural light, the tree bathed Stomatus in a perpetual golden twilight. Henrik took a moment to appreciate Stomatus' glory, for he seldom had the chance to wander the surface. Damage from the witch attacks had been fixed, though the hasty repairs were more clumsy than the city's original builders. Many buildings appeared lopsided, while others were still missing large sections of their outer walls. The towering crystal palaces near the center of the city, however, remained beautiful and unscathed.

"To the wall," the Alchemist ordered, straightening and dashing between two buildings. Dakota followed without hesitation, but Henrik stood still for a moment. A distant light from the center of the great tree momentarily blinded him. The golden beam flicked on and off like a flash of a strobe light, and Henrik wondered whether he might have imagined it. He frowned, feeling exposed in the empty street.

Dakota and the Alchemist were no longer in sight, so Henrik chased after them. Only one path wound to the outer wall from where he stood, and the Alchemist soon came into view. The ancient man stood upon the wall's highest reaches, his gaunt frame bright against the black dome. Henrik shook his head, wondering how the man had already climbed the wall. Dakota was still running up the narrow wedges cut into white stone.

By the time Henrik reached the top of the wall, his heart beat against his ribcage, and he sat to collect himself. The Alchemist ran one bony finger along the inner surface of the dome, which rose from the ground only a hand's width from the wall. He muttered to himself, tapping each finger against the dark surface before pushing his entire face into the dome.

"What are you doing?" Henrik asked.

"He's determining the dome's composition so that we may leave," answered Dakota.

The Alchemist pulled a short rod from within his cloak. The delicate instrument reminded Henrik of his attackers' wands on Earth. Minuscule glass chambers protruded along the golden stick's length, each filled with a colored substance. The old man pressed the rod against the dome, which triggered the chemicals to glow within their translucent bubbles. A compact section of the dome's unforgiving surface bubbled, then melted into a puddle of viscous sludge at the Alchemist's feet. Henrik reached towards the dome's edge, but the Alchemist grabbed his wrist.

"That'll be hot enough to sear your skin for another minute."

"So you catalyzed a chemical reaction?" Henrik asked, bending closer to examine the Alchemist's handiwork. The edges didn't glow red, but an intense heat singed his eyebrows. "Your wand is like a miniature chemistry lab. Wonderful technology! You'll have to show me how it works."

"Yes," spoke a calm voice from below. "You will." Henrik craned his neck to locate the source, but he soon fell back as a sheet of rock slid in front of the hole in the dome. Inside the wall, below Henrik, stood five cloaked figures. Another ten figures approached from both sides, boxing in Dakota, the Alchemist, and Henrik.

The center figure removed his hood, revealing a trimmed wave of blond hair and a handsome face. Henrik recognized the young man as Astor, the Perianth trainee Priven had entrusted with guarding Dakota and Henrik upon their arrival.

"You will come with us," Astor said, motioning the figures on the wall to advance. For the first time, Henrik noticed Dakota's face had become creased, furrowed in uncertainty. The small boy didn't move, but the Alchemist stepped forward.

"We're leaving Stomatus," the Alchemist said. Henrik didn't see how, though.

Astor took a step back, but the other fourteen men raised their arms from within their cloaks, stone hands forming affinite bonds with hundreds of small rocks which flew towards the Alchemist at tremendous speed. Dakota and Henrik dove to the ground while the Alchemist brandished his wand, jumping high into the air and planting his feet against the dome. He pushed off the inflexible surface, propelling himself forward like an arrow from a bow, straight off the edge of the wall and towards his assailants. The golden wand spun in his hand, delicate motions causing the liquids inside to intermingle in calculated amounts until a rush of heat blasted out ahead, throwing the stones back at Astor.

The men on the wall, ignoring Dakota and Henrik, sprinted down the stairs towards Astor, reaching their master just as the Alchemist somersaulted onto the ground. In unison, they leaped at the ancient man from all sides, rock fists raised to strike. The Alchemist ducked down, pushing his wand into the stone below his feet. Dirt rose like a shield, throwing back all but one of the men.

Astor smashed through the stone shield as his men scrambled to their feet, and his hard fist made contact between the Alchemist's shoulder blades. Gasping in pain, the ancient man fell to the ground, scrambling for his wand. Astor kicked the thin instrument away and stepped back, yelling, "Now!"

Another five men rushed into the opening with a golden amber cage. Astor's Ethereal Hand lifted a slab of rock and scooped the Alchemist's limp body into the cage before swinging the door shut.

"We should run while they're distracted," Henrik whispered to Dakota, who still lay next to him.

"Escape must come later."

"Damn it, boy. You'd rather turn yourself over to them than at least try to run?" Henrik's outburst only brought a slight downturn to the corners of Dakota's mouth.

"It is not a question of preference. That young man has a measure of control over Stomatus' population, and neither of us has the skill to fight even one Perianth soldier. Run if you please, but you will wind up in a cage within seconds after you initiate your escape attempt."

Henrik pounded his fist into the stone, wincing in pain. But Dakota was right. The foreign land on an unfamiliar planet posed too many challenges, even for a genius from Earth. Henrik had been so busy with his work underground that he'd almost forgotten where he was, but the situation rekindled the sinking helplessness he'd known as a boy. Where would he run? What chance would he have on his own in a strange land where men and women controlled elements with their minds? Forcing a modicum of calm over his roiling emotions, he stood and trudged after Dakota, who'd already begun his descent to the cage where the Alchemist lay unconscious.

Once they reached the ground, Astor said, "Put leaves in those two." Strong hands grabbed Dakota and Henrik by their arms, guiding them towards the great tree in the center of the city, where soldiers would insert little golden leaves in their necks. Henrik had witnessed what those leaves did, how they stripped away individual thought. The blank look in the soldiers' eyes was proof enough; the darting inquisitiveness, the sense of depth in any human's eyes—all replaced by a cold, robotic menace, evidence of another will, a stronger mind overriding the men's consciousness, their souls.

"Your intention will not offer the result you seek," Dakota said, directing his statement at Astor. To Henrik's relief, the soldier to his right relaxed the iron grip on his arm, and Henrik turned.

"With the leaves in your neck, I can control you from the tree," Astor said, closing the distance between them.

"To what end?" Dakota asked. Henrik noted the look of smug superiority written across Astor's handsome face. The young man believed himself unimpeachable, a notion that might betray his ambition to Dakota's clever mind.

"I know what you've been doing down there. You're fixing a ship, a weapon Stomatus will use to wipe the witches off this planet for good. With Jaffa gone, none will stand between me and total control over Stomatus."

"You believe we will finish the project."

"I know you will. Once you're under my control, I'll force you. You'll have no choice."

"Ah, but that's not how the leaf works. Independent thought and mind control are opposite concepts. If you control us, your ability limits our knowledge. You cannot order us to complete a task you cannot complete."

"Then I will persuade you in other ways," Astor said, frowning.

"That was no doubt already your intention. I estimate an over ninety percent chance that you would have stopped the leaves from entering our necks in a dramatic fashion to persuade us of your compassion. When that failed, you would confine us, deprive us of food and water, and torture us in other ways. But let us skip ahead, shall we? Send us to your dungeon. Do what you will, but we will not complete the ship's construction—no matter the persuasive technique you use."

Astor's face had turned red, and his entire body shook with uncontained rage. Henrik wondered how the youth's wish for control had led him to a point where only absolute submission by all around him would bring satisfaction.

"Fine," he said. "Off to the dungeon, as you say. I'll check on you in a few days. Perhaps you'll have changed your mind." With a smirk, Astor returned to the Alchemist's hole, leaving his soldiers to escort Henrik and Dakota deeper into Stomatus.

"You realize Astor will torture us," Henrik whispered to Dakota. The soldiers guiding them didn't flinch, so he said, "Maybe you can hold out against torture, but as soon as a soldier with a hammer breaks my fingers, I'm going to be inclined to help them."

"Torture is preferable to allowing a leaf to connect our minds to the Elders in the tree. Sevron's darkness would contaminate our essence, and all hope for a brighter future will be lost. Flesh can heal, but consciousness must stay untainted. I will teach you to ignore physical pain. As the son of our father, you should be capable of detaching your mind from your body."

"If you say so," Henrik muttered. He'd read the news describing the horrible acts humans committed against one another. Even his government took part in inhumane acts of torture. Yet such barbarisms were a distant concern from his tower of wealth and technology. Now Dakota had entangled him in an unfathomable situation, and he grew dizzy not from fear but from his extreme helplessness.

"Watch your step," Dakota warned. They'd arrived at a hut in the Dumrolls, and the soldiers shoved them through its crooked door. Broken glass bottles littered the floor, and had Henrik known more about Stomatus' history, he'd have recognized the place as Mogen's laboratory, where he'd concocted a protection against the leaves.

A soldier pointed to a hole in the room's corner, and Dakota clambered inside. A moment passed, and the soldier prodded Henrik.

"Fine, I'm going." Henrik sat on the ground and eased himself into the tunnel. The slick mud propelled him down a steep chute onto a pile of wet rags. A single crystal lit the room from above, casting a cool glow on his muddy surroundings. Dakota stood near one wall, examining a pile of rags, so Henrik joined him.

Henrik's eyes widened when he saw they weren't rags but a person, thin as a skeleton and barely able to move. Another young man beside the first, though he wasn't as skinny. Henrik had only briefly met the two, but he recognized them.

"Hey," Robinson said, struggling to sit. "You didn't sneak any food in here, did you?"

Chapter Seventeen

Cayden nodded at Leyna, then turned to face the cave entrance. He'd expected a grand doorway, perhaps lined with primitive, tribal markings warning away trespassers. Instead, he met a crack in the hillside, barely large enough for two men to walk shoulder to shoulder. The hill was unremarkable, but Leyna insisted they had arrived at the Blood Caves.

After escaping Jaffa, Cayden allowed himself a week to recover from his injuries. He hadn't just repaired the damage, though. Using his Ethereal Hand, he'd also modified his body, strengthening his bones and reinforcing his joints, then building up new muscles to support his increased weight. Leyna never commented on the changes, but she radiated disapproval as though shouting her displeasure in his face. She'd only held her tongue because her insistence on the Blood Caves' importance forced them both onto a path Cayden resented.

"Since we're here, we might as well go in," Leyna said, responding to Cayden's unspoken thoughts. He nodded, sending his Ethereal Hand ahead to search for danger, but his senses dulled the further his Hand traveled into the confined space. *I don't like that,* he thought. Only the great tree's amber sap had ever blocked his abilities, so the danger ahead would be new and unpredictable. They'd have to explore the old-fashioned way—with their five traditional senses—so he pulled the light crystal from his neck, using the energy inside his body to cast a gentle glow before stepping into the dark. Leyna followed him, hand on his shoulder.

"Leyna, you're afraid," he whispered as they walked forward, ducking to avoid low-hanging outcrops of rock. Her arm trembled against his skin, and she breathed in short, anxious gasps. "I've never seen you so scared." Through all the dangers they'd faced together, she'd never shown a hint of terror, but now the emotion pulsed from her mind.

"There's a silence here I've never experienced. When you or Mogen were not tying my consciousness to reality, the noise from those around me, even distant minds, overwhelmed my senses. Despite our bond, I can still hear the noise—but it's far away, remote. The sound is like the roaring ocean beside your hometown, ever-present but unnoticed. Now, I hear almost nothing. The further we walk into this cave, the dimmer the noise becomes. All is silent except for your mind."

"And that's why you're scared?"

"It's silly. You wonder why I don't welcome the silence, but it's like losing one of my senses. Imagine if you lost the ability to use your Ethereal Hand. Wouldn't you be frightened?"

"Actually, my Ethereal Hand is much weaker in here. The cave's walls block the tree's energy, limiting my reach. Perhaps we should turn back since we decided to explore based on your intuition alone."

"Don't be absurd. When has fear stopped us?" Leyna turned, straightened her shoulders, and strode with deliberate steps further into the deep. Only the sound of their shuffling feet on damp rock broke the overbearing silence as the cave walls grew narrow. They crawled under towering outcrops of stone, and Cayden trembled to consider what would happen if a single rock shifted above them.

Time piled up like a physical barrier, every minute increasing their distance from the entrance. The air grew heavy with chill humidity, seeping through Cayden's clothing and soaking him to the bones.

"We've reached a cavern," Leyna said at last. Cayden prepared to brighten the light crystal to illuminate the space ahead, but the moment his foot entered the wide area, he froze. Fear coiled around his heart, tightening his chest and weakening his knees. Leyna trembled beside him, sinking to the ground. Cayden fell, too, pressing himself against the stone wall near where they'd entered. He opened his mouth to speak, only croaking out a meaningless gurgle.

The slap of solid footsteps echoed across the chamber, and a shape emerged from the darkness to loom just outside the reach of Cayden's faltering light. It stalked forward and emerged from the gloom, showing its true form when it stood not ten feet away. Cayden recoiled, for he recognized it as an animal from pictures he and Charlie had seen as children: a bear, its fur as black as a starless night and standing on its two hind legs. It towered over them, a pillar of solid muscle, its eyes filled with an intricate, almost human intelligence.

A muscular man, who rivaled Priven in size, arrived at its side and stood in judgemental silence for ten unbearable seconds. Leyna's hand shot to Cayden's arm, and she squeezed so hard that his fingers lost sensation. He stared in frozen horror until the bear sunk to its paws.

"We know… you," the man said in a strained whisper, as though he forced each word from a parched throat.

"We've not met," Cayden said as his paralyzing fear eased.

"Not… you…" The man bent to examine Leyna.

"Not me, either," she said.

"We followed you… many years ago… in your village. You called… for us… but an ancient man interfered."

"Mogen. I touched him, and—"

"He formed the sacred bond. Human anchoring human… an impossibility, or so we believed. Now, we welcome you… but not the stranger… you lead to our home."

"I'm no stranger," Cayden said. "The ancient man, Mogen, died at the hands of the witch queen Jaffa. I bonded with Leyna. I am her anchor now."

"No. Another… presence… lurks below your mind's surface."

"You can sense Lysander?" Cayden asked, surprised.

"More than sense. He stands before me… as bright as your flesh. But… he is broken. A fragment lives in your golden eye… but a larger piece dwells within the book in your satchel."

"I have so many questions," Leyna said. "I'd always thought I was alone."

"No questions, no answers… not yet. We will speak elsewhere, but first… we must cleanse the dark presence from the boy before it enters our… community."

"You can do that?" Cayden asked, shocked. Ridding Lysander from his mind was an outcome he'd pursue to any end.

"It is possible… though you might not survive." *Yep,* thought Cayden. *Too good to be true.*

"It's not worth it," Leyna said.

"Yes. It is. If we don't cleanse my brain, Lysander will control me the moment my guard drops. Dying is preferable to watching my life through Lysander's eyes, so we need to accept any offer that has a chance of erasing this curse."

"Excitement clouds your judgment, Cayden, which is understandable. But we must understand the risks and how they plan to remove Lysander before deciding."

"You follow," the man said, turning with the great bear at his side.

"Only one way to find out." As Cayden followed beside Leyna, he marveled at the bear's movements. Though its wide legs supported a torso that must have weighed a thousand pounds, it nevertheless picked its way across the rubble-strewn ground with effortless grace. Yet he sensed the ferocious power beneath its careful steps, and he understood one swipe from its pointed claws would tear his body in half. *If only Charlie were here,* Cayden thought, remembering when his world was smaller, when he would joke with his best friend about mythical bears.

They crossed the vast chamber and entered a smaller tunnel, ending at a flat wall. The bear rose and pressed its mighty paws against the smooth surface. Muscle rippled under fur, and a door groaned inwards, slowly at first, before swinging wide.

Warm light flooded the tunnel, powerful and bright as the sun. Cayden once had trouble adjusting to sudden changes in light because the pupil in his golden eye refused to contract, but now he exerted such control over his own body that he could tighten the iris as easily as one might make a fist. But though he could see, he had trouble interpreting the spectacle before him.

They stood on a bluff overlooking verdant pastures, flowing blue streams, and trees brimming with natural leaves. The landscape extended for miles. It was hard to remember they were still underground. Far above, a powerful light source cast a shadowless glow across the land, though when Cayden tried to see past the light, all he could detect was darkness. He tried to reach up with his Ethereal Hand, but he could not extend his Hand more than a few inches from his body, no matter how hard he pushed.

"Isn't this wonderful," Leyna said beside him, and when he looked at her, all his analysis, all his calculations evaporated. Her pale face glowed in the light beneath a frizzy band of hair blazing red over thin shoulders. A smile broke out across her face, and then she laughed. Her melodic giggle was childlike and filled with wonder, so different from the coldness that had been growing in Cayden's worried thoughts.

Most would view Cayden as a child. At thirteen, he should have been free to play, free from the cares that burden adults as they accumulate responsibilities. Lately, danger dominated Cayden's every moment. Instead of playing, he plotted. When he should have been learning about himself, he focused on Jaffa, Dakota, the Alchemist, and Sevron's darkness in the north. He had become obsessed and single-minded.

Here, with Leyna and her unbridled joy, overlooking a breathtaking underground vista that had no right to exist, Cayden relaxed. *I can let myself enjoy this moment with her,* he thought. But even as the thought appeared, worry rushed to consume his joy, and Cayden shook his head. *It's not time to relax yet. There's so much I need to do. I'm the only one who can rid the world of Sevron's darkness.*

"Jaffa or the Perianth king might share your self-importance," Leyna said.

"You're saying I'm like them?"

"No, you're not. But you're not the same boy I met a year ago, either."

"Everyone changes," he said, shrugging. To his surprise, Leyna hugged him, touching her lips to his cheek before pulling away and blushing.

"I still like who you are, and change is good. Just remember that Jaffa's obsessions and the Perianth king's ambitions resulted in chaos. Our world is at risk because of their mentality. While we strive to make good decisions and rid the world of Sevron's influence, our actions will also have consequences. Let's try not to lose ourselves in our mission."

Cayden didn't know what to say, so he stood in silence, letting his eyes follow the path of a nearby stream as it wound around a series of gentle hills into a valley far below. Their guide returned, this time without the bear.

"The old one… will see you." The nameless man broke into a jog, leading Cayden and Leyna through the most beautiful display of natural color, a veritable garden of novel sights. Flowers bloomed here and there, while groupings of golden bushes dotted the hills. The air smelled fresher than any meadow Cayden had ever tread.

Soon, the man slowed, stopping near the base of a massive tree. Though Stomatus' tree dwarfed this venerable oak, its trunk eclipsed any other in the forest. A grouping of gray tents lay at its roots, while hundreds of footprints—some human and others beastly—compressed the soil as evidence of a recent gathering. Only one man sat within sight, elderly but not as ancient as Jaffa or her quarreling brothers.

He wore a simple tunic, which hung from his bony shoulders as he leaned against a tree root. The root moved, and Cayden jumped, for he had mistaken the man's animal companion as part of the tree. Its gray-brown hide bore uncountable wrinkles, while each of its legs could encompass a grown man's torso. Strangest was its fifth appendage, which hung from its head like a limp arm and cradled the resting man.

The animal stomped towards Cayden until it stood a foot away. Its fifth arm snaked out, wrapped around Cayden's waist, and lifted him so he hung at eye level. Large, rheumy eyes roamed over Cayden's body, examining every part of him. He didn't squirm, and the creature soon set him down and returned to the man.

"This is... a wise man," said their guide. "He will speak. I... leave." And with that, he turned and ran past the tree, vanishing from sight. Every society looked to respected elders for advice, a wise council capable of guiding or ruling the population. *Experience is valuable,* Cayden thought as he examined the elderly man, *but Lysander's folly proves that age doesn't always bring wisdom.*

"And even the youngest can find wisdom," the man said, his voice clear and his enunciation flawless. Cayden blinked, more surprised that the man could talk than at his apparent ability to read thoughts. "But your mind houses more than wisdom, doesn't it? An evil presence prowls beneath your golden eye."

"Yes," Cayden said. The man closed his eyes and inhaled. After a few seconds, he spoke.

"I sense four separate consciousnesses, though my eyes see two. Asha insists your mind houses a sinister spirit," the man said, resting his hand on the animal. "Ah yes, you must be unfamiliar with a beautiful animal such as my Asha. She is called an elephant, as you are called a human... though I see too that you are not quite human, either."

"He's as human as I am," Leyna insisted.

"I appreciate the sentiment, young woman, but he is not. There is a lack of substance to his form, or perhaps I'm viewing part of a whole. Whatever the case, within him lays a creature of foul purpose. You want this creature removed?"

"Not exactly. We came here because Leyna—my friend—was drawn to the Blood Caves."

"Yet you stand before the only person who may draw the evil from you like poison from a wound."

"Our guide suggested removing the evil might kill Cayden," Leyna said.

"That's one risk, yes. There are two risks and one certainty. Come, sit beneath the tree's shade while I explain."

Cayden looked at Leyna, and she tilted her head. *I don't sense any danger*, she said in his mind, and Cayden nodded. He didn't expect any threat either, so they both joined the man, sitting on the ground as he did with their legs crossed.

"You've already learned that children may develop a psychic ability, like an allergic reaction to the leaf. For hundreds of years, the Perianth Empire hunted these special children. They were insane, uncontrollable, and therefore useless to the king. Then there was me: Harken. By a chance so slight it approaches the realm of impossibility, strange events fell into line, starting with my reaction to the leaf and ending with all the wilderness you see here.

"Leyna, you've heard the minds of an entire world… and beyond. A single consciousness, exposed to the world's ocean of tumultuous thoughts, cannot support individuality. Only an anchor which acts as a motionless point within the raging sea can keep you stable. Your anchor tethers your consciousness."

Leyna nodded. "That's what I did with Mogen when he touched me and then Cayden when Mogen… when Jaffa murdered him."

"Before your bond with Mogen, I considered it impossible for another human to act as an anchor, for the average human mind already supports a considerable burden. When I was a child, the Perianths came to my village and implanted the leaf, but it drove me insane. My insanity lasted for hours, but before a disposal team arrived to kill me, a shadow fell. It was a baby elephant, separated from her mother by a pack of attacking hyenas. She reached out with her short trunk, making contact at the back of my neck where the leaf had been. At that moment, my mind entered hers through our physical connection. As Mogen became your anchor, Asha became mine."

"It must have been so different from my connection with Mogen," Leyna said. "I absorbed his memories, but I also took on bits of his personality. He was ancient, but his thought patterns were familiar."

"For a time, I became less than human. Chaos faded, but Asha's thoughts and emotions suppressed my immature consciousness. It took a year for Asha and me to find our balance; I became mostly human, and she mostly elephant. Still, bits of us remain inseparable. Primal fears, joys, and curiosities can overwhelm me to this day, taking over the rational part of my brain and transforming me into a much more primitive being. We are two, but we are halves of the same whole."

"It's the same with Leyna and me," Cayden said. "We're careful not to let one personality overwhelm the other."

"Perhaps so. I'm not sure how it works when two humans form this bond. Because I discovered Asha, I set out to rescue others like us. A dark influence crept into the minds of many across the Empire, including the animals, who were affected deeply. They killed one another without mercy until none survived, save those who formed bonds with others like me, those we lead to this protected forest."

"It must have taken an extraordinarily powerful Ethereal Hand to build this place," Cayden said. "And the cave's walls block power from reaching my Hand."

"Ah, well, I'm afraid my knowledge runs out there. I did not create these caves, nor have I discovered their architect. I only happened upon it by chance, drawn by Asha's curiosity at the smell of blood during our wanderings across the Perianth Empire. Thousands of animals congregated and filled the outer chambers with blood. Asha waited outside until I found a pathway large enough for her to enter. Together, we walked to this place of silence and tranquility under rock and mountain.

"Asha wanted to help others like me, so we spent six decades scouring the Empire. We rescued many, helping to form bonds between humans and animals, but when the world became too dangerous, we retreated here with all those we'd rescued. I collapsed every cave entrance save one, and many of our kind have forgotten about the troubles beyond these walls. Because we speak into one another's minds, many have lost their ability to speak aloud. Here, we are safe and content to rest while the world crumbles."

"We're trying to stop that from happening," Cayden said.

"While we have been talking, my friends have been examining your mind." Only now did Cayden's attention shift to the men and women who lurked among the surrounding trees, each with an animal of their own. He counted birds, snakes, dogs, and creatures so strange he didn't have a name for them. "We can guide the dark presence within you, Cayden, into the vessel you carry in your pouch, but we must carve the path. I will be its path."

"You're talking about Lysander's journal. You can pull Lysander out of my head and put him in the journal?"

Harken did not respond, and Leyna directed her entire focus upon him for the first time. Her surroundings had been so overwhelming, and she'd been so pleased to meet others of her kind that she'd overlooked Harken himself. Now, she aimed her thoughts at Harken, ready to fight through his mental barrier. Instead, she saw a developed plan in his mind as plainly as if it were on paper. Leyna understood Harken's intent, and she gasped.

"Why would you offer this to a stranger?" she asked him.

He smiled without humor. "You are no stranger. Though we have lived apart, you are one of us. The Blood caves have taught us much, and for a decade, we developed a plan to alter the world's events with our power."

"What power is that?" Leyna asked.

"Don't tell me you have not sensed this ability within yourself."

Puzzled, Leyna said, "I can see inside the minds of those around me to a limited degree. I've only done it a few times, though."

"Be honest with yourself. Sight is the least of your abilities. With training and focus, you can alter others' minds by assigning new meaning to that which they hold important. For instance, we once stopped a Perianth soldier from killing a boy by pushing his love for his child to the center of his thoughts. With our mental prodding, the boy became as precious to him as his son, and he disobeyed the great tree's will. We tried to use our power to clear the evil from the corrupted minds in this world, but unfortunately for us, the evil originating with the Elders in Stomatus was far beyond our ability to combat. We have been powerless to affect change. Until now."

"That doesn't explain why you'd be ready to make this sacrifice."

"What sacrifice?" Cayden asked, puzzled. He struggled to make sense of Leyna's thoughts, but they skittered away.

"You are young, Leyna," Harken said, ignoring Cayden's question for the moment. "It is always difficult to explain the thought patterns that develop as one ages. Though I don't claim wisdom, I insist that my long life has gifted me with a limited vision capable of helping save the world. Your friend, your anchor, is like the evil that threatens our world, yet his intent is not evil." Leyna saw Harken's thoughts about Cayden, and she quailed at the vision of Cayden's body drifting apart in the breeze as the force that bonded his molecules lost cohesion, and his consciousness departed.

"You expect he can fight this bodiless evil by surrendering his body," Leyna said.

"Just like the Alchemist told me," muttered Cayden, shuddering as the tiny hairs stood up on the back of his neck.

"And you believe that removing Lysander is the key?" Leyna asked.

Harken said nothing, keeping his expression carefully neutral.

"If removing Lysander means I have to give up my body, I don't think I'd want to do it."

"I won't let you risk Cayden's life," Leyna said, standing up and stepping in front of Cayden. "You're selfish, just like all the others. You only want to use Cayden for your purposes. I see now that it was a mistake to come here, and it's even more foolish because we've made the same mistake over and over again—leaping before we looked. Let's get out of here, Cayden!"

"Alright," Cayden said with confusion. "We'll go."

"I'm afraid the decision is not yours to make," Harken said. Many hands grabbed Cayden, pushing him to the ground so his face pressed into the wet dirt. The bear they'd seen earlier wrapped Leyna in his massive paws tightly enough to prevent movement but not so tightly as to hurt her. Cayden tried to summon his Ethereal Hand, pushing with all his will to form an affinite bond with anything he could use as a weapon. But no bond would hold, and he soon felt a cool fingertip at the back of his neck, calling up a memory of when he'd been in a similar position on Mogen's floor, powerless to move as Mogen examined him as if he were a lab animal. Harken removed Lysander's journal from his satchel and placed it near his head while the world outside faded to black.

Cayden sank into his mind down to the barrier that held Lysander. He'd explored that barrier plenty of times—a wall keeping Lysander in check—though now, a third presence appeared alongside Cayden and Lysander, a golden tapestry flowing through the currents of his thoughts. He sensed Harken and Asha in the warm light, but as he unraveled the intricate patterns playing off the surface of the tapestry, the threads binding it unwound. Jagged golden lightning twisted and reformed, solidifying into a thin, glowing cable. The cable plunged to the deepest part of his subconscious and stretched up to his outermost thoughts before traveling all the way out of his golden eye and into the journal beside him.

Golden beads of light danced along the thread, puncturing Lysander's cage. Cayden tried to pull away from Lysander as he surged outwards. At first, Cayden shrunk from Lysander's gleeful shouts as he flowed up along the cable, shattering his prison and racing towards the surface. Then Lysander slowed, and Cayden felt Lysander's joy turn to dread. Lysander pulled back, trying to burrow back into his cage, but now the golden beads of light tugged at him, pulling. The progress was slow but ceaseless, tugging at a now writhing Lysander, forcing his dark presence to flow along the cable and into the journal.

When it was done, Cayden sprang up as if jolted by electricity, rubbing violently at his burning left eye while trying to blink the world back into view. Gradually, his surroundings came into focus, brightening around him until he came to rest in the conscious world. To his left, Harken lay beside his massive elephant companion, Asha. Cayden reached out to touch the man, already knowing what he would find. Both Asha and Harken were dead.

Released from the bear's grasp, Leyna rushed to Cayden's side.

"Are you okay?" she asked, and Cayden could feel her probing his mind with fearful intensity.

"I… I think so." Cayden closed his eyes, directing his thoughts inwards. With nervous excitement, he bounced around his mind, searching for any sign of Lysander, a hint of the darkness that had called his mind home for thirteen years. But he detected no trace of Lysander. "He's not there," Cayden whispered, almost unable to believe it, while struggling to make sense of what had happened, and why Harken lay dead at his side.

"Not gone," said the man with the bear. "In there." He pointed at Lysander's journal, and Cayden saw the cover glowed with an amber intensity. He reached out to touch the book but stopped short, for the heat radiating from the book was as hot as fire. The residents of Harken's underground paradise dispersed, scattering in every direction. Cayden and Leyna watched them go in silence, until they stood in the little grove alone, accompanied only by the bodies of Asha and Harken.

"Harken used his consciousness to guide Lysander from your mind," Leyna explained, trying to hold back tears. Despite what she'd said earlier, calling Harken selfish, she knew that she'd just witnessed the most selfless act imaginable. "Harken gave his life, turning himself into a bridge so the others could force Lysander into the journal without causing you harm. They united both halves of Lysander within his journal, though the version of Lysander that emerges may be evil or good."

"But why?" Cayden asked, eyes fixated on Asha's hulking body. "Why did Harken give his life?" He could not tear his eyes away from the two lifeless forms as he tried to comprehend the magnitude of Harken's sacrifice.

"He sacrificed himself for you," Leyna said, "because he believes you have the power to cleanse the world of Sevron's evil."

"There are so many people counting on me," Cayden said, turning towards the glowing journal. The ground turned to burnt ash, and it glowed ever more brightly in the shade of the tree. "Whether they know it or not."

Chapter Eighteen

Naya strode into the anteroom of councilman Doris' office, but a bulky man dressed in a gray jumpsuit slid in front of the entryway. His body blocked the arch, which glittered with rare gemstones embedded in its bone-white surface—a reminder that not only was Doris a councilman but also that he owned great personal wealth. Naya had intended to barge into the councilman's office, throwing Doris off guard, though she saw now her rage-fueled plan would no longer be possible.

"And who might you be?" Naya asked the man, crossing her arms and allowing Afterlife's star pendant to swing from her wrist.

"I'm Mr. Doris' secretary."

"His secretary," she repeated, eying him. "You look more like hired muscle, maybe hired to stop me from entering unannounced?"

"If you say so, ma'am."

"My title is 'Ruler,' so please use it next time you address me. Now, I order you to stand aside." Naya did technically have authority to issue specific commands to any of Afterlife's occupants, though she seldom used it, and now that she had, she expected this brute to move aside. When he didn't budge, a familiar swell of desperation quickened Naya's heart. She approached a crucial test of her leadership; failure would collapse all the delicate political maneuvers she'd executed over the past months.

Cayden and Leyna's unexpected visit had upended Naya's world as her daily routines became meaningless in the broader context of reality. News of extreme turmoil in the outside world created a problem not faced by any Ruler in centuries, so Naya had taken to visiting the Departed in Afterlife's central spire. At first, she'd only gone intermittently, meditating on all she'd learned of the events swirling around the Perianth Empire.

Her visits grew in frequency with her worries, and she'd communicated with those whose consciousnesses lived within the tower. The star pendant she wore as a sign of rulership served a more practical purpose, allowing her to speak with the Departed in the tower. The minds of Afterlife's citizens throughout its history—even from the days it had been part of Stomatus—lived on in the tower, and the more they told her, the more unease replaced the quiet confidence she'd grown up knowing.

Afterlife's founding principle of independence revolved around complete freedom from the Perianth Empire's grasp. As its leader, Naya ensured external forces remained separate from the lives of those within the city's walls. Since the Alchemist founded Afterlife a thousand years ago, its isolation was absolute. Cayden's arrival prompted the Departed to turn their vision outward, and their sight extended farther than any natural eye.

Naya peered through the eyes of the Departed for weeks, studying all they sensed of the Empire and its surrounding lands. She saw the witches gathered around Stomatus, which was covered by a black dome. She perceived increased pressure from the evil laying wait in the north, like a wind composed of ill will, blowing towards the Empire. Amid the chaos sat Cayden, an immovable anchor that resisted the sea of change swirling across the globe. Gradually, and against all better judgment, Naya accepted that the turmoil would destroy Afterlife's independence. War would consume her beloved city, whether or not they chose to rejoin the Empire.

So now she waited outside the office of Councilman Doris, one of seven officials elected to represent the interests of each of Afterlife's districts. With Doris' "secretary" blocking her way, Naya felt like the little girl she'd once been, trying to enter her father's study while he dealt with city business. But her parents were both dead, killed in a meaningless accident before they joined the tower. With difficulty, Naya shook thoughts of her parents from her head, focusing on the task at hand.

Doris sat behind his crystal door with the other council members in a meeting he called without her knowledge. Such a gathering meant that the council intended to impeach her. She didn't blame them, either. Her speech the previous day outlining an aggressive intervention in the affairs of the outside world stood against centuries of teachings. Despite conventional wisdom, Naya held to her judgment, so she turned to the stubborn guard. Her face grew stern, and she summoned every bit of authority she could manage.

"You will step out of my way," Naya commanded. "Or I will forcibly remove you. Either way, I will enter." Conviction lent Naya's voice a power that sent tremors down the man's spine, and his eyes darted around the antechamber as if seeking reassurance. The room gave him nothing, so he stepped aside. "Thank you," Naya said before he changed his mind.

After a deep breath, she pushed open the door and entered. As she'd suspected, all seven council members squeezed around Doris' table, with Doris himself seated in his plush, white chair. His thin frame took up less than a quarter of the chair's width, while his smooth face was the only one to remain expressionless upon Naya's sudden appearance.

"You cannot call a council meeting," Naya said, determined to control the conversation. "Without my presence, as stated in Afterlife's consti—"

"That rule does not apply if our topic is impeachment," Doris cut in smoothly. Naya didn't expect him to cut to the issue, so she stammered and fell silent. That was the thing about Doris, though. Barely older than Naya herself and younger by at least twenty years than anyone else on the council, his mind sped along more quickly than anyone else Naya had ever met. He'd dominate any discussion, cleverly routing conversations through twists and turns until others agreed with his personal goal. Usually, the goal was to gather more power for himself.

"On what grounds are you calling for my impeachment?"

"Have you no sense of tradition, girl?" asked one of the older councilmen, his bony finger quivering as it pointed at Naya.

"Quite right," Doris continued. "This meeting is about your utter and reckless abandonment of the traditions that have kept Afterlife the sacred home of our people. You suggest we rejoin the Perianth Empire, the tyrannical regime from which we escaped. Would we trade freedom for shackles? Independence for subjugation? Are the lives of Afterlife's citizens worth less than your selfish desires?"

"You have lost your mind, Doris," Naya said through clenched teeth as her temper threatened to control her words. "While I respect our people's history, I have seen things you can't imagine. You might not sense it, but enemies surround us. The Departed foresee no scenario in which Afterlife may be independent and intact. When the fighting escalates—and it will—we must ally ourselves with the winning side. My willingness to abandon traditions will preserve Afterlife. Doris, if you insist upon grabbing power… well, enjoy your short-lived authority for the last few days of your pitiful life."

"We've heard enough," Doris said, grinning.

"If you'd just give me a chance to explain…" But Naya looked at the faces of the other council members, whose expressions had hardened during her speech. She had fallen into Doris' clever trap by giving a show for the elder members. He wanted Naya to barge in, to behave like the petulant child he'd told them to expect. She sputtered, unable to think of anything to say without playing further into Doris' plan.

"Let's cut to the vote, shall we?" Doris asked, taking advantage of Naya's hesitation. "All in favor of impeachment, place your right hand on the table."

Rules demanded a private vote, but the councilors' emotions ran so high that even the most tradition-bound among them placed their hands on the table. Naya looked down at their hands, covered in veiny wrinkles and dark, textured spots. Cloudy eyes glared at her from around the room while Doris kept his expression politely blank.

"Very well. We'll arrange a meeting to elect a new leader. In the meantime, this council will command Afterlife. If our business is concluded, I'll stroll through our beautiful—and independent—city. After all this stress, we should all consider stretching our legs."

Fury raged within Naya and skewed her vision. She turned to leave, but Doris said, "Leave the pendant." Naya stopped as suddenly as if she'd run into a wall. Her hand went to her wrist, where the star pendant hung, her connection to the wisdom and vision of the Departed and the symbolic artifact that marked her as Afterlife's ruler. With shaky fingers, she unlatched the golden chain, turned, and flung the heavy stone at Doris' head. He neatly caught and pocketed it.

Although Doris had only taken her bracelet, Naya felt exposed, as if living a dream in which she forgot to dress before leaving her house. Her title mattered little, but the link to the tower had become a necessity. Without it, her vision narrowed to what lay before her eyes. The hurricane of forces scrambling for control of the world was now invisible, though she knew they remained potent and deadly despite her inability to sense them.

She wandered up through the city towards Afterlife's central tower. The Departed existed within its opaque walls, yet communication was impossible without her pendant. Still, the familiar structure comforted her raging emotions and allowed her to process the day's events with clarity.

Her legs carried her up the stairs, taking the steps two at a time until she ran with her full strength, bounding higher and higher into the heart of Afterlife. Despite herself, a smile inched across her face, the pure adrenaline from the sudden burst of energy filling her mind with hope for the future. Doris was a power-hungry monster, but she would outlast him in a contest of wills.

"Thank you, mother," she said, leaning against a pillar at the top of the stairs to catch her breath. Her mother had taught her the value of hope and how it powered one's determination and resilience in adversity. With a final, calming sigh, she turned to the tower but stopped when she heard Doris' unmistakable voice.

"I don't see them," Doris said. Not wanting to offer him the chance to gloat so soon after his triumph, Naya slid into an alleyway between two buildings, pushing herself into a crack to hide. A moment later, Doris passed, followed by another man she didn't recognize. Squat and desperately panting, the stranger struggled to match Doris' leisurely pace.

"You don't see them because they are below the ground," the stranger wheezed. "As I've explained, they are quite good at tunneling." After they passed, Naya tiptoed after them, a sense of nervous dread pooling in the pit of her stomach. She followed them to the pillar where she'd been moments before, and when they rounded the corner, she peeked her head around the stone. Both Doris and the stranger stepped through the entrance to the tower, and Naya crept forwards until she crouched just outside, where she could spy on their conversation.

"This is a risk, quite a risk for me," Doris whispered. Naya was pleased, for his voice never betrayed uncertainty. "You understand?"

"And you think I risked nothing by abandoning my brothers? War invites risk, and every venture might result in small failures—which we will ignore so long as the outcome is favorable. Our agreement will deliver children to the witches, while you will become Afterlife's hero. When we conquer Stomatus, Jaffa will let your city manage its affairs. The time for second thoughts has passed. It's time we act."

"Of course you're right, Dugal," said Doris, his voice regaining its familiar confidence. "My people deserve a future that resembles our storied history. The alternate sacrifices are even worse to contemplate."

"Then lower your defense. Expose Afterlife to our forces, and this sordid business will be over in mere hours."

Naya almost rushed in to stop Doris from enacting whatever he'd planned, but she held herself in check. She was outnumbered, and Doris could use the amulet to disable their defenses as soon as he caught sight of her. No, better to alert Afterlife's guards from the watchtower. At least her people wouldn't be caught unaware by the assault Doris had arranged with this stranger, Dugal.

The watchtower sat three stories below the spire, but Naya didn't dare risk taking the stairs. Thinking back to her childhood days, when she'd scurried over rooftops and archways with other children in dangerous games of tag, she planned a route to keep her off the street. But as she turned to leave, her foot kicked a pebble, which careened into the tower's outer wall, sending up an echo through the hollow interior where Doris and Dugal stood. A moment later, Doris appeared in the doorway, sharp eyes snapping to Naya. For the briefest moment, neither spoke a word, but soon Dugal barreled through the door behind Doris, shouting, "After her! Don't let her get away."

Naya turned on her heel, pushed off the top step, and leaped recklessly down the stairs four steps at a time. Doris fell behind her, grasping at her collar before she hooked her arm around a drainage pipe and used it to swing herself into the alleyway where she'd been hiding moments ago. Doris cruised by, cursing as he tripped and giving Naya the precious seconds she needed to climb a ladder to the squat building's rooftop.

From the roof, she spotted the watchtower a few buildings over, a rounded stone structure poking up amidst the surrounding buildings. Running almost more swiftly than her legs could handle, she took a flying leap off the roof, landing on the next building. She rolled to her feet before dropping to a lower structure. Like a wild animal, she scrambled up walls, a potent mix of desperation and adrenaline giving her the superhuman strength she needed to reach the watchtower without touching the ground. Three near-falls later, she clambered into the tower through a window above her head.

By the time she plunged into the tower's dark interior, she lacked the strength to climb the last steps to the guardroom. Breath tore from her lungs, and a debilitating tightness constricted her chest as she tried to draw in more air. Half crawling, half stumbling, she arrived at the guardroom, where the warning bell lay in arm's reach. She sank to her knees on the cold stone floor, allowing herself two seconds of rest before raising her head to locate the loudspeaker.

Before her stood Doris, out of breath but doing his best to hide it. He smiled at her, and Naya let out an involuntary moan. Doris grinned.

"Well, well. Thought we'd raise the alarm, did we?"

"Why…" Naya sighed, too tired to speak.

"Why what? Why did I ally Afterlife with Dugal and Jaffa? Why have I lowered our defenses? Why, perhaps, have I removed you from your seat of power?"

"You've doomed us all." Doris' face straightened, and any look of haughtiness or superiority vanished.

He said, "I'm no villain, Naya. I've saved Afterlife. I've preserved Afterlife. Your argument against neutrality was brave and correct, for the world's turmoil will cross our borders. However, we must take every step to preserve our independence. No cost is too great to guard our future."

"You're surrendering our children," Naya said, forcing herself to her feet as her chest loosened. "The witches will turn them into gremmels!"

"Yes, and our sacrifice will reverberate for generations. Only a concession of this magnitude will safeguard our freedom."

"You must be mad if you believe anyone will be happy after the witches tear their crying children from their arms? Will Dugal even keep his word? What if Jaffa conquers Afterlife itself?"

"The details are bound in blood," Doris said, waving his hand dismissively. "We will be left in peace."

"With you as Afterlife's ruler, of course."

"Of course. I will have saved the city."

"You're an intelligent man, Doris, but this craven wish for power has warped you. You're not thinking clearly. Three powers vie for authority in our world: the Perianth Empire, Jaffa's witches, and the evil in the north. Afterlife must stand with one of these powers to survive. I've spent hundreds of hours communing with the Departed, seeing what they see, so trust me when I say the Perianth Empire is the least of the three evils. We cannot continue as we have been."

"Jaffa will protect Afterlife once she conquers the Perianth Empire. By joining the Empire as you suggest, we would have already lost."

Naya saw no point in arguing further, for the damage was already done. Her only priority became reaching the alarm before the attack commenced.

"Well, you've decided for me," she said, taking a shaky step forward. "I tried to beat you at your own game, but you won." Another step. "If this is our path, then I must do my part." One more step. Now Naya stood within arm's reach of Doris.

"Finally, you show maturity. It's too late for you, but at least—"

Naya fluttered her eyes and fell forwards as if fainting. Reflexively, Doris reached out to catch her, but Naya spun as she fell, raising her elbow and letting her momentum carry it into Doris' pale temple. Doris stumbled but didn't fall, so Naya regained her balance, formed her left hand into a fist, and punched Doris in the nose. She felt bone crunch beneath her fingers, and Doris fell to his knees, blood pouring from his nostrils.

"You," Naya said, kicking him in the groin, "are dead wrong." She aimed one more kick at his temple, and he fell still. "And you may have doomed us all."

Stepping over Doris' inert body, Naya reached down to reclaim her amulet from his pocket, securing it around her wrist. Next, she limped to the loudspeaker, which amplified her voice through a series of clever echo chambers. Drawing in a deep breath, Naya yelled, "Priority one! This is not a drill. Repeat: this is a PRIORITY ONE ALERT! All guards prepare for immediate assault. The enemy is underground and will attack from outside the walls. Take your positions and remember your training. Defend your city. Defend Afterlife!"

Naya's heart beat from her chest as the adrenaline thrashing her body took its toll. She leaned over, resting her elbows on the console. The city stretched out ahead, beautiful and white. Afterlife was home, and she loved it almost as much as her memories of her long-dead parents.

Down on the streets, she was pleased to see guards sprinting to their positions along the city's outer ring. Other citizens barred their doors and closed their blinds to protect their families. "Good," Naya said. "I can only hope the witches take no children today."

Then a crack snapped the air, followed by a dull boom. Far away, the ground broke open, solid earth flying hundreds of feet into the air. From her position, Naya could just make out the ant-like gremmels pouring from the holes and rushing the walls. Intricate tree-like siege contraptions followed along with a tangle of vines, which crawled towards the city, giving the gremmels easy access into Afterlife. The assault had begun.

Chapter Nineteen

"I've never been this relaxed," Cayden said, spreading his arms so wide they touched both sides of the cave walls.

"You're happy," Leyna said, squeezing him with a quick hug. They stood just inside the Blood Caves' entrance after two blissful weeks in the underground paradise. Neither Cayden nor Leyna wanted to leave, so content had they been sitting under the artificial sun and exploring the bond they shared. Without the constant threat of Lysander's resurgence, their connection deepened to a level Cayden hadn't imagined possible; they'd grown as close to merging into a single person as two individuals could. Leyna's thoughts floated into Cayden's mind as if they were his own, though they were still separate. *Hers have a unique flavor,* he decided. *Like golden caramel. I wonder what mine tastes like to her?*

"Like rotten fruit," Leyna said in answer to his unspoken question, and they laughed. The more their bond solidified, the less real everything else seemed until the outside world had become a distant point to which they'd someday return, a land of desperate worry far apart from their time together.

But Harken's sacrifice loomed above them like a dark cloud, a constant reminder of the expectations placed upon them by the dead man—and so many others. Cayden admitted the only way to repay his debt was to rejoin the world and direct his power towards stopping Sevron's evil. The unseen malice twisted minds across the Perianth Empire and beyond, spreading war and inviting untold death. With a heavy heart, Cayden trudged from the cave and into the blinding sun.

An unexpected rush of energy coursed through Cayden's body, the force of it bringing him to his knees. The Blood Caves' walls blocked Stomatus' power, but the open air carried the great tree's potent energy into Cayden's quaking limbs. His Ethereal Hand raced around him, out of his control for a minute before he steeled his mind, willing his Hand back to his body. *I'm stronger than ever,* he decided, wondering if it was just an illusion after the weeks in the cave or if Lysander's absence reinforced his Hand. *Well, I had to exert constant mental energy to prevent him from taking over, so maybe I'm tougher now that he's gone.*

"Cayden, look," Leyna said, cutting through Cayden's thoughts. He knew where to turn his head without her pointing, sensing what she had spotted through their shared connection. Far overhead, several Perchidian airships raced north, and for a moment, Cayden wondered about their destination. Then he remembered.

"Afterlife," he said. "I told the witches about the children in Afterlife." The ships raced with the wind, moving faster than the clouds, their massive, ringed structures tearing through the air more quickly than Cayden had known possible. They'd soon be overhead, and Cayden cast out his Ethereal Hand, reaching for one of the retrieval pods near the bottom of the tree ring. To his surprise, the distance posed no challenge, and he formed an affinite bond with the pod's control panel, activating its automatic launch protocol.

The pod shot down from the ship, propelled by a coiled spring. It crashed ten feet from where Cayden and Leyna stood, a tightening length of vine trailing up to the airship behind it. Cayden jumped over to the pod to pry its door open, and Leyna lowered herself into the padded interior. He swung himself in behind her, slamming the door shut. The pod could only be reeled in from the ship itself, so Cayden once again reached up with his Ethereal Hand to the control panel, this time activating the return mechanism—a system of gears powered by a wind turbine that captured energy from the tree's movement.

Cayden's insides dropped as the pod swung into the air, ascending one thousand feet to the airship over a minute. The capsule swung from the dangling cable like a fish on a hook, and they bumped around its padded interior. Finally, the pod clicked into the airship's docking bay, and Cayden kicked the door open, only to find himself at the wrong end of a dozen glinting spearheads.

"Hey," Cayden said, falling onto his rear and holding his palms up to show he was unarmed. Heavy footsteps approached behind the Perchidians, and they parted, revealing a familiar face Cayden was relieved to see. Balint stalked forward, a frown upon his face, which soon turned into a smile and a laugh.

"Cayden, my boy! I didn't expect to see you again after you entered the Blood Caves, but here you are. You escaped?"

"Escaped? Not quite. It'll take a while to explain," Cayden said, struggling to his feet. Leyna was a bit bruised but was otherwise unscathed from their rapid ascent, and she soon stood beside him. "I take it you are off to help Afterlife?"

"Do you read minds now, too? Just hours ago, we received word from a scout that the Jaffa and her witches besiege the city."

"How many airships did Jericho send? Will they be enough to lift Afterlife and carry it to Stomatus?"

"We'd better talk," Balint said, puzzled.

Cayden agreed. "The sooner, the better."

***

Cayden would have preferred to meet in the open air instead of Balint's tight cabin, but the airship traveled fast enough for the wind to knock over anyone who left the ship's interior. Balint sat on his bed, a shelf of wood extruded from the wall that reminded Cayden of the bunks he'd slept in beside Tonius and Robinson in Stomatus' great tree. Cayden leaned against the doorframe while Leyna sat comfortably in the room's single chair, a woven nest of pliable branches rising from the floor. Cayden forced himself to focus despite the constant roar of the wind, which penetrated the tree ring's thick hull.

"How does the airship move this fast, anyway?" Cayden asked. Leyna sensed uncertainty emanating from Balint, and Cayden hoped to put the large man at ease with a familiar conversation. Leyna smiled, aware of Cayden's effort.

"What do you mean?" Balint asked, expecting Cayden to explain how he'd boarded an airship traveling at great speed from such a distance.

"Well, the ship is a massive tree bent in a circle. I know it stays aloft from helium produced in various pockets, but how does it move? I don't see any engines or propellors."

"Ah, that would confuse an outsider," Balint said. Leyna shot Cayden a look, for Balint had already relaxed. A childlike question made Cayden appear more human in Balint's eyes. "Valves dot the surface of the tree, like those in your heart that pump blood." *You'd be surprised to see my heart*, Cayden thought, recalling his modifications to his most vital organ. "One of these valves cannot pump much air, but together, they create a fierce wind that propels the ship in any direction we choose. It's how we steer, too. We adjust the flow from the valves, turning the ship how we please."

"That's amazing! The sun powers the valves?"

"The sun gives us much energy, but the ship also needs to refuel on a hyper-rich nutrient field every so often. Perchidians tend these fields, and the airships take root for two weeks, refilling their depleted energy reserves."

"Then your ships must be capable of incredible lifting power."

"Ah, so we return to the central subject. You were asking how many airships it would take to lift Afterlife." Balint had lowered his guard, and Cayden was free to proceed with his plan. *On second thought,* he told Leyna, *why don't you explain?*

"Afterlife is a valuable target in the war," Leyna said, smoothly cutting into the conversation. "The Empire, the witches, or Sevron's forces would capture it as the conflict consumes every inch of our world. Naya, Afterlife's leader, is stubborn. Her people are more set in their ways than even your people, Balint, so they would not willingly alter their isolationist policy and reunite with Stomatus. Only an existential threat would provoke them into action…"

"You told Jaffa about Afterlife," Balint guessed.

"Cayden did, yes. Afterlife's large child population is a glittering lure. With proper timing, the Perchidians will save Afterlife from the witches by returning the city to Stomatus' Dumrolls."

"That's quite a risk. What of the timing? We may already be too late."

"There's risk in everything we do from this point forward," answered Cayden. "How far are we from Afterlife now?"

"We are close, very close. We will reach them within the hour, though we did not plan on hoisting an entire city. Our ships are strong, but I won't guess how many we need for such a monumental task. Besides, anchoring to Afterlife's moorings will leave our fleet vulnerable to witch attack."

"Leyna and I will protect you," Cayden said. "Commit your ground troops to repel the witch attacks while your ships lower their tethers. If Afterlife falls, the witches may have enough troops to overwhelm Stomatus, and we cannot let that happen. For centuries, the Perchidians have acted as our world's peacekeepers. This is your ultimate test, the largest contribution to peace you will make in your people's proud history."

Balint sat for a time, staring down at his feet. "You've grown, Cayden," he said, and Cayden held his tongue. "Very well. I'll discuss the matter with Jericho. He is our leader, and the final decision rests with him. Wait here, and I will return with an answer." Once he'd decided, Balint moved quickly, exiting his quarters and disappearing down the corridor.

"You're troubled," Cayden said to Leyna.

"Of course. We've set in motion an ambitious plan with a dozen or more moving parts, any one of which might fail and ruin everything. I worry we're not doing the right thing."

"I understand, of course, but I don't see another path. Afterlife and Stomatus must unite if we hope to rid the world of Sevron's influence."

"And what of the witches? They're not likely to join the Empire."

"No. I'm not sure what we'll do about them. Jaffa has nothing in her heart besides hatred and a desire for vengeance. Like Mr. Reynolds always said, you have to take things one step at a time. Hopefully, something will come up before Sevron's army of dead souls is strong enough to destroy us."

Leyna nodded, but she closed her eyes and withdrew her thoughts. Cayden lay on the ground, allowing his mind to relax into a short sleep. As he drifted off, he examined his body, so different from the one he'd possessed a year ago. Most of his frame was muscle and bone, with a more efficient heart to carry blood to his extremities and strengthened lungs. Little remained of his digestive system, for he absorbed all the energy he needed from the tree in Stomatus. Soon, sleep took over, and he fell into a troubled world of turbulent nightmares.

"Wake up!" Balint shouted, and Cayden and Leyna jumped to their feet, hearts beating. "We have reached Afterlife, and Jericho has agreed with your plan. You should join the rest of the troops at the landing bay."

Shaking the sleep from their heads, Cayden and Leyna followed Balint, using the airship slides to make their way down to the bottom of the tree ring. Over fifty Perchidian soldiers in full armor stood on the central platform, ready to be lowered into battle.

"After we drop you by the outer wall, we'll reposition over the nearest of Afterlife's anchors. Please do everything you can to keep the witch projectiles from hitting our ships. We can't afford to lose a single airship if this plan is to succeed."

Cayden nodded. He stood behind the soldiers, feeling as small as the day he met Tonius and Robinson. Then a boy among teenagers, now a teenager among men. *I could increase my height in the same way I've changed my internal structure,* he thought, but the idea repelled him. Altering his appearance made him uneasy. Strengthening muscles was one thing, but modifying his face or lengthening his legs was another matter entirely.

The platform swayed as it lowered from the bottom of the tree ring on cables, and Cayden's heart sank when the field surrounding Afterlife came into view. Hundreds of witches, more than he'd ever seen at once, commanded an army of writhing vines and trees grown into catapults capable of sending massive bundles of tangled branches sailing over the walls of Afterlife, where they latched onto the buildings and crushed stones into a fine rubble.

Cayden spotted eleven other airships hovering above Afterlife, spreading out in a circle around the city as they dropped soldiers onto the battlefield. After depositing the Perchidian warriors, the ships maneuvered over the hooks surrounding Afterlife's ring wall.

With a thud, the platform upon which Cayden stood hit the ground, cables snapping away from Balint's airship as it sailed towards the nearest crystal hook. Even the most battle-hardened Perchidian soldiers quailed in the face of thousands of gremmels backed by an impenetrable line of witch embattlements. Cayden turned towards Afterlife itself, where many gremmels were already streaming up the sides of the vine-covered walls like spiders, flipping into the city and scrambling towards the tower of the Departed.

"Leyna, we must stop those gremmels from reaching the central tower. I don't know their plan, but I'm certain it's not good."

"You're right. We'll let the Perchidians defend their airships. If Jaffa destroys Afterlife from within, there'll be no point in flying the ruined city back to the Dumrolls."

"Soldiers!" Cayden yelled to the Perchidian regiment surrounding him. "Form a perimeter around Balint's airship and protect it with your lives. We need to buy your airships a few minutes." The soldiers looked at Cayden but didn't move, so he said, "Don't fight for Afterlife, and don't fight for me. Fight to protect Balint, who has served your people with honor for decades. Our goal isn't to defeat Jaffa's forces, only to defend your ships."

Without another word, Cayden and Leyna raced towards Afterlife's outer wall, hoping the soldiers would find the courage to fight. *It's not courage they lack,* Leyna thought to him. *They are uncomfortable with a boy issuing orders.* Cayden had to agree, though he was frustrated that he lacked time to share knowledge of their impending doom. *If they shared my vision,* he thought, *they would listen.*

Nearby, gremmels continued to scale Afterlife's walls, and though Cayden couldn't scramble up vines, he could form an affinite bond with organic material. He used his Ethereal Hand to shape one of the thick vines into a rough set of stairs that he and Leyna used to climb the wall. Amidst the chaos, something strange struck Cayden as he surveyed the battle: two forces charged Afterlife's guards. The gremmels were the obvious enemy, but a group of men dressed in black with masked faces and glittering swords also attacked.

"Afterlife's citizens are helping Jaffa's forces," Leyna said. "Those masked fighters are from Afterlife, yet they are fighting against their own people."

"I'd better lend the guards a hand," said Cayden, jumping from the wall and throwing himself headfirst between two groups of fighting men. Forming an affinite bond with the stone road, he tossed chunks of chipped rock at the masked men. The flurry of hail knocked down at least a dozen fighters, giving Afterlife's guards time to secure the traitors' limbs with rope.

Watch your left, Leyna thought, and Cayden ducked under three gremmels who had leaped at him, their bony, clawed fingers ready to rip into his flesh. The gremmels landed on all fours, spinning around to launch themselves once more, but Cayden guided several loose shards of stone, using the rock to pin the creatures to the ground by their ragged clothing.

"We don't have time for this," he said, eying Afterlife's tower in the distance. "I can't fight every group of soldiers."

"Why don't we use that?" Leyna asked, pointing to a tangle of vines spreading from a nearby building. In her mind, she projected an image of him catapulting himself from the witches' lair a month ago. His previous effort nearly killed him, but renewed energy gave him the confidence to try again.

"Are you coming for the ride?" he asked as he formed an affinite bond with the vines, bending them into a stiff yet flexible column.

"Promise to catch me when we fall. I'm no Airwalker, remember."

He nodded, using his Ethereal Hand to flex the vines back, almost to their breaking point. He and Leyna sat atop the end, which Cayden had fashioned into a cup. *Hold on to me,* he thought, and Leyna wrapped her arms around his waist. When he released his grip on the vines, they snapped up, hurtling Cayden and Leyna like human missiles high into the air. At the apex of their flight, Cayden saw the entire city, and he used his Ethereal Hand to shape the surrounding air, guiding them as they fell towards the base of the tower. Just before they reached the ground, Cayden buffeted them with a gust of wind strong enough to slow their descent for a smooth landing. He'd wanted to land on his feet, but he instead tumbled with Leyna in an awkward pile.

"Incredible," said a familiar voice, and Cayden noticed Naya approaching from the east. She held a gremmel's limp arm in her fist, but she dropped it to pull Leyna to her feet and into a hug. Cayden stood, dizzy from the effort, and Naya shook his hand.

"Much happened since we left?" Leyna asked.

"A bit," Naya answered, matching her carefree tone.

"So, uh, we should probably…" Cayden said.

"Right," Naya said. "I fought my way up to the tower so I could re-enable our defense. With all the Ethereal Hands waving around everywhere, I couldn't use my pendant from outside the tower, and the Departed can't access the continuity shield without the consent of Afterlife's Ruler. Which I suppose is me, again."

"What do you mean, 'again'?" Leyna asked.

"Trouble with Doris. I'm sure you remember him. Nothing I couldn't handle, though."

"Go inside and talk to the Departed. Get them to raise the shield."

"Right. It won't do much good unless we can move Afterlife, though. I think Jaffa and Dugal have a pretty good idea of where we are. Can you protect the airships while I work on the shield?"

"Of course," Leyna said. "Cayden will protect the airships, and I'll gather guards to defend the tower while you work." Then, mentally, she said, *Don't worry, Cayden, I'll be careful.*

Who said I was worried? Cayden asked, grinning.

"Alright," Naya said, turning to the tower. "Good luck, you two."

Leyna ran towards a quieter section of Afterlife, where she might find unoccupied guards, while Cayden sprinted toward the witch attack. At the city's edge, Balint's airship struggled to maintain altitude above a swelling mass of gremmels and witches as more and more vines latched onto the tree ring, dragging it inexorably to the ground. Knowing the loss of a single airship would signal defeat, Cayden ran faster and faster, using his inhumanly firm muscles to propel himself past groups of fighting guards and gremmels, under arches of white crystal, near the occasional witch attacker, and to the city wall.

Down below, ten witches controlled a growing mass of vines, whipping more up to Balint's airship with every passing second. A small group of Perchidian fighters held off a ring of gremmels surrounded by the vine-controlling witches, so Cayden dove straight over the gremmels and into the midst of the witches. It took the women a couple of seconds to register his presence, enough time for him to disable three of them with a simple affinite bond to the dirt below their feet. Cayden pulled the witches underneath the ground, leaving only their heads above the hardened, rocky surface.

The seven remaining witches released their grips on the vines and spun towards Cayden, who had already crouched low to prepare for their attack. Instead of the flurry of vines he'd expected, the witches turned and ran away from Cayden and the airship. The gremmels, too, scrambled away from the fight.

Cayden stood, puzzled, until he saw it. A massive projectile glinted in the sun overhead, arcing high above Balint's airship. Almost half the size of the airship itself, this rock fortress glided improbably in the sky, casting a shadow across Cayden and much of the surrounding battlefield as it fell. For a second, Cayden's arrogance told him the witches and gremmels fled when faced with his menacing skill, but he now saw they ran from the blow that would end the Perchidian plan to lift Afterlife.

Cayden reached out to slow or at least alter the solid stone projectile with his Ethereal Hand, but it took only a moment to realize that the witches had constructed the weapon out of thousands of different compounds to resist affinite bonds. The projectile reached its zenith and plummeted, leaving fewer than fifteen seconds for Cayden to act. *Change the shape of the target,* Leyna thought, for she had been keeping tabs on Cayden from her position near Afterlife's tower.

It's so absurd it might work, Cayden thought, laughing to himself while he worked. Jericho's airship had attached itself to the crystal loop on Afterlife's outer wall with thick vines ending in a hook. With a hasty bond, Cayden pushed the hook from the loop, and as the airship rose, he grasped several of the witch vines in his Ethereal Hand, many of which still hung from the uppermost portion of the tree ring. He tied the ends of the vines to the solid crystal at Afterlife's base, causing the tree ring to lurch as it rose. The top of the ring, now anchored to

Afterlife, remained in place. The bottom part of the ring swung up, and Cayden grabbed hold of several vines hanging from the lower section of the airship. The Perchidian sailors shouted, and he just hoped they'd had time to grab onto something as their ship tilted around them. The ring leveled out, its once vertical loop now forming a massive circle horizontal to the ground.

In the last moment, before the witch's projectile struck, Cayden tightened three vines while loosening six more to shift the airship's position. Squinting, he watched the massive stone weapon sail through the center of Balint's airship, striking Afterlife's crystal bed. A frightening clap tore through the air when the stone hit and split down the middle. One half fell outside Afterlife's wall, while the other fell into the city, crushing a nearby grouping of small structures.

I did it, Cayden thought excitedly. A plume of dust rose from the ground, and by the time it cleared, Cayden had reattached the airship's hook to Afterlife's crystal loop while cutting the witches' vines he'd used to change the ship's position. The airship swung up into its natural, vertical orientation, and it pulled against Afterlife's weight with the other eleven Perchidian ships straining upwards around the city.

But Afterlife didn't budge. Cayden sensed that the soil beneath Afterlife's crystal bed was wet, creating a suction effect that gripped the city. *I can solve that problem,* Cayden thought, forming an affinite bond with the unwanted moisture. He focused on the liquid, allowing it to become part of his consciousness. He pulled the moisture down, deeper and deeper, giving the soil near the surface a similar consistency to the dryest desert dune.

It worked. Afterlife rose, just an inch, speeding up until Cayden could see clean through beneath the city. He grabbed onto a vine and swung up into the city, which now rose with the full force of twelve Perchidian airships propelling it into the sky. Many gremmels and witches remained in Afterlife, fighting alongside Doris' traitors, but no new attackers could now enter.

Tell Naya to order her guards to clear the city of the remaining forces, Cayden said to Leyna. *I'll find Balint or Jericho and help coordinate the Perchidian soldiers. Now that no new troops can enter the city, we'll win this fight.*

Chapter Twenty

Robinson's head sagged against his sunken chest as he phased in and out of hallucinations. Memories from his childhood in the Dumrolls overwhelmed him, and his dead parents beckoned him from beyond their graves. He toiled alongside them, scraping bark and pulling leaves from the branches of muddy trees, which would later be shipped off to the great tree for consumption. His father's sure arms moved in a tireless rhythm while his mother's gentle fingers sorted through leaves of various sizes. Robinson looked up at his father's round face and took comfort in his presence.

Then, his father stopped moving, bent his head down, and said, "Wake up." Robinson's mouth dropped open in surprise. His father never spoke. No one in the Dumrolls spoke. "Open your eyes," said a high-pitched voice out of his father's mouth. "Now!" shouted the voice.

Robinson's eyes fluttered open, and he stared at Dakota, who was chained across the room, his thin arms stretched over his head.

"Why are you shouting?" Robinson asked, looking around the chamber as he struggled to gain his bearings. While Astor's rock-fisted soldiers dragged the Alchemist to an unknown prison, Robinson, Tonius, Henrik, and Dakota remained together, chained in a small cell for two months. Every other day, a soldier brought just enough food and water to stave off death, though Robinson never complained about the short break from the endless grinding of shifting rock. Tonius suspected the noise originated with Astor's minions, whom he'd tasked with expanding the small prison into a dungeon.

On the day all fell silent, Robinson could hardly believe his ears. For a few blissful minutes, the absence of noise allowed him to listen to his breaths, the shuffling of Tonius' clothing moving over his thin body as he raised his head, and even the faint hint of other voices from nearby cells. Then the room lurched alongside a dozen booming explosions, which permeated the dense rock. Hours passed, and the room still shook with fury. Robinson imagined a massive battle was taking place in Stomatus. When the shaking subsided, silence descended, and a patter of many footsteps echoed down the corridor.

Priven appeared before them, and for a moment, Robinson's eyes widened. But the giant man dripped blood from a thousand cuts, and his right arm hung from his shoulder. Astor's men pushed Priven forward, and many injured Perianth soldiers followed.

"Astor must have taken control of the city," Tonius said. Then Astor himself stepped up to their cell, grinning for a moment before following the battered Perianth soldiers. Since then, they had seen no sign of Astor, Priven, or anyone other than the silent soldier who brought them food. A foul mood had descended upon them, and no one uttered a word—until today, when Dakota shouted.

"You have refused to speak for two months," Tonius said, for he had attempted to converse with Dakota many times.

"I was thinking," Dakota replied.

"For months?"

"It was a complex train of thought in which I attempted to follow events as they unfold in the world above so that we may take action."

"Your Ethereal Hand reaches so far?" Robinson asked.

"No, not at all. I have been using all the knowledge I gained before our imprisonment to predict events as they unfold aboveground."

"Impossible," Tonius said. "There are too many variables to predict the future. It's not possible."

"For a human. But I share my father's gifts, which inform me that we must act. My brother Lysander will have informed Cayden that he must cleanse Sevron's evil by seizing Stomatus' great tree and using its incredible power to forcibly unite the planet."

"You're suggesting Cayden will conquer Stomatus?"

"Exactly. An impossible task without help. Jaffa's siege is absolute, requiring a Perchidian airship to carry his forces past her army. Cayden will likely arrive at Stomatus within the next month with one or more Perchidian airships. There is a sixty percent chance they will arrive in Afterlife. In either scenario, I estimate a ninety percent chance that Jericho's airship will be among those to arrive. We must ensure that the dome opens to allow them entry upon their arrival."

"Even if you're right, the dome's controls lay out of reach," Henrik said.

"If we can access the controls, and if I were to offer the proper recognition patterns, can you program the dome can to open upon sensing Jericho's airship?"

"Yes…"

"Good. Then you will instruct Robinson on how to work the machinery. He will input your instructions in the control room, then return to his cell."

"Uh. What?" Robinson asked. "If you haven't noticed, we're chained. I can't form an affinite bond with this metal, and I can't escape."

Dakota's body convulsed, and for a moment, Robinson thought the boy was having a seizure. But then he coughed, and a golden ball, the size of a child's fist, flew out of Dakota's mouth and rolled across the floor, stopping at Robinson's feet.

"I believe this will enable your escape," Dakota said as blood dripped from his mouth onto his chest.

"You've been hiding gold in your throat for months?" Tonius asked.

"On the day of our capture, I removed a golden leaf from a soldier's uniform and swallowed it. I guessed we would need to perform a necessary action outside our prison before Cayden's inevitable return."

"Why didn't we use this to escape sooner?" Henrik asked, struggling to understand.

"And go where? With Astor's forces hunting us within Stomatus and Jaffa's witches surrounding the city, our re-capture was a near certainty. No, our place is here, where we can sway events from within the city."

"For Christ's sake," Henrik whispered fiercely, "We might have hidden in the Dumrolls. Anything is preferable to this."

"That would have been a needless risk. We know with certainty that Astor will not kill us until Cayden returns. Remaining here has guaranteed our survival."

"Your logic is flawless," Tonius said, though he shuddered at Dakota's attitude.

"Of course," Dakota said, either ignoring or failing to notice Tonius' tone. "Now, Robinson, you must free yourself. This gold will cut through the metal that binds your wrist and ankle cuffs to the chains. Henrik, please explain what he must do."

"Why me?" Robinson asked. "Henrik can go himself."

"You have been the least weakened by lack of sustenance, as your body had copious fat reserves upon which to feed."

"I see."

***

Robinson crept through Astor's dungeon, cursing under his breath. He had almost rejected Dakota's instructions, but if the boy's claim was true—if Cayden needed his help—then Robinson would go to any length to lend his aid. Even so, Robinson bristled at the thought of the soulless Dakota ordering him as if he were one of Henrik's machines.

"Damn that tiny cell," Robinson said, finding the simple motion of walking a challenge. His knees wobbled, and he hugged the rough wall for support. Months of confinement had whittled his body to the size of a healthy Tonius, though excess skin hung off his bones like a dry leather coat. At least their cell was one of the first Astor had built, sitting near the exit to the dungeon and limiting the distance he'd need to travel.

As Dakota had predicted, the halls stood abandoned. Most of Astor's soldiers awaited his orders in the streets of Stomatus. Behind Robinson stretched hundreds of cells hewn from stone, while ahead lay stairs leading to the surface. Since Astor's goons had shoved him into the dungeon, workers had refined the chute originating in Mogen's old hut, widening it into a serviceable staircase. Taking one step at a time, Robinson climbed, each push upwards a fight against gravity.

About halfway up, a rattle stopped his ascent, and he stopped behind a door hewn from the wall. Robinson readied Dakota's chunk of gold in his shaking hand, and after taking a steadying breath, he lurched around the corner and burst through the door. Instead of a guarded passage, the room was little more than a storage closet. The noise originated from overhead pipes, which carried pebbles into woven baskets. Robinson noticed the stones bore a resemblance to Astor's rock arm.

Clenching his teeth to steady his nerves, Robinson gathered energy to walk the rest of the way up to the Dumrolls. Then he stopped and stared. A dozen loaves of bread sat wrapped in white cloth, tempting him from one of the closet's shelves. Almost not believing the food was real, Robinson lifted one loaf, feeling its fresh, yielding texture beneath his callused fingertips. His mouth watered as he took a tiny bite. Compared to the moldy bits of scrap he'd been eating for two months, the bit of bread exploding across his tongue was a veritable cascade of flavor and sensation. He chewed before swallowing, for he knew his stomach had shrunken. Still, he felt strength flow back into his exhausted limbs, and the little jaunt Dakota had sent him on didn't seem so bad.

He reached the prison exit a minute later, poking his head through the cloth covering the doorway to see Mogen's rebuilt laboratory. Dim light filtered through cracks in the wood, just enough to highlight hundreds of clear bottles sitting along uneven shelves. He'd expected at least one guard, but the room was empty.

Outside, he crept across the Dumrolls with the confident ability of a native. Distant childhood memories bubbled up, especially when he neared the tree processing area where his parents had toiled till the Perianths snuffed out their brief lives. A lump rose in his throat, and tears washed thin lines down his encrusted cheeks.

He scolded himself, brushing the tears away. He had a mission and plenty of time to reminisce once he returned to Tonius and the others in Astor's dungeon.

Henrik had said the nearest elevator to the tunnels beneath Stomatus would be in a stone structure southeast of Mogen's hut. Robinson knew where to look, for there were precious few stone towers in the Dumrolls, and he soon saw the building's white peak sticking up amidst the rotting wooden hovels. Mud stained the tower's lower half a dull brown, just as its sullied all the unlucky souls who called the Dumrolls home. Robison noticed with dismay that soldiers had boarded the door, but upon closer inspection, he found an open area someone had clawed aside.

He squeezed through the space, something he'd never have been able to do before his stint in the dungeon. Inside, a section of the floor dropped away to uncover a narrow crawlway. Henrik hadn't described the elevator's precise location, only that its door would be marked by a golden surface. Robinson gingerly dropped into the hole, grunting from the pain in his stiff knees, and crawled. The space soon widened into a room holding a golden mirror surrounded by an intricate stone carving depicting hundreds of leaves attached to a curved vine.

He still held the bit of gold from Dakota's stomach, and he shaped it into a key, following the outlines of a drawing Henrik had scratched into the dirty floor of their cell. He ran his hand around the mirror's perimeter until he noticed something strange: his reflection wasn't moving with him. The version of himself he saw in the mirror was him from a year ago, fat and happy, rather than the skeleton he'd become during his captivity.

"What is this?" he asked, not expecting an answer. But the other Robinson in the mirror spoke.

"Hey, don't be rude," the reflection said. Robinson recognized his voice, though it sounded strange, originating from a place other than his throat.

"I'm not. I mean, who are you? Is this a trick?"

"If it is, it's a pretty neat trick. I think I'm you… at least, I'm you as you see yourself. Speaking of which, you've got to work on your self-image, man. I'm pretty overweight."

"Great. I'm hallucinating. I've been locked up for so long that I've gone mad."

"Don't be absurd."

"Quiet! I'm looking for a keyhole to help Cayden save the world. It's important."

"You ran your hand right over it earlier, but you were too foolish to notice."

Now that the reflection mentioned it, Robinson remembered one leaf wobble a bit as he'd passed his hand over it. Which leaf was it? He pushed and prodded until a leaf budged. With a bit of force, he pried the carved leaf from the decoration to uncover a small black hole. He inserted the key, and the golden mirror slid down into the floor, taking with it his reflection or hallucination.

Robinson stepped onto the elevator, which descended into the maze of tunnels below Stomatus, and he followed the path Henrik had outlined. Lights flickered to life, dimming as he passed to chase him with absolute darkness. Many corridors shone with clean, new metal, though he spotted two passages where dirt poured in through rusted holes in the walls.

When he came to a large, open room, he recognized the panel featuring a red button standing in the center of the floor. He searched the room until he located a console outlined in dashed yellow paint. The console lit up, and he input Henrik's code. The next step was more difficult. He had to describe Jericho's airship so that the pattern recognition sensors, as Dakota called them, could detect the Perchidian tree ring if it arrived at Stomatus. The process took half an hour, and Robinson wiped rivulets of sweat from his brow when he finished.

He retraced his steps back to the elevator, exiting through the space left by the golden mirror. When the mirror slid closed behind him, he looked again at his healthy reflection. He opened his mouth to speak to the figure, but he decided it was best to hurry back to Tonius and the others.

His walk back to Mogen's hut was as uneventful as the walk to the control room, and Robinson soon reached the inconspicuous structure. He stopped in his tracks, though, when he saw the guard. The teenager wore rags as a disguise, but he'd forgotten to paint his face or arms with mud, so he stood out from the other Dumrolls residents like a sore thumb. Robinson waited, kneeling in the dirt behind a short fence, but Astor's soldier showed no sign of moving. Robinson knew he couldn't fight the soldier, even if he had the strength. A missing soldier could arouse Astor's suspicions, ruining the entire plan.

"Think," Robinson said to himself. A distraction might draw the young soldier's attention, so Robinson crawled towards the nearest processing station. Two Dumrolls workers picked leaves from a tree, placing each leaf in a gelatin solution for preservation until the great tree could absorb their nutrients to generate its signature golden leaves. Robinson knew the workers would pay him no attention, just as he knew the gelatin had beneficial explosive properties.

The gooey substance, if left in the open air, would harden into blue stones capable of producing a powerful flame if struck. He lacked the time for careful preparation, so he hit two rocks together and ignited the volatile gel. The sides of the crate contained the resulting explosion, and the force of the blast shot upwards over two hundred feet. Robinson limped back to Mogen's hut, finding that the soldier had left his post to investigate the explosion. Robinson didn't waste any time. He scurried into the cabin and made his way as quickly as he dared back into the dungeon. He did pause at the storage closet to get another piece of bread before he re-entered his cell, sealing the gate behind him.

"Look what I got us," Robinson said, holding up the food.

Tonius reached out to take it, but Dakota said, "Attach your shackles. Now we must wait."

Chapter Twenty One

A jagged breach in the rear wall of Jericho's meeting hall left the room exposed to the corridor, where Cayden watched Perchidians scurry in a frantic rush to repair the airship. Cayden tried to bring his attention back to the conversation, but he focused only on the groaning of the ship as it struggled to maintain altitude. Afterlife's unfathomably massive weight hung below as every ounce of power in Balint's wounded ship fought gravity.

The energy Cayden required to power his Ethereal Hand during the battle had taken a heavy toll. The witches hadn't damaged his body, but his mind had grown so fatigued and sluggish that everything around him had blurred. *It would be so much easier to fall asleep,* he thought wistfully.

You'll soon have some time to rest, Leyna thought back. Gritting his teeth, he forced his eyes to focus on the gray stone table. He'd first sat in this meeting hall about four months ago, after Jericho had rescued him from the first witch attack on Stomatus—though far fewer Perchidians crowded the room now. Gone, of course, was Dugal. Also missing were most of the Perchidian Flying Council members, leaving Jericho, Balint, Naya, Cayden, Leyna, and two other airship captains to plan their next move.

Leyna gave Cayden a mental nudge, helping him direct his attention back to the conversation. As he stared at the table and allowed his mind to recover, he watched and listened through Leyna's eyes and ears.

"If you considered the attack at Afterlife bad," Jericho was saying, "Jaffa's forces surrounding Stomatus are far more organized and fortified. We'll never break through the blockade, especially while we can't maneuver. We're already struggling to fly." His broad shoulders stooped, and his thick arms hung by his sides like idle oars on a boat. Cayden had never seen the Perchidian leader appear so defeated.

"Best to just set Afterlife down in a remote area where it'll be safe," Balint said. He'd planted his fists on the table, but his arms dripped blood from a patchwork of angry marks left by gremmel claws. A rough cloth stemmed the worst of the bleeding, but the makeshift bandage did nothing to soothe the underlying wounds. *Gremmel nails dig deep*, Cayden thought.

"No," Naya said, her voice quivering from the ceaseless flow of adrenaline that refused to subside. "There's no point in running. If you don't reunite Afterlife with Stomatus, you may as well drop us from the sky and leave us to our deaths."

"What's your suggestion?" Jericho asked. "How do we circumvent Jaffa's forces?"

"We rise as high as we can manage, then drop straight down upon Stomatus," Balint said. "The witches' weapons won't be able to reach us until the final moments of our descent."

"Need I remind you that an impenetrable dome protects Stomatus?" Jericho asked. "Are we to count on them opening it for us? Our descent will be final since ascending will deplete all our remaining energy reserves. Once we've hit the ground, we won't fly again."

"When Cayden and I left Stomatus, we asked two of our friends to stay behind and help return the city to order," Leyna said. "You've met them before—Tonius and Robinson. There is also a man named Henrik and a boy called Dakota, whom we count as allies in this fight. Among the four of them, I'm certain one will open the dome. If you're still worried, send Cayden and me down in one of the landing pods before you begin your plunge, and we'll get in touch."

"We have little choice," said Jericho, bitterness edging into his voice. "And I believe our lack of choice isn't by chance." He turned his stern brow towards Cayden, who still struggled to keep his mind on the conversation. "Cayden has plotted this path since first we spoke. He told the witches of Afterlife's location, ensuring we would be called to help and knowing our obligation. You may hold the Airwalker inside you, but I won't lead my people by the deceitful whim of a child."

"Cayden hasn't hidden his wish to unite the Perianth Empire and restore peace," Leyna retorted. "I don't see how his plan conflicts with your duty as peacekeepers. Look around you. The world is at war. Keep the peace. Do your duty." Leyna glared at Jericho intensely, but Cayden noticed something else in her stare, something he grasped through their connection. She was pushing at him. All her thoughts bombarded Jericho, willing him to see the situation as she saw it. A frown creased Jericho's sturdy cheeks before his mouth relaxed into a steady line. *"You can change the minds of those around you by assigning new meaning to that which those minds already hold important,"* Cayden recalled Harken saying—and Leyna was now turning Jericho's pride in their favor. His deep-seated desire to appear as a noble peacekeeper helped Leyna push his thoughts into alignment with hers.

"Very well," Jericho said, eyes widening in slight surprise at the words coming from his mouth. Balint turned towards him but held his tongue.

"It will be as you say," Jericho continued. "Make yourselves ready, as we have scant hours until we hang over Stomatus like a spider too heavy for its web. When we fall, Stomatus had better open its arms to accept Afterlife." He and the other captains strode from the room. Cayden sighed and allowed Leyna to lead him to a secluded cabin near the inner part of the tree ring, far from the bustle of activity.

Cayden sat cross-legged on the floor, leaning his head against the coarse wall to let his mind settle into an all-encompassing state of worry. Any confidence he'd had in their plan evaporated with each passing moment. Though he struggled to pinpoint the reason, a danger just out of sight taunted him, threatening to topple their efforts.

Let's not second guess ourselves, Leyna scolded, and Cayden refocused on her. Leyna's hair had become a wild tangle in the fight, but he decided he preferred it that way since it was how she'd worn it at their first meeting in the dead forest more than a year ago.

"Then we'll discuss how to open the dome covering Stomatus," Cayden said. "Its material resembles the tree's amber sap, which resists all interference from my Ethereal Hand."

"We'd better hope Tonius and Robinson succeeded."

"I guess, but it's been so long since we left. I'm worried about them."

Leyna closed her eyes for a moment, then said, "When you took Lysander's journal, you used a liquid to burn through the amber. With the proper formula, we might fashion a similar method."

"The formula is lost to time, or otherwise locked within the Alchemist's broken memories… or…"

"You can't mean—"

"Yes, I do." Cayden unfolded his satchel and removed Lysander's journal. He'd not communicated with Lysander since the day Harken sacrificed himself to extract the man from Cayden's mind, and reconnecting his mind with Lysander's consciousness turned Cayden's stomach. *But who else is there to ask?*

After Harken's extraction, Lysander's journal had burned red hot for a day before it flickered and cooled. Lysander's pure side lived within the journal's pages, preserving the man who had sacrificed his life to offer peace to his brother's Perianth Empire. But Sevron's evil tainted the version of Lysander who once dwelled within Cayden's golden eye. Harken's reunification of Lysander's dueling personalities might have resulted in either gaining dominance—though Cayden didn't dare guess who won. He didn't want to risk communicating with Lysander again, so he'd wrapped the book in his satchel and slung it over his shoulder to be dealt with another time.

Now is that time. Cayden placed his hand on the book's cover—which was still warmer than his fingertips—and guided his consciousness into contact with the material. Lysander grasped him, creating a connection with his mind. Cayden nearly jerked his hand back, but Lysander didn't exert any pressure. The man remained inside the book and made no blatant attempt to retake his position in Cayden's mind.

Cayden, where are we? spoke Lysander's familiar voice. This time, to Cayden's relief, the voice originated externally, sounding very different from the evil whispers to which he'd grown accustomed.

We're on a Perchidian airship, Cayden said, careful to keep his mind wrapped in his Ethereal Hand. *Afterlife is in tow, and we're returning to Stomatus.*

I see.

There's a dome covering the city, though. We need to get inside, and I have no one else to ask. Will you help? The longer Cayden maintained the connection, the more nervous he grew.

Cayden, you can relax. I've quelled the corrupted part of my personality. You don't have to worry about me leaping into your mind. I am myself again.

I can never relax around you, Cayden said, reflexively strengthening his mental barrier further. Even the remote possibility of Lysander taking root inside him again brought a rush of panic.

I understand, and… I'm so, so sorry. An overwhelming sense of remorse emanated from the journal, but Cayden pushed it back, keeping it far from his mind. Lysander had proven himself a more than capable liar, and Cayden promised himself not to fall into any traps.

You can repay me in part by helping me now.

I wish I had an answer worthy of your question, but Stomatus' dome is impenetrable. Its designers, including myself, built the dome to withstand space travel at speeds approaching that of light. Such strength is not readily undone.

What of my Ethereal Hand? No material is impervious to affinite bonds, not unless the substance itself is conscious. Perhaps I can communicate through the dome and speak with my friends?

Release your physical form, and your consciousness might pass through the dome. This route would mean a permanent separation from your flesh, something only my father Sevron has achieved.

You're not the first man to suggest I walk this path, Cayden said, straightening. The Alchemist's words still echoed in his thoughts.

It's not like I'm ordering you to do anything, Cayden. You asked me how to breach the dome, and this is my answer.

You manipulated me for months. What's to say this isn't another trick?

Fair enough. I understand why you cannot trust me. Lysander fell silent, and Cayden wondered whether he should continue the conversation. The notion of severing his consciousness from his body repulsed him on a primal level, but Lysander's knowledge tempted Cayden into asking one further question.

Why can I exist without form while no one else can? Cayden asked.

As I said, my father can also exist in this manner.

You're his child, though. Shouldn't you share his abilities?

Sevron created his children, myself included, with an Earth woman, so while our bodies hold a measure of his substance, the world of solid matter tethers us to our physical forms. I created you from the tree of Stomatus, the purest vessel of my father's corruption. You arose from a grain of my father's consciousness—directed by my Ethereal Hand—and though your consciousness resides within your current form, no rule locks you within any prison of flesh. Like my father, your consciousness is inhuman and powerful beyond my reckoning.

Cayden's eyes flew wide, and he blinked twice before locating Leyna, who sat on the floor. Panic gripped him, an out-of-body sensation washing across his limbs. He looked down at his hands as he'd done three and a half months ago when facing Lysander's father, Sevron. *This isn't me,* he thought, compressing his fingers into a tight fist. *This flesh is not me.*

"Are you okay?" Leyna asked.

"No," Cayden said, trying to calm his breathing. "No, I am

definitely not okay."

"Let go of your fear," she said, placing her cool hand on his neck. "Tell me what Lysander said since your panic clouds my ability to live your memories."

"Lysander said…" Cayden said, unable to form the words. *I feel like any other human,* he thought before asking, *but how do I even know how other humans feel?* When he moved his hand to wipe the sweat from his brow, his arm seemed distant, an extension of someone else's body in which he lived as an unwelcome guest. *I'm just as much a foreigner in my brain as Lysander.* Cayden's breathing sped up, out of his control, his chest tightening as the world closed around him, and he blacked out.

Awareness remained, and he sensed Leyna tugging at him, returning him from the abyss. He allowed himself to float to the surface of consciousness with her.

"You had a panic attack," Leyna said, helping Cayden rest his back against the wall. He dared a glance at his hand, relieved to find the panic subsiding, and his breathing slowed.

"Lysander told me I am not human."

"We've been over this, Cayden. You are your own person, just like anyone else."

"No, not like anyone else," he said, forcing himself to relax so she could access the memory of Lysander's words.

"I warned you not to talk to him," Leyna said. "His torture didn't teach you any lesson?"

"He didn't intend to upset me. Quite the opposite. All his words were designed to please me, to make a small payment against his past atrocities." Leyna raised an eyebrow. "Yes, yes, you suspect another trap… but I do trust him, despite everything. When another consciousness lives within your head, you learn how it operates. The icy edge in Lysander's voice that once sent chills down my spine is missing. His wicked self wouldn't have been able to speak with such genuine kindness even if he wanted."

"You're not suggesting we follow his advice, are you? You won't detach your consciousness from your body."

"Of course not," Cayden said, gulping. "I can't imagine anything forcing such a drastic step. We'll just have to hope the dome over Stomatus opens for us and that Tonius and Robinson were successful."

Cayden stood and pressed his face to the window, finding reassurance in the solid wood under his feet. Angling his head, he spied Afterlife below the airship, and the sheer improbability of what they'd already accomplished brought a smile to his face.

Chapter Twenty Two

Cayden looked through the porthole beneath his feet and squinted. Far, far below, a black circle showed Stomatus' position, the surrounding land a wreck of upturned earth and splintered trees. His insides dropped as their pod detached from the bottom of the airship and passed Afterlife, which hung underneath twelve Perchidian tree rings.

Across from him, Leyna sat strapped in, her body jerking this way and that as gusts of wind buffeted the landing pod. The pod was equipped with a special parachute, a massive sheet of fine, leafy material that would deploy during the last five seconds of their flight, cutting their momentum before the pod hit the dome while not allowing the witches enough time to intercept them. At least, that was the idea. It'd still be a rough landing, so Cayden prepared to extend his Ethereal Hand around the pod to further cushion their descent.

Within the blink of an eye, the dome covering Stomatus grew to fill Cayden's entire field of vision. Focused on their impending landing, he didn't notice the wooden projectile hurtling towards them until Leyna's alarm penetrated his consciousness. It was too late for him to act, so he braced for impact.

At the last moment, another golden projectile intercepted the wooden one, splintering it into thousands of pieces, which rained upon their pod. The parachute deployed, and Cayden expanded his Ethereal Hand, forming an affinite bond with the air to further slow their descent. Two seconds later, they hit the impenetrable dome with enough force to stun them both.

Leyna slammed her hand against the release button, and the pod split into four sections, releasing Cayden and Leyna from their restraints. Cayden rolled to his feet, but Leyna slid down the dome's curve away from him. Forming an affinite bond with the nearest section of the broken pod, Cayden swung it around Leyna, using it to halt her slide and then push her towards his position. He grasped her arm, helping her to her feet.

Far below, he heard the high-pitched screams of dozens of gremmels, and he turned his attention to the broken field surrounding the dome. A group of men, split into two columns, charged at the dome. Hundreds of gremmels ran between the two columns, speeding on their short legs towards Cayden. *Wait, those aren't gremmels,* Cayden realized. *They're actual children.*

"Mr. Reynolds," Cayden said, almost too stunned to trust his senses. Against all odds, Mr. Reynolds had followed through on his mission to gather children from the outlying training camps and guide them to the capital. *Is it a coincidence they're coming now?* Cayden wondered. *No, they must have seen the Perchidian ships overhead and figured now's their only chance.*

"You'll have to pull them atop the dome," Leyna said. "Jaffa's forces will slaughter them."

"Jericho's airships have begun their descent, and we still haven't figured out a way to open the dome."

"One thing at a time, remember?" Leyna asked, motioning towards Mr. Reynolds.

Cayden nodded. It was Mr. Reynolds who'd taught him the value of tackling life's problems in manageable pieces. "Wait here."

Cayden vaulted onto a section of their shattered pod, surfing down the dome's steep side at ever-increasing speed. When he neared the ground, he pushed off the dome with all his strength, using his momentum to somersault into the air. He landed a dozen feet from the dome and ran, racing to meet Mr. Reynolds before the gremmels reached the line of children. Cayden's vision narrowed at ground level, so Leyna gifted him sight from where she crouched high above the field. Cayden counted eighteen witches dotting the landscape, standing taller than the surrounding sea of gremmels. Their powerful Ethereal Hands represented the real threat.

Cayden was almost a mile from the dome when he reached the children. Mr. Reynolds held the lead position, keeping a pace so swift that many malnourished children stumbled. Cayden motioned for Mr. Reynolds to keep running, as the man almost stopped at the sight of him, and Cayden fell into step beside his old mentor.

"Good to see you, Cayden," rasped Mr. Reynolds in between

breaths.

"I'm so happy you made it here. But we're going to have a problem once the witches reach us. I assume your men can handle the gremmels?"

"Yes."

"Good. I'll deal with the witches. Keep heading towards the dome."

"And then what?"

"You'll see," Cayden said, though he still hadn't figured out a way to lift hundreds of children onto the dome before the witch attack overwhelmed them. *That won't matter unless I can stop the first wave of witches,* he decided. With one last reassuring smile, Cayden broke off from the group and shot down the column's left flank.

A line of gremmels approached, and Cayden prepared for a swarm of dozens of the creatures, but to his surprise, the gremmels split around him, allowing him passage through their ranks. The witches slowed to a halt, and Cayden almost returned to protect the frightened children until Leyna spoke in his mind, *Ignore the gremmels. Deal with the witches first.*

But they're trying to separate me from Mr. Reynolds and the children.

Trust Mr. Reynolds to deal with the gremmels. You're the only one who can tame Jaffa's witches. Plus, they brought an old friend you'll want to greet.

The gremmels had all run past him, and eighteen witches gathered ahead while more streamed from the forest to bolster their ranks. With a cursory glance, Cayden noticed the "old friend" of whom Leyna spoke.

"Why am I not surprised to see you?" Cayden asked as Neflina stepped forward.

"Because you know I must repay you for the last time we met. You should have realized that the Perchidian prison wouldn't hold me." She raised one thick arm and screamed, "Sisters, NOW!"

Eighteen thick vines sprang from the solid ground near Cayden, and before he had time to move, they snapped down on him hard, pinning him to the ground. The sheer force would have crushed his former body, but amidst the pain, he noticed with pride how well his reinforced bones stood up under pressure. Neflina's mouth dropped open in surprise, and Cayden used that precious moment to probe the Ethereal Hands controlling the vines. Their bonds were too numerous to break at once…

"You expected your toys to kill me?" he asked, startling the witches who had hoped to kill him outright with the attack. "I'll give you one warning only. Release me, or I will crush each of your Ethereal Hands without mercy. Judging by the strength of your affinite bonds, you may die from the experience."

One vine loosened and fell to the ground as a witch yelped and sprang backward. "Sisters," Neflina said, "hold tight. I will kill him myself." She strode forward, a dagger leaping to her chubby fist.

Cayden knew he'd only have one chance to save himself, but still, he hesitated. Fear was his only weapon, for even his impressive power would fail before Neflina reached him. His hope lay in arousing absolute terror.

You have no choice, Leyna said. *You know what you have to do.* Neflina had closed half the distance between them, her glittering weapon ready to strike.

"Fine," Cayden said. He reached out with his Ethereal Hand, feeling for the strongest affinite bond among the witches. His Hand slapped against a tight cord of woven steel from a thin witch with gray, windblown hair and pale cheeks. Cayden gathered every ounce of strength in his Ethereal Hand and broke her bond with the vine. He didn't merely break it, though. He crushed it methodically, starting from the point nearest his body and ending with the section wrapped around the witch's neck. Her scream echoed across the sky with unspeakable agony that brought tears to Cayden's eyes. Then her heart stopped, and she dropped to the ground, dead.

The other witches loosened their grip on Cayden, and he spun free of the vines, jumping high over the knife Neflina had just flung at him. He stood tall and calm, eying Jaffa's force with disdain as if they meant nothing more to him than the dirt below his feet. Many witches fled, unable to face the terrifying man-child who had slaughtered one of their sisters. Cayden readied himself for Neflina's next attack, but the fat witch fell to her knees, sinking into the muddy ground.

"Go ahead," she said, holding out her wrists. "Kill me."

"I'm not a killer," Cayden said, turning away.

"And yet you just killed one of my sisters."

"Only in self-defense and to save hundreds of others." *Why am I arguing with her?* he wondered. Far away, Mr. Reynolds neared Stomatus' dome with the children.

"You find it so easy to pass judgment on my lady Jaffa," Neflina said, rising to her feet. "Do you perceive her goals as more evil than yours? Cayden, you are no saint."

"No," Cayden said with genuine sadness. "I'm not." He turned his attention towards Stomatus, and an insane idea took shape. He formed an affinite bond with dozens of vines, using his Ethereal Hand to lift them over his head before running towards the dome. Neflina stood alone in the field, mouth agape, awaiting the witches and hundreds of gremmels who would soon join her on their way from the forest. Above, the tiny dot of Afterlife had grown to the size of Cayden's outstretched fist as the Perchidian airships lowered the giant city closer to the black dome.

Fifty vines writhed through the air around Cayden, and he wove them into a single, long vine, bonding the ends together. By the time he reached Mr. Reynolds, who stood before a group of children with the other town protectors, Cayden had created a ladder by splitting off hardened, brown portions of the vine from the main branch.

"Mr. Reynolds, you and your men instruct the children to grab onto the brown parts of the vine while I raise it," said Cayden, eying Jaffa's army as they drew closer. "And hurry. We only have a couple of minutes." Cayden pushed thoughts of the sea of gremmels from his mind to direct all his attention toward the massive ladder. To guide it up the dome without flinging children to their deaths, he established an affinite bond with its impressive length. Leyna helped, lending her vision to Cayden to make sure he didn't crush anyone while his Ethereal Hand worked to create more spots for the children to grasp.

Cayden hoisted the vine as quickly as children jumped aboard. Then the first line of gremmels struck. Mr. Reynolds had set up his men in defensive positions around the vine, and though they didn't have the razor-sharp leaves from a Perianth soldier's uniform, they'd created makeshift golden weapons, which they used to hold back the gremmels. Finally, the last child hopped onto the vine, and Cayden shouted, "Everyone else, grab hold!"

The town protectors retreated, two at a time, while their partners defended against the unrelenting gremmels. With all the strength Cayden had poured into his affinite bond, he lacked the power to help the men fight, and he saw four fall under the growing onslaught. He continued to slide the children up the dome, teeth gritted in concentration, curling the vine into a neat coil high above as Leyna helped the children hop off.

At last, Mr. Reynolds and Cayden stood at the dome's base. In seconds, the witches would overtake their position, but Cayden had let a thin rope drag behind the vine, and, wrapping it around both his and Mr. Reynolds' waists, he tugged both of them out of harm's way with his Ethereal Hand. The wave of gremmels crashed into the dome, but Cayden and Mr. Reynolds already stood in relative safety with the other survivors.

"Now what?" Leyna asked.

"We figure a way into Stomatus before the witches catch up with their gremmel pets."

And you have no idea how to do that, Leyna added silently.

None whatsoever.

Afterlife cast an ominous shadow, and the Perchidian airships would soon lose enough altitude to place the flying city within arm's reach. Cayden pressed his Ethereal Hand into the dome, but it was just as impenetrable as ever. A wave of hopelessness overcame him. To have come so far and have everything fail now.

Then the dome opened, and Cayden fell beside Leyna, the children, and the town protectors. They plummeted into Stomatus, near the westward side of the tree, and though Cayden tried to envelop everyone within his Ethereal Hand, he didn't have the energy or the time. The ground approached, so he put his arms out before him to prepare for impact. But to his surprise, he landed in a net, bouncing a few times before coming to a rest. Similar nets caught the others and lowered them to the ground. *Tonius and Robinson's work*? Cayden wondered.

Before he could stand, a golden bubble slammed down over him, rolled to the side, and snapped shut. *Leyna,* he called out, but he heard only silence. Looking around in confusion, he saw, through the bubble's golden-amber surface, Leyna being dragged away by soldiers with a crest depicting a clenched rock fist embroidered into their uniforms. Light struck him from above, and he snapped his attention upwards. The dome had opened, forming a large enough gap to allow Afterlife passage along with the Perchidian airships. The city descended majestically, and the ground rumbled as Afterlife settled atop the Dumrolls.

When he looked back down, neither Leyna nor Mr. Reynolds nor the children were in sight. He reached out with his Ethereal Hand, but it couldn't penetrate the golden material holding him. *It's the sap produced by the great tree,* he realized. With relief, he remembered that he still had Lysander's book in his satchel.

I have to calm down and make a plan, he thought, until Astor's face appeared in front of his cage. All calm thoughts fled his mind as a thick cloth fell over the cell, blocking his view.

Chapter Twenty Three

Utterly helpless, Cayden smashed his fist into the golden amber so hard the skin over his knuckles split. The iron scent of blood flooded his nostrils as pure rage pumped hot through his veins, but a quiet, internal voice said, *Don't lose control.* When he kicked the impenetrable wall, the pain amplified the voice: *You can't succumb to rage.*

He shouted with incoherent madness, but the voice scolded him. Cayden forced himself to breathe, eyes closed, until his body ceased vibrating. The roar in his ears quieted to be replaced by another noise, muffled sounds from outside his cage.

Each city sector had a different smell and sound, something he'd learned well during the dozens of times he'd patrolled Stomatus with Tonius and Robinson. Now, he focused on the sounds, and judging by the diminishing noise, he grew certain that they were moving him into the center of the city, towards the great tree.

Time passed in seconds, each one a struggle to stay calm against the animal instincts urging action. But any action would only further deplete his strength, and he could not afford to miss a chance at escape —if they ever gave him one. He tried to slow his breathing, using the absolute least amount of air to keep conscious. *I wonder when the air will run out.* He barely had enough room to sit, let alone lay. *Probably not very long.*

All grew silent, and from the uneven footsteps jolting his cage, Cayden sensed his captors carried him down a flight of stairs. Then, with a thud, the soldiers dropped the amber pod and lifted the cloth veil. Cayden's eyes bulged, and he almost bit his tongue clean in half. His fists hammered at the cage without conscious consent, all his calm evaporating instantly.

Just ahead, six amber pillars rose from the stone ground into a low, uneven ceiling. Tonius, Robinson, Leyna, Dakota, Henrik, and the Alchemist were each tied, hands stretched high over their heads, to the unbreakable pillars. Leyna thrashed against her bonds, the wild, inhuman look Cayden had seen twice before dominating her face. The amber material holding Cayden had severed their connection, and without an anchor pinning her to reality, she'd fallen into madness.

Tonius appeared more skeleton than human, though his eyes shone clear, while Robinson had shed every ounce of fat, and his head hung low against his shrunken chest. The other three didn't register to Cayden, who still pounded at the amber, channeling every bit of energy into his Ethereal Hand to penetrate the golden barrier. He swung his arm back again, reinforcing his flesh with his Ethereal Hand before slamming it forward.

Astor slid in front of Cayden's fist, and Cayden smashed his arm into the amber in front of Astor's face. Astor smiled through a smear of Cayden's red blood, laughing so his voice penetrated the cage.

"Let them go, Astor!" Cayden yelled. "You have me. Why do you need them?"

Astor stopped laughing, but his grin widened far enough to mar his otherwise handsome features. He clenched his stone fist to his chest, displaying the prize he'd earned after Cayden had accidentally severed his arm almost a year ago. In place of the golden leaf Perianth uniform, a crackled grey material stretched across Astor's body and merged with his rock arm. Hundreds of tiny bands, like veins of glittering ore, shone across the garment in a dashing display of shifting, silver light. Cayden squinted, trying to locate within Astor's eyes any shred of decency or evidence of the human bully he'd once known. He saw only wild eyes and a hatred-fueled craziness.

Astor pressed his lips to Cayden's cage and said, "Today, you will pay the price for shaming me." Backing up, Astor spread his arms wide. "Bow before your king, ruler of the Perianth Empire." Cayden looked beyond Astor, for the first time realizing the size of the underground chamber. Members of the merchant circle stood alongside a hundred soldiers bearing Astor's stone-fist banner. The walls held carved cells containing at least a hundred captives. The religious caste and Perianth soldiers were absent.

"Do you recognize me as your king?" Astor asked in a tone aimed at the entire chamber. Though only muted sounds penetrated the amber cage, Cayden was sure everyone else fell silent. Eyes turned to him, imploring, tearful, or angry. None appear content, Cayden noted, thinking sadly, *I can do nothing to help you.*

"Whatever you say, Astor," Cayden said. "You are the king." Cayden shouted this last sentence to ensure his words reached Astor's ears, but his voice was limp and without energy. *I'll tell Astor whatever he needs to save my friends.* His eyes traveled to Leyna's delicate face, contorted into a warped mask of agony as the thousands of minds in Stomatus pummeled her unprotected consciousness with their billions of thoughts. *To save Leyna.*

"Then bow!" Astor yelled, his eyes burning.

"I'll bow—look, I'm bowing," Cayden said, bending low at the waist while keeping his eyes locked on Leyna.

"I don't think you mean it!" Astor screamed back, waving his rock hand. At the signal, one soldier thrust a gold-tipped spear into Tonius' arm. His muffled scream bounced against the walls of Cayden's cage.

Cayden raged, crying out with enough force to tear his vocal cords, and he sank to his knees. "What do you want from me?" he asked. "I'll give you anything." Blood poured from the wound in Tonius' arm when the soldier pulled back the spear. It pooled at his feet as the color drained from Tonius' already pale face.

"What do I want, you ask?" Astor touched Cayden's cage, running his hand over its smooth surface. "I want what I am already getting. I want to watch you as I kill your friends before your eyes. Then I want to watch you die as you run out of oxygen, knowing you have failed everyone you love."

"Astor," Cayden said weakly, struggling to explain his anguish. "You bullied me in the Academy, but you weren't a monster. You don't have to walk this dark path."

"Have to? HAVE to? I WANT to walk this path and claim my place as KING of the Perianth Empire!" Astor's face twisted into a grotesque caricature of human features, and Cayden's eyes widened with new understanding. His gaze drilled past Astor's flesh and discovered the darkness seething below the surface. *Astor isn't human,* Cayden realized. *Somehow, Sevron's evil has consumed him.* Cayden lost all hope of reasoning with Astor, and he collapsed.

With tears streaming down his cheeks, he watched with impotent fury as Astor turned from the amber prison and leaped up to snatch the bloody spear from the soldier who'd wounded Tonius. He watched Astor yank back Robinson's head, slash him across the cheek, and, because he got no reaction, plunge the spear into Robinson's gut. Robinson jerked as blood streamed out through the gaping hole in his abdomen. Then Astor moved on to Leyna. She tried to squirm away, but Astor pinned her shoulders.

"Where shall I cut first?" he asked. "How about here," he said, drawing a line of blood along Leyna's arm. She reacted as any animal would, howling and thrashing even more violently against her restraints. Astor raised the weapon above his head and swung at Leyna's frail chest.

A warmth boiled near Cayden's stomach, getting hotter and hotter until his burning flesh snapped his attention to his satchel. He tore it from his waist, and Lysander's scalding journal spilled out. Cayden grabbed the book, and time slowed. Astor's spear stopped a foot from Leyna's chest while Lysander faded into existence next to Cayden.

"What's happening?" Cayden asked, confused because everyone in the room grew as still as figures in a painting.

"I had to attract your attention." Lysander's face glowed with a serene peace Cayden had never seen before, and when he spoke, his words were deliberate. "Fury has clouded your mind, Cayden, but you must focus on me now if you want to save your friends."

Cayden sobbed. "There's nothing I can do. It's too late."

"No, it's not. In your mind, I've stretched a single second into minutes, giving us leeway to discuss your predicament."

"Even so, Astor's attack will kill Robinson, and he's about to slaughter Leyna. My cage blocks the tree's power, so I'm struggling to breathe, let alone escape."

"You are right that you cannot save your friends in your current form. But if you separate your consciousness from your body, breaking all ties to your physical form, you can pass through the amber as though it were not there."

"The Alchemist gave me the same advice, but I never listened."

"As flawed as my brother has become, he is right. Disembodiment is your sole path towards crushing the forces my father left behind, and it's the only way you can pass through this cage to reach your friends. I know you still don't trust me, and I can hardly blame you after the suffering I inflicted. But you must trust me, my brother, or, better yet, yourself. Life presents moments of infinite choice, but it also offers tests for which there is but one answer."

"Without my body, will I be human?"

"I wish I knew. Sevron was born as he is, but your transformation will be unprecedented. The balance between what you lose and gain is not predictable, for although you may inhabit flesh again, it will never imprison your consciousness. My best guess is you will not be the same person you were before. Whether that makes you more or less human is unclear."

Cayden considered Lysander for almost a minute. This authoritative man had terrorized his mind for months, and his twin golden eyes glowed with an ever-present danger. Yet Harken's sacrifice may have drained Sevron's malice, leaving behind only wisdom and kindness. Cayden wanted to trust Lysander, but past pain clouded his judgment. Still, none of that mattered in the face of Astor's spear, which hung above Leyna's retreating chest.

Lysander faded, and Cayden wrapped his consciousness in his Ethereal Hand as he'd done so many times before to explore faraway places, to form affinite bonds with thousands of materials, and to support his connection with Leyna. As much as he'd altered his body over the past two months, he'd always remained tethered to his physical form, using the brush of air passing through his lungs to keep him grounded.

Now, as he carried his consciousness upwards, he focused on the connection to his flesh. He visualized the connection as a rope, and he unwound the rope with his mind. Layer after layer he peeled off, dissolving the strands into nothingness until only a thread, as thin as any thread one might use to reattach a button, remained. With fear gripping his thoughts and the image of Leyna held in his mind, he let the last string dissolve, and all fell silent.

Even on the stillest of nights, the gurgles of Cayden's own body kept him company, but now an all-consuming hush fell across his senses. *That's not quite right,* he thought, for though he lacked ears, he could track the subtle shifts in the air caused by soundwaves. He sensed the thump of his former body collapsing atop Lysander's journal. The human form, his home for thirteen years, became foreign, as if it were a piece of meat on a butcher's counter.

"Astor!" one soldier shouted as time resumed, pointing at Cayden's prone body in the amber cage. Astor stopped his arm mid-swing and whipped around, eyes wide.

"It can't be," he said when his eyes found Cayden. "You can't die yet."

"I'm sorry, sir," the soldier said. "He shouldn't have run out of air. Perhaps he's faking?"

"It wouldn't help since we don't know how to open the cage once it's been closed. Playing dead won't do you any good, Cayden!"

Cayden directed his consciousness towards Astor, feeling not so much as a tingle as he passed through the amber barrier. To save Leyna, Cayden knew he'd need to tie his consciousness to a solid form but lacked the confidence to control sand or stone in the way of Sevron's agents. *I need something organic.* A quick survey of the surrounding area uncovered several dead bodies, dissidents executed by Astor's soldiers.

This will be gruesome, Cayden thought as he entered one of the bodies, grimacing at the unsettling nature of what he was about to attempt. The corpse's brain pulled him in like a magnet, providing familiar ground to anchor his consciousness, and while he settled into the brain's neural pathways, he reshaped the body in his image. Bones broke and reformed, muscle rippled, then solidified, and the face melted like butter, solidifying to match the one Cayden abandoned in the amber cage. As he stood, his left iris turned from brown to gold.

No one noticed when the body rose from among the pile, and no one turned a head to watch the boy walking towards Astor. All attention lay on the cage until Cayden pushed past two merchant class members into the open. A handful of merchants screamed, and one fainted, toppling onto the stage. Astor pried his eyes from Cayden's caged body to locate the source of the commotion.

"Hello, Astor," Cayden said, continuing his deliberate pace towards the stricken teenager.

"But… how?" Astor asked. Then a grin spread across his face, for in his twisted mind, Astor saw a chance to smite his enemy in front of his subjects. Astor plunged his fist into the stone ground, pulling up a great slab of rock twelve feet long. With a sneer, he brought it down upon Cayden's head.

"Not this time," Cayden said. With the full power of his anchored Ethereal Hand, he smashed Astor's affinite bond with the rock, cutting it off with such vicious force that part of Astor's stone arm fell from his body. Before Astor could utter a sound, Cayden split the slab of rock down the center, forming his own affinite bonds with each section. He knocked Astor high into the air and, with the other slab of rock, swatted him into the wall like one might squash a fly. Astor crumpled into a quivering heap of broken bones.

Cayden turned to the other soldiers, both eyes burning with golden fire. For five seconds, the entire room lit up like the sun, and Astor's soldiers fled towards the stairs, too frightened to face the terrifying demon before them. They didn't make it far, for a regiment of

Perchidian spearmen, led by Naya, Jericho, and Balint, flooded into the dungeon. Cayden snarled, gathering his energy for another strike until a cry from Tonius extinguished his fury.

"Robinson's dying," Tonius said as he clutched his arm, and Cayden blinked, locating Robinson's lean body at his feet. His preoccupation with destroying Astor's soldiers almost sent him trampling over Robinson. Shaking a dose of clarity into his head, he touched Robinson's stomach, probing the wound using his Ethereal Hand while severing the bonds tying Tonius, Dakota, and Henrik to the pillars. With more than a twinge of guilt, he kept Leyna restrained, for she required more nuanced care.

Blood continued to escape through Robinson's wound, but Cayden sighed with relief when he saw the spear had nicked none of his vital organs. Relief gave way to panic, however, when he tried to reform Robinson's skin only to find his Ethereal Hand rebuffed. He applied more energy, but the stronger his attempt, the more aggressively his Ethereal Hand rebounded.

"I don't understand," Cayden said in frustration. He'd repeatedly repaired his own body, but a force prevented him from saving Robinson. Maybe someone is blocking my Hand, he thought, searching for Astor's body amidst the chaos.

"Ask his permission," Dakota said, stepping in front of Cayden.

"Huh?" Cayden still struggled to locate Astor, peering around Dakota.

"Stop trying to find Astor and listen to me. You must ask for Robinson's help, for though you may guide his Ethereal Hand, you cannot affect the flesh of another living being. None may break the affinite bond between one's mind and body. You cannot bond with Robinson's flesh because his control is absolute." Thoughts of Astor faded from Cayden's mind, and he nodded his understanding, recalling a time when he failed to heal Mr. Reynolds for the same reason. He then grabbed Robinson's head between his small hands.

"Wake up, Robinson." His friend didn't move, so Cayden shouted, "It's time for lunch! Open your eyes." Robinson's eyes blinked open, and Cayden spoke before he lost consciousness again. "I'm going to help heal you, but you must stay awake and let me guide your Ethereal Hand. Got it?" Robinson nodded weakly, so Cayden didn't waste any time donning Robinson's Hand as though it were a surgical glove. The precision required to mend flesh—especially without direct contact from his Ethereal Hand—dwarfed that needed to swing massive slabs of rock, and Cayden struggled to hold the entire structure of Robinson's abdomen in his mind while he worked. Only the gentle pressure from Tonius' hand on his shoulder gave him the concentration he needed to continue. Ten minutes later, he finished repairing Robinson's abdomen.

"Sleep, my friend," Cayden whispered, and Robinson mumbled something inaudible before he drifted into a fitful rest. "He'll recover," Cayden told Tonius. "Now, let's see what I can do about your arm."

"You have more pressing matters," Tonius said, stopping Cayden. He'd wrapped a length of cloth around his arm to halt most of the bleeding, so Cayden nodded gratefully, allowing himself to focus on Leyna.

Gone were any signs she'd been struggling against her bonds. She sagged forward, and though her red hair obscured her twisted face, it left the nape of her neck exposed. Cayden could just detect her gentle pulse against bare skin when he guided his Ethereal Hand inwards until it contacted the golden leaf. He recalled violent and searing pain from when he'd first formed their bond, and he braced himself for the oncoming shock. Instead, their connection snapped back into place with no ill effect. If anything, their renewed bond brought with it a sense of giddy joy. *I'm whole again,* Cayden thought.

"We're whole again," Leyna said, and Cayden grinned despite himself, pulling Leyna into a tight hug.

"I thought I'd never be able to save you, but Lysander... he helped me. He helped me save you." Leyna dove into Cayden's mind, replaying his memories of the past hour, and Cayden reveled in her touch.

"Cayden," Balint said, placing his hand on Cayden's shoulder. With a struggle, Cayden forced his attention away from Leyna. He saw the Perchidians had successfully corralled Astor's remaining soldiers into a corner, where they sat with hands tied behind their backs. Aside from a few scratches, Balint looked no worse for the wear.

"What is it, Balint?"

"We received word from a Perchidian scout ship just before we descended into the dome covering Stomatus. The witches surround the city."

"I already know this."

"Yes, but they discovered another force approaching from the north. It can be seen only in a subtle ripple across the landscape."

"It's Sevron's darkness, the captured dead souls who now have the strength to take physical form."

"What do we do?" Balint asked, fear showing in the large man's eyes. Cayden frowned. Beyond rescuing his friends and securing Afterlife within Stomatus, he had no clear path forward.

"I think my brother has something he'd like to say," Dakota said, pointing to the amber cage holding Cayden's former body. Inside, Lysander's journal glowed red hot once again.

Chapter Twenty Four

Cayden surveyed Stomatus from high in the branches of the great tree. To his right, the Dumrolls were no longer visible, buried under Afterlife's crystalline foundation. Its massive tower almost scraped against the upper reaches of the dome, and only the tree in which Cayden now stood rivaled Afterlife's tower in height. Indeed, Stomatus appeared much as it had a thousand years ago—though he didn't imagine the Perchidian tree rings, which now lay in lifeless piles across the city, were part of the original design.

He hoped the Dumrolls' bewildered residents had time to flee Afterlife as it descended into their ruined town, but he admitted many might have perished. He decided not to probe Afterlife's underbelly with his Ethereal Hand because some facts are better left unconfirmed.

Cayden forced his attention to his immediate surroundings, where he'd been vaguely aware of the debate that had been raging on behind him. He turned to face a meeting hall filled with familiar faces. Leyna, Tonius, Robinson, Naya, Dakota, Henrik, Balint, Jericho, Mr. Reynolds, the Alchemist, and Priven sat around a long, wooden table grown from the floor. The Perianth throne, a tall, golden chair, stood unoccupied at the end of the hall. Cayden observed their weary faces, especially those of Tonius and Robinson, who had endured unthinkable tortures at Astor's hands. *Perhaps I should never have left them in Stomatus,* Cayden thought. *If I had only known about Astor.*

"We cannot fight the dark force in the north," Balint said. "We've established this fact." Cayden rubbed his hand across his forehead, wiping the beads of sweat pooling just above his eyebrows. Lysander had dumped a monumental stack of information upon him over the past five hours. With his hand on the journal, Lysander had spoken with precision, outlining his plan. The proposal set a towering responsibility atop Cayden's slender shoulders, and its urgency sent him into a paralyzing spiral of despair.

Leyna offered no opinion, for every alternative threatened perilous consequences. Cayden didn't blame her. *I have to follow Lysander's advice,* he decided. *Especially since I'm the only one capable of carrying it out.* Knowing that he, alone, among the billions of humans in the Perianth Empire and on Earth could rid Sevron's influence from their planet nearly broke his spirit. Despite all his growth over the past year, his consciousness was less than fourteen years old, and such responsibility promised countless unpredictable results. *No matter,* he thought. *The decision is made.*

"I can offer one defense," the Alchemist said, voicing a bit of knowledge that surfaced in his broken mind. "But Sevron's army will overcome the obstacle within an hour."

"A plan without an objective is without merit," Cayden said, turning his full attention towards his friends and allies. "Damek suggests we channel our Ethereal Hands through diluted amber to shield Stomatus from Sevron's army of souls. He used this tactic to defend Afterlife, but Sevron's forces have since grown and would shatter our Hands in seconds."

"How did you know about the amber—"

"An explanation demands time we don't have," Cayden said, cutting off the Alchemist mid-sentence. Now that he'd decided what to do, his words flowed as if he'd spoken them many times. "We will have to work faster than Sevron, so listen closely."

"I don't take orders from a boy," Priven said. "Astor taught me the peril in obeying the foolish fantasies of a child. The title of Airwalker alone will not persuade me to cooperate."

"Then I'll confine you to prison until my task is done," Cayden said. "This goes for all of you. My plan will erase Sevron's wicked presence in our world, but his incoming assault pushes us to act without fully understanding our strategy. If you value the Perianth Empire, you will cooperate." Priven's expression relaxed, though his hand stayed close to his axe's hilt. "Until we eradicate Sevron's army, you're either my ally or enemy. If you choose not to cooperate, I will imprison you until the danger has passed." Cayden looked around the room, his golden eye daring anyone to respond. Priven opened his mouth but shut it in the face of Cayden's determination.

"Cayden has proven himself a friend," Tonius said. "I, for one, intend to stand by him."

"Me as well," Robinson said.

"I, too, vouch for the child," Balint said, but Cayden thought, *This might be the one time you shouldn't trust me.* Leyna, who sensed Cayden's guilt, averted her gaze. Naya and Mr. Reynolds nodded their assent, so Cayden continued.

"Very well. Our immediate goal is to create a physical connection between the tower of the Departed in Afterlife and the tree in Stomatus."

"Won't that corrupt our city?" Naya asked. "Sevron's disease ravages your Elders."

"Let me worry about that," Cayden said, attempting to project a false air of certainty. "Dakota, I suspect you're capable of directing this effort. You understand my meaning?"

"Yes, you require a bridge between the neural pathways of the tree and those in Afterlife's tower."

"Right. Jericho and Priven, the Perianth soldiers and the Perchidians must work together to follow Dakota's instructions. Henrik, you will return to Stomatus' underbelly and open the dome in two hours, forty-five minutes from now. Tonius, you and Robinson will work with the Alchemist and Mr. Reynolds to protect the city from the gremmels until the Perianth, Perchidian, and Afterlife soldiers join you. The city will be vulnerable for five minutes after Henrik opens the dome. I trust you have enough town protectors to arrange a suitable defense?"

"Yes," said Mr. Reynolds.

"Good. Leyna will gather her strength while I try to reason with Jaffa." *The witches deserve one last chance,* he thought. *And I have a spare moment before Dakota readies the connection.*

"They will kill you on sight," Balint said.

"They might find that task beyond their capabilities. Now go. I trust you all to carry out your tasks, and if all goes well, I will greet you on the northern city wall within three hours."

Cayden turned and leaped through an open window, plummeting to the streets and cushioning his fall just before landing. The effort used to exhaust him, but manipulating air no longer affected his concentration. As soon as his feet touched down, he asked, *Leyna, are you sure you are up for this? You will need to support my mind in a tight embrace—even tighter than when you pulled me from Lysander's control.*

I will do the best I can, she answered, but he sensed her extreme reluctance. He knew, deep down, that she'd only agreed to help him because of their connection. Despite the consequences that would result from Cayden's inaction, Leyna still didn't accept the path Cayden now walked was correct.

I can worry about this later, he decided as he ran through the city, whipping past buildings and people who stood aside, stunned at his speed. His enhanced legs pumped below his torso, and he soon reached the city's outer wall. Not bothering with the stairs, he jumped atop the wall, where the dome touched the wall's upper reach. As Henrik had instructed, Cayden located a control panel, tapping the requisite buttons to iris open one section of the black material before shutting it behind him.

Taking a quick survey of his surroundings, Cayden noted that tens of thousands of gremmels surrounded Stomatus, but the witches had retreated beyond the forest's edge. The gremmels parted before Cayden, allowing him passage while subtly controlling his direction through their movement. They led him to a dense patch of woods, where Cayden knew Jaffa would be waiting. As he advanced, the gremmels closed in behind, blocking off any chance of escape. Or so they expected.

Cayden stepped through a veil of trees, and he saw the witches had constructed a fortress matching their primary base, a woven tangle of branches and vines several feet thick. With his Ethereal Hand, Cayden noted more Hands controlled the walls than he could count. *They still believe I am walking into a trap.*

You are walking into a trap, Leyna replied from her perch in Stomatus' tree.

True. But a trap must be stronger than its prey to be effective. And theirs is not.

You sound arrogant, Cayden. Are you certain you are not overconfident in your abilities? There are over a hundred witches. Not even you can fend off a hundred Ethereal Hands.

But I'm not me anymore, remember? I'm much more connected to, well, everything.

Leyna sighed, and Cayden shrunk from the worry pulsing across her mind. He sensed two layers of concern within her thoughts. She not only worried for his safety, but she also worried about the transformation that occurred when he left his original body behind in the amber cage. Neither of them yet knew the full implications of abandoning his body. For now, Cayden was satisfied that forfeiting his flesh had saved Leyna's life.

Gremmels crowded him as he drew closer to the witches' base, some even grabbing his shirt tails. By the time he reached the vines, it seemed every gremmel had arrived to form an angry sea behind him. He ignored them, focusing his attention on a mass of vines woven together in the shape of a squat building. Near the center of the structure, above his head, a section of the wall moved, writhing opened to expose the witch queen Jaffa.

She stood tall and straight, looking more majestically royal than Cayden expected. Delicate vines hung from her body like a gown, and she wore a crown of thorns above sunken eyes. Her face and bearing projected a fierce confidence that few mortals could ignore. All those around her bowed low to the ground. Cayden felt an unexpected urge to bow as well, but it passed when he reminded himself of her true nature. He blinked away the regal vision to witness the cruel witch who murdered Mogen.

"Welcome, Cayden," Jaffa said cooly. "It's good to see you again. Have you changed your mind and brought me the book? I can't fathom you'd come for any other reason since it's obvious we won't let you depart without surrendering the journal."

"Why do you want the book, anyway? You never told me." Cayden noted with minor trepidation that more than a dozen witches walked in a wide semicircle among their gremmel children. No doubt they hoped to block off any chance of retreat.

"I would use the book to crush the Perianth Empire, of course. The book holds the remnants of my brother Lysander's consciousness. His Ethereal Hand is a domineering power that rivals even the strength of our father, Sevron. Through the book, I can channel my Hand, strengthening it enough to crush your precious Stomatus under the weight of the ground itself."

"Tens of thousands would perish."

"So? The Perianth Empire is a disgrace that my brother Adam should never have founded. It is a source of pure evil."

"Pure evil flows from many wells," Cayden said under his breath. "I promised you'd never own the book, Jaffa. You killed Mogen, a great man working to free the citizens of Stomatus from the king's grasp, and that act alone is enough to prove you should never hold such power."

Jaffa's eyes darkened. "Then what are you here for, boy?"

"To offer you one last chance to save yourself."

"From what do I need saving?" She laughed, and the other witches joined her in a raucous display of wicked merriment. "We have surrounded Stomatus, and they will choose to open the dome rather than starve. Our forces will flow across Adam's city like a cleansing flood, scraping my brother's work from this world. And I will feed upon his despair as he watches his kingdom fall and his tree burn to ash."

"The Perianth king is alive?" Cayden asked in surprise.

"Oh, yes. We took him the day we attacked Stomatus. And I've kept my brother alive—barely—so he could bear witness to my destruction of his life's work."

She has nothing but hatred in her thoughts, Leyna said to Cayden from afar. *I sense her evil, and I doubt she can change her mind any more than a stone can roll itself uphill.*

"A force approaches from the north," Cayden said. "Your father, Sevron, seeded this army years ago, and it has gained strength ever since. The Ceremony of the Spirits, which Adam invented to keep the portal to Earth closed, failed, letting your father's influence into this planet. You lack the knowledge and weapons to battle a foe who can approach as a sandstorm and transform into iron blades in the blink of an eye. Within two hours, you will die... unless you agree to work with me. Put your hatred aside, Jaffa, for it will kill you in the end."

"Let's supposed I trust you, Cayden. What power do you have that I lack? How can a boy defeat your supposed army?"

"War and hatred lend power to Sevron's influence, so we must abandon all hostilities and face your father as a united planet. The Perianth Empire, Perchidians, Afterlife, Blood Caves, and witches can coalesce into an unstoppable force and raze Sevron's influence from our world. Come, Jaffa, release a thousand years of hatred and embrace unity. Be better than your brother."

For the briefest moment, Jaffa furrowed her brow in doubt of her own beliefs, but the moment passed almost as soon as it had begun. "I will never join you. I would rather see this force destroy my people and Stomatus with it than see the Perianth Empire survive."

Her mind is set, Leyna said, and a terrible rush of sadness overcame Cayden. It took him a moment to realize the emotion originated from within Leyna, for she had understood the consequences of his trip to see Jaffa even before he'd left the city. Cayden hoped he might persuade the ancient witch by forcing her to accept that the path forward required her to abandon her hatred. But hate had become her reason for being. Her malice grew for a thousand years, and not even the leaf's mind control could overpower her illogical resolve.

You've avoided considering the inevitable consequences, said Leyna. *Only one path leads to victory*. Cayden's head sank. Without complete unity, even the most nuanced application of power could not erase all traces of Sevron's evil. Jaffa alone, among the hundreds of thousands across the Empire, possessed a will capable of resisting Adam's mind control. Her mind would break rather than release its hatred. *She murdered Mogen*, Leyna said. *She has transformed countless thousands of children into monsters. She's caused more harm than a million Astors could. If anyone deserves death, she does.*

"Yours is the only mind on this planet too stubborn to change," Cayden said. Then, through a wrenching sob, he continued, "I'm going to have to kill you."

Jaffa laughed, a shrill, throaty sound that bounced around the husks of dead trees. Dozens of witches stepped forward, and Jaffa jumped down from her perch to take her place at their center. The witches raised their arms, and the entire wall behind them rippled, thousands of interlocking vines twisting together to form a serpent as wide as a house. Jaffa brought the massive structure crashing down with such tremendous force that the ground quaked for miles.

The molecules composing Cayden's body blasted apart into millions of pieces, but Cayden remained aware of every atom that had composed his solid form. *I truly am no longer attached to any physical body*, he thought, the implication of his transformation in Astor's dungeon becoming clearer.

Cayden willed his body to reform around his Ethereal Hand, and, in an instant, stood behind Jaffa. Every molecule of his body had snapped together under his command so that he dwelled within flesh and blood once more. Jaffa turned, preparing to strike him again, but he was too fast. He willed his arm to transform into a silver blade and thrust it through Jaffa's back and into her heart. She died instantly.

Chapter Twenty Five

Back in the great tree of Stomatus, Cayden lay his head upon Leyna's lap. *I am a murderer,* he thought, tears welling up in his eyes.

"Yes, you are," Leyna answered aloud. "You killed in cold blood." Cayden's eyes grew moist with the horror of his act against Jaffa, and he searched Leyna's rigid face for solace or understanding. She said, "True, you had little choice, but the fact will always be that you killed to serve your purpose—whether or not historians judge your purpose as worthy."

"That's not making me feel any better," he said, sitting up.

"It shouldn't. You've done something terrible today, Cayden, and you're about to commit an even more heinous crime."

"Yes," he whispered. Then, louder, he shouted, "Do you think I forgot!?"

"I'm just being realistic. But I don't mean you should have acted differently. We stand together, and today's events will burden us in equal measure. You've sensed my reluctance, and I've shared your guilt—but you are right. This must be done." Cayden lacked any response to her cold, logical words. *She's trying to wrestle with her feelings,* he thought. *I'll allow her to handle her trauma as she pleases.*

A scraping along the floor marked Dakota's arrival as he trailed a thin, crystalline cable behind him. Flexible yet hard, the translucent line reached back to Afterlife's tower. Dakota surveyed Cayden and Leyna, noting Cayden's red eyes and Leyna's drawn cheeks. Of course, Dakota's face displayed no signs of emotion.

"Connect this cable to the tree," Dakota said. "With Damek's help, we converted the material from one of Stomatus' old towers into a flexible conduit through which Afterlife's Departed may flow."

"And Naya has instructed the Departed?" Cayden asked, struggling to his feet and wiping the tears from his eyes.

"Naya is within Afterlife's tower, and she will direct her Departed as you commanded."

"Good. Dakota, I should tell you I didn't create this plan. He did," Cayden said, lifting Lysander's journal from its place on the table.

"Ah, I see." Dakota's eyes glistened for the briefest moment. To Cayden, that seemed the most passionate display of emotion he'd seen from the boy. Then his face relaxed into a mask of impassivity. "May I say goodbye to my brother?"

"You can have a couple of minutes." *Dakota knows what we intend to do,* Cayden thought. *Though I guess I shouldn't be surprised.*

"Very well." Dakota stepped forward, placed his hand on the journal, and closed his eyes. Before Cayden had time to wonder about their secret discussion, Dakota opened his eyes. "Lysander deserves your complete trust."

Cayden nodded, lifting the journal while Leyna took the cable from Dakota's outstretched hand. Together, Cayden and Leyna walked past the golden Perianth throne and into a dark passage leading to the tree's heart, leaving Dakota in the meeting hall. Cayden stopped at a dead end to place his palm against a cold slab of gray metal. Lysander had explained that the king had programmed the panel to recognize his mechanical hand, so Cayden closed his eyes and dug through his memories of the king. Once he had a good mental image, he willed his flesh to reform into a replica of the king's hand. His flesh turned to gold as his fingers separated at the joints, segmenting into tiny struts connected by complex ball bearings. When the transformation finished, a voice said, "Authorization accepted."

A hidden door slid open, and a more intense golden light than any Cayden had seen spilled forth, blinding both him and Leyna. After his eyes adjusted, he faced a claustrophobic chamber with a golden core. A gnarled pillar of amber sap converged in this room, descending from the tree's millions of leaves to form a control panel.

"This is the room from which the Perianth king commanded his Empire," Cayden said.

"It's also where Sevron's evil corrupted Astor."

Cayden nodded gravely. Their actions would soon decide the Perianth Empire's future, but before he committed to their plan, he wanted to consult Lysander one final time. Cayden remembered Harken's death, for which he still felt overwhelming guilt. A stranger had sacrificed his life to pull Lysander from Cayden's mind, all so he might banish Sevron's evil. Now that the decisive moment had arrived, Cayden needed reassurance that Lysander's plan would honor Harken's death.

"I'm certain that Harken accepted his death might not have meaning," Leyna said, responding to Cayden's thoughts.

"He was wise. It's just that without Lysander and me, none of this would be possible. I must trust that Lysander is ready to release his life, or Harken's sacrifice will have been for nothing."

Cayden focused on the journal and said, *You may change your mind. Are you sure you're ready?*

Of course. Lysander appeared before Cayden's open eyes as a ghostly apparition, and he spoke with calm confidence. *I decided to end my life a thousand years ago to save the Perianth Empire. Today, my decision will hold weight, though I expect we will rescue far more than my brother's Empire.*

Then I will do what I can to cleanse this planet of your father's influence.

And after that?

If I survive, then I have no choice, right?

There is always a choice, Cayden. But if you choose life over death, then no: I'm afraid only one path remains open to you.

Well… good luck. And… I suppose… thank you.

Lysander inclined his head before fading, and Cayden pushed the journal into the golden pillar, which yielded against the book like viscous, melted rubber. He understood that, regardless of what happened inside the tree, he would never again speak to Lysander. For so long, Lysander's dark presence threatened to take over Cayden's mind, but now, at the moment of Lysander's demise, Cayden was reluctant to say his last goodbye. Lysander's pure form differed so much from the dark presence in his golden eye, and Cayden judged him an honorable man. The finality of Lysander's decision weighed upon Cayden, but he steeled himself.

"Leyna, hand me the cable." She hesitated, anticipating the looming dangers. Though tears filled Leyna's eyes, she did not look away as she pressed the end of the cable into Cayden's hand, and he grabbed her wrist, pulling her into a tight hug. They'd embraced many times without a second thought, but as their embrace endured, they realized this time was different. Cayden enjoyed the warmth of Leyna's body pressed against his, and he also observed Leyna hugging him through their shared connection. As much control as Cayden had over his body, he could not prevent his cheeks from turning the brightest shade of red.

Cayden let go, turned impulsively, and pressed the cable into Lysander's journal. He kept one hand on the book and the other on Leyna. The room snapped out of existence, leaving Cayden in utter darkness. Pure, unbridled malice swept over him, threatening to pull him under as it had done all the Elders of Stomatus who had entered the tree through the Caretaker's chamber. His consciousness now lay bare and unprotected within the complex pathways that flowed through the tree like chains of neurons in a human brain. He steeled himself against the dark forces tearing at him as Leyna's mental grip tightened around his consciousness. Then, just as he slipped into the black, Lysander glowed into existence.

Lysander whispered, "Goodbye, Cayden," before his body exploded outwards into the brightest light imaginable, illuminating countless shapes lurking in the shadows. Another point of light appeared before Cayden, marking the gateway through which Afterlife's Departed could enter Stomatus' tree via the cable. Thousands of glowing forms materialized behind Cayden, winking into existence one after another.

Get ready, Cayden thought, and Afterlife's Departed citizens lined up, prepared to unleash their combined strength against the thousand-year-old darkness within the tree. As Lysander had instructed, Cayden extended his Ethereal Hand around the haze of light that was Lysander's consciousness, and he led the Departed towards the nearest grouping of dark figures.

Inky shapes swarmed towards Cayden, only to be frozen in the light and then torn to shreds by the Ethereal might of Afterlife's Departed. Cayden swung the light to and fro, pressing through the tree's neural pathway and destroying any darkness he detected. The further he descended within the tree, the more Lysander's light shrank. For each group of dark figures absorbed, a bit of the light dissipated, and the darkness grasped at Cayden. Leyna's mental grip on him grew even tighter so that no shape found purchase upon his consciousness. Holding onto Leyna's mind like a life rope, Cayden continued to swat away the misty figures with his Ethereal Hand, funneling them into Lysander's consciousness to be absorbed and then destroyed. Onwards and downwards, he thought.

Time passed without notice. Minutes, hours, or days might have passed. Such was his singular focus on blasting every dark figure he found into oblivion. Eventually, when all in sight shined with a clean, white light, he allowed his mind to relax. He expanded his consciousness throughout the tree, trying to catch a tiny glimpse of Sevron's darkness, any sign that the evil hid in a deep, undiscovered section. But he uncovered nothing.

I guess that's it, Cayden said to the Departed. *Thank you.* The misty figures bowed with solemn respect, filing back through the cable that had led them to the tree. Cayden imagined they must be at least as tired as he, for the fight—if one could call it that—had been mentally draining. Only a golden spec remained of Lysander's consciousness, and even that flickered beyond the unknown veil that separated the living from the dead. Cayden mourned Lysander, who had wiped away his father's darkness in the ultimate act of defiance. Stomatus' Elders were also gone, and the tree blossomed into an image of its original glory.

As tired as Cayden was, he allowed himself a bit of time to examine the intricate beauty of the tree's interior. Of course, everything before him was a fantasy, a representation his subconscious created to give shape and substance to the tree. Even knowing this, the glowing diamond walls were beautiful to behold. *It's more than that,* Cayden thought. Floating mid-air as a point of consciousness, he enjoyed the tree's essence flowing over his mind like the purest breeze. I*'d love to live in this paradise,* he realized, suddenly understanding what life must be like for those who dwelled in Afterlife's tower. *It's like a constructed heaven.*

Leyna nudged him, guiding his thoughts back to the world outside the tree. Cayden knew Sevron's army of evil souls approached from the north, so he channeled his consciousness back into his body through Leyna's lifeline. He found his body stood where he'd left it, his left hand still on Lysander's journal. Cayden beheld the worn book, which now contained only words. Then he looked down at Leyna.

"You're exhausted," he said, his throat almost too dry to speak. Leyna crouched by his feet, pressing her fists against her temples, which glowed white even in the warm, golden light of the chamber.

"So are you," she answered, squinting up at him.

"How long was I in there?"

"Almost two hours. You should take a brief rest."

"No," Cayden said, shaking his head. "Henrik will open Stomatus' dome, and I must prepare."

"I don't like this."

"But we agreed it must be done."

Leyna remained silent until, with a sudden burst of energy, she rose to her feet and said, "Let's return to the Blood Caves. Sevron won't reach us there, at least for a time. We'll live our whole lives without dealing with any of this ever again!"

Cayden took her hand, remembering their embrace before he'd cleansed the tree. His body against hers. Their closeness. That special moment almost persuaded him to flee with her. More than any reward, he wished to spend more carefree days with Leyna alone. Then Tonius' words popped into his mind. "There's a difference between right and wrong," he'd said months ago after their visit with Tonius' parents. "You can choose to ignore it, but it's still there."

I know, I know, Cayden thought.

"You know we can't leave now," Cayden said to Leyna, forcing himself to release her hand.

"Yes," Leyna said. "I... I don't know what I was saying." But they both understood her lie. They foresaw the future she'd envisioned for them, just as they watched it fade with every action.

Before he changed his mind, Cayden turned from Leyna and reconnected with the tree through a simple affinite bond to the golden pillar. This time, instead of entering the tree's core, he directed his thoughts to the outer branches, spreading his consciousness throughout the tree's exterior structure.

He sensed the stagnant air around the tree's branches as if they were his arms. Pushing himself even further, he located thousands of golden leaves hanging from their connections to the tree, each one a potential channel through which the Elders of Stomatus had directed their wills. Lysander destroyed the Elders, and the witches held the king as their captive. Perianth citizens were free—but only for a few minutes.

Far below, Henrik directed the dome to open. *It's time,* Cayden thought, steeling himself for one final effort. Feeding upon the tree's energy, Cayden guided his Ethereal Hand into hundreds of thousands of leaves, which fluttered as though caught in a breeze. He grasped every leaf as his appendage, and it took all his attention to control them like fingers.

Lysander had taught Cayden that under normal circumstances, a dozen years of brainwashing softened the mind enough to accept the leaf. Institution prepared children to release their free will and submit to the control of the Perianth king and Elders. But these were not normal circumstances. Cayden's consciousness was stronger than any on the planet, and the precision with which he directed the leaves exceeded human ability. Still, Cayden accepted the limits of his power, which translated into unwanted casualties.

Cayden comforted himself with his goal to unite their world. *Absolute unity is the only way to end Sevron's plague.*

***

"To the walls!" Priven roared, his steel axe glinting ever brighter as the dome cracked open. Mid-day light burst into Stomatus, bathing the white and gold city in harsh sunlight for only the second time in many months. Priven commanded the few Perianth soldiers strong enough to fight after their release from Astor's dungeon, while Jericho and Balint rallied the hundreds of Perchidian spearmen who'd survived their treacherous descent into Stomatus with Afterlife. Mr. Reynolds had already organized the town protectors in a defensive ring around Stomatus as Cayden had requested, while Afterlife's guards, armed with bows and led by Naya, stood below the wall awaiting the command to fire.

The moment the dome's top ridges cleared the uppermost sections of Stomatus' towers, projectiles sailed into the city. Far overhead, clusters of vines spun through the air, latching on to repaired buildings and crushing them into piles of rubble. The witches long-prepared their assault, and though Jaffa's death shattered their organization, they made up for her absence with sheer numbers. Soon, their vines filled the sky and eclipsed the sun. As the dome retreated below the wall, the full might of the witch attack bore down upon Stomatus.

Gremmels rode over the wall on great tree-like platforms controlled by witches in waves of hundreds, jumping upon any exposed target. They bit, tore, and clawed at unarmored flesh. Though skilled, the joint Perianth and Perchidian forces retreated as they attempted to repel the gremmels.

"Look," Tonius said. He stood with Robinson atop a tower away from the front lines. Robinson tore his attention from the fight and aimed his eyes at the forest where Tonius pointed. A broad swathe of land had opened just beyond the fight now that the witch and gremmel forces were clear of their encampments near the forest. Robinson groaned when the land rose as if a hand pressed up the soil. Gray soil turned black, and an army of dark figures arose. The figures flowed in one coordinated mass towards Stomatus, faster than any human had ever run.

"Sevron's forces," muttered Robinson, whose head still spun from the blood he'd lost.

"Yes. I hope Cayden has enough time."

"For what? He never shared his plan."

"But he gave us these," Tonius said, holding out the two metal ingots Cayden had handed them.

The air reverberated from tinkling metal, and Tonius pointed towards Stomatus' great tree. Every golden leaf fell from its branches and flew towards the horizon in every direction, covering the sky with a golden blanket. Leaves fell like hail upon the battlefield, and both Robinson and Tonius pressed the metal ingots to their necks. Mogen's substance, which had protected them from the tree's control, slipped from their flesh, attaching to the ingots.

***

Within a moment, Cayden's Ethereal Hand grew in strength, magnified through the tree's branches a hundredfold. His consciousness ballooned with the storm of leaves and spread across the planet faster than the swiftest wind. The battlefield surrounding Stomatus became just a tiny part of the picture as all his thoughts focused on one directive.

Seek flesh, he commanded, and the leaves obeyed. They darted and burrowed into exposed necks not already containing a leaf. Cries echoed across the planet from the unexpected pain of golden leaves burrowing into the spines of unsuspecting farmers, warriors, and merchants. Hundreds of lives blinked out of existence, casualties of an imperfect binding process. Hundreds of thousands more, though, joined the tree's planetwide network.

In a few minutes, the leaves had done their jobs. Every human, witch, and gremmel on the planet who'd survived the procedure became part of a single entity.

Sevron's army fell upon Stomatus, so Cayden had to act more quickly than he would have liked, projecting his will across the world with one directive: stop fighting and release thoughts of conflict. The effect was instant. Tens of thousands of people fell still. All animosity evaporated, forced from every mind like water wrung from cloth. Those whose minds writhed with hatred grew dull and unresponsive, while others subtly adopted the directions.

Sevron's dark army of souls found themselves without fuel. Like a hot air balloon without flame, the terrible soldiers deflated. A minute later, all traces of their existence vanished.

Chapter Twenty Six

"It's over," Leyna said.

Cayden backed away from the tree's golden core, his head reeling as he struggled to readjust to a single point of view. *Being human limits my vision,* he realized, and Leyna frowned in response. After expanding his consciousness across an entire planet, containing his thoughts within one body seemed inadequate. For a few seconds, he fought the desire to shed his human form like a set of wet clothes, to abandon all earthly concerns and soar off into the sky. But as time inched forward, he forced himself to see the hair moving across his arms and focus the touch of Leyna's hand against his skin. Thousands of tiny sensations added to create a physical connection to the world around him, something he'd no longer be able to experience without a body. The urge to flee subsided, and he opened his eyes.

"Yes," he answered. "It is done." He took Leyna's hand and walked with her to meet Dakota, who led them through the tree and into the city. Though fires burned in the windows of many buildings and rubble littered the streets, an eerie silence had settled over Stomatus. Cayden's feat hung over him like a haze, with all consequences of his battle against Sevron's forces hidden and unknowable.

They spotted Tonius, Robinson, and Henrik sitting atop the outer wall, their legs swinging over the edge, while gremmels wandered below in idle confusion. Cayden's instructions still pulsed from the great tree, suppressing the wills of any who tried to oppose his recent orders. Even the witches, who had led the attack, now sat amidst the shattered battlefield, eying him incuriously as though they were inhabitants of the Dumrolls.

"They halted their assault about ten minutes ago," Tonius reported, standing to greet Cayden.

"It was wild," Robinson said. "One second, the gremmels were trying to pull the skin from my back, and the next, they fell still."

"Yep," Cayden said. "I inserted leaves in everyone's necks, then hijacked the Perianth king's tree to broadcast my commands."

"So that's why my neck stings as if a cow poker stabbed me," Henrik said. "I hope you plan on removing them."

"Unless the king has an idea, I'm afraid the process is irreversible," Cayden said, adding, "I didn't seek this power, but if I hadn't acted, we'd all be dead now, killed at the hands of Sevron's forces."

"Are you absolutely certain?" Tonius asked.

"Before interfacing with the tree, I still had doubts. But guiding the leaves taught me a bit of Sevron's methods, which reassured me that my decision was right. Sevron's goal is control, and his weapon is division. Open war between Jaffa's witches and the Perianth Empire allowed Sevron's darkness to spread among the minds of all who fought. It gave strength to the souls under his command."

"The soul is an antiquated concept," Dakota said.

"Fine. Then you can call them the captured, bodiless consciousnesses of the deceased. I'll call them souls, souls of the dead who bring form to Sevron's will. In any case, the greater the conflict grew, the stronger the souls became until they were strong enough to kill us all—had I not forcibly erased all division. Without conflict, Sevron's disease had nothing to feed on and lacked the energy to spread."

"If it's as you say," Tonius said, "we can begin producing the substance Mogen created to block the tree's signals. Now that we've destroyed Sevron, there's no need for the tree's control."

"Won't everyone just go back to fighting, though?" Robinson asked. "Maybe my understanding is wrong, but Cayden didn't destroy Sevron. He just, like, wiped out whatever darkness Sevron left here."

"That's true," Cayden answered. "Sevron left traces of his influence on Earth to worm into the minds of the population. Lysander explained how events here would have ended as they've ended on thousands of other worlds under his father's control. His children—Henrik and Dakota excluded—came here to escape their father and pursue their own goals, but we all learned what happened next."

"If Earth is the source of Sevron's darkness, then we should sever the connection," Tonius said.

"We could do that…"

"You must," Naya snapped, walking up behind them. Her clothing hung in bloody, shredded strips from her body, but she stood tall and strong. Cayden suspected much of the blood matting her hair originated from the gremmels. "You can't expect us to live with these abominations in our bodies."

"Of course you're right," Cayden said, though he wasn't sure. "Tonius, how long before we can produce leaf blockers for the entire population?"

"If we had the raw materials, it'd take many months. Unfortunately, many of the elements required are quite rare. The Empire doesn't store enough to build more than a couple dozen leaf blockers."

"And what of the gremmels and witches?" Leyna asked. "They'll begin fighting as soon as we suppress the leaves."

"So let them stay under the tree's control, or kill them," Dakota said. "Either way, they're evolutionary dead ends that do not need to exist in their current forms."

"We'll figure out what to do about them when the time comes—but we're not killing them," Cayden said. "Enough people have died already." Dakota raised his slender shoulders in a shrug.

"It doesn't matter, as long as they're not on the ship when it leaves the planet."

"Now, hang on a second," Robinson said. "You agreed not to run if Cayden booted Sevron from our world. Look around, buddy. Sevron's gone. We need Stomatus so we can help the injured recover."

"Agreed," Cayden said before Dakota could respond. "Tonius, will you return to the tree and compile a materials list for the leaf blockers?"

"Sure. I'll also pillage the storerooms."

"Great. Anyone else who's willing, let's split up and go help—" A boom rattled the wall, and a flame streaked overhead. *What now?* Cayden sighed as lashes of wind whipped across the city. He reached high into the sky with his Ethereal Hand, discovering a core of hot iron hiding beneath flames. The burning iron hurtled towards the ground, its light growing in intensity until it cast a harsh glare over everything in sight. *That'll destroy everything within miles if it hits,* Leyna thought, prompting Cayden to jump from the wall and onto the subdued battlefield. Leyna leaped after him, followed by Robinson, Henrik, Naya, and even Dakota.

Iron accepted affinite bonds, but even with a strong bond, slowing such a large projectile demanded tremendous energy. Cayden channeled power from the fusion reactors beneath Stomatus as quickly as they supplied it, using the extra force to sap momentum from the iron. Two Ethereal Hands couldn't control the same material, so Leyna and the others stood by as the object neared the ground a hundred yards away. Cayden had killed much of its velocity, but its impact still sent up a volcanic plume of dust. A moment later, the ground shook hard enough to toss them onto their backs.

"Is everyone okay?" Cayden asked, helping Leyna to her feet.

"A fireball just about blew us up, but I'm doing great," Robinson said. Tonius just groaned, holding his injured arm.

"It is called a meteorite," Dakota said, brushing dust from his shirt.

"Whatever it is, it's moving." Still shrouded in dust, a shadowed silhouette shifted ominously within the impact crater. Cayden crept forward, motioning his friends to keep quiet and preparing himself for anything. But what emerged from the crater stopped him in his tracks. Of all the creatures he'd seen in Harken's cavern, this monstrosity made the rest appear tame. A fleshy sphere writhing with thousands of tiny fingers like amoebic flagella sat atop three brittle legs. The legs lacked joints, and the creature lurched in awkward, stuttering jolts. It stopped six feet away, forcing Cayden to look up, for it towered overhead. Black oil dripped from its slick carapace, and the putrid scent of sulfur flooded Cayden's nostrils.

"Greetings," it said, gargling like a diver attempting to speak underwater.

"What are you?" Cayden asked, keeping his limbs tensed and ready.

"Do you mean 'who'?" Cayden spotted no mouth, eyes, or other recognizable features from which the sound might emanate, though he noticed the flesh ball vibrating as it talked.

"Fine. Who," Cayden corrected himself. Leyna joined Cayden, followed by Dakota and the others. *Be careful,* Leyna warned. *I can sense no thoughts coming from this thing.*

"I was the Seer responsible for a region of space containing the world upon which we stand. It is one of several hundred worlds I oversaw."

"My father controls you," Dakota guessed.

"Indeed, I have the honor of serving Sevron, he who commanded me here to deliver a message to you, Dakota, and his other children." The creature's legs spread out in a triangle below it, scraping through the dirt as the fleshy sphere lowered itself to eye level. "Your petty experiments have come to Sevron's attention."

"I see."

"And your father is returning to correct his mistakes that led to these experiments."

"Is that all?" Despite the bizarreness of the creature, Dakota's face displayed no emotion, and he spoke in his usual mechanical cadence.

"That is all." The creature raised itself back onto its legs, reaching a height of at least fifteen feet.

"Hang on, it's telling you that Sevron is returning to kill you," Cayden said, surprised that even Dakota wouldn't display more emotion under the circumstances.

"There is no need to restate its words."

"Your father is coming to kill you, Dakota. Don't you have more to say?"

"What else can I say? I agree with your assessment of the situation, Cayden. Though, I am wondering: Seer, you must have other duties aside from delivering messages if indeed you handle hundreds of worlds."

"No longer. My only remaining duty was to deliver that message. Now I will await Sevron's arrival and continue to serve him in whatever way he sees fit."

Cayden, Leyna whispered in his mind, *look at the creature from my perspective*. Cayden let his senses merge with hers until he shared her cognition. The Seer's mind, if it had one, didn't vibrate with emotion like a human or animal; instead, it appeared to Leyna like a stone, impermeable and inanimate. She shifted her attention to the minds of Dakota, Tonius, and Robinson, which seemed off somehow. Different. Changed. It took Cayden several long seconds to sense the disturbance, but once he did, he recognized the source.

"Everyone, back away from the creature!" Cayden yelled, the pit of his stomach dropping. *I can't lose everything I've worked for,* he thought desperately. "You, creature. Stop broadcasting Sevron's will, or I'll kill you." Cayden blinked in surprise at the force of the threat he'd just shouted and how capable he was of carrying through on his threat.

"I am what I am," the creature said, standing immobile, its flagellum undulating complex patterns in the gathering wind as fetid oil soaked the soil beneath its feet. Through Leyna, Cayden watched Sevron's influence seep into his friends, pushing through their minds like an eager disease. *I can't let it happen again,* he decided, gathering the might of his Ethereal Hand before him. Forming a hasty affinite bond with a slab of nearby stone, he swept the legs out from under the creature. It fell into an awkward pile and didn't attempt to rise. Still, darkness pulsed from its core, threatening to reestablish Sevron's will in the Perianth Empire.

"I'll give you one more chance," Cayden warned, his voice breaking. "I will kill you if you don't stop." The creature fell silent, and its flagellum became rigid.

"End this," Leyna urged. "Robinson's mind is already falling into the abyss, and the others will soon follow." Cayden quickly looked at Robinson, who'd fallen to the ground. He banged his head against the dirt as if attempting to knock the invading force from his mind. Cayden realized he couldn't delay any longer.

With a cry, Cayden brought the stone down upon the creature's vulnerable flesh, crushing it against the ground as one might squash a bug. The creature perished, but a pitch-black presence screamed from its body, charging at Cayden. He flexed his Ethereal Hand around himself like a shield just as the darkness hammered against his improvised barrier. Cayden's Hand weakened more quickly than his shapeless foe, every passing second further sapping his strength.

Keep it up, Leyna encouraged him. *I can see the darkness thinning.* Propped up by her words, and with the lives of his friends in the balance, Cayden let out a determined hiss through gritted teeth. His Ethereal Hand blossomed outwards, growing stronger than he'd imagined possible. For the briefest moment, the air shimmered as if the Hand gained material form. But he knew that to be impossible. The fight lasted only seconds, and soon the last wisp of darkness exhausted itself against Cayden's renewed strength. The black fog dissipated into nothingness, and Cayden sank to his knees.

"That was—" Cayden blacked out. Minutes later, he came to with his head on Robinson's lap. His friend's gaunt face stared down at him, eyes wide with concern.

"I had… to… get rid… of it," Cayden said.

"We understand," Robinson said, helping him into a sitting position. "Leyna already explained."

"I didn't realize how difficult it would be to destroy." Cayden shook his head, remembering the eradication of Sevron's disease from the great tree. He'd had help then, but still… "The darkness on this planet was nothing compared to whatever that creature held. It nearly destroyed me, and without Leyna's help, it would have."

"A virus is always most potent when fresh," Dakota said. "And my father behaves like a virus."

"A virus we cannot stop unless we are united. It just takes the smallest gap, the tiniest of breaches in one person's mind, for this darkness to spread."

"Cayden, you must free everyone from the leaves," Leyna said, sensing the growing determination in his mind.

Cayden didn't answer. Every soul on the planet housed a golden leaf, and while still possible to overpower, the leaves provided significant protection against Sevron and his minions. If they used Mogen's recipe to block the leaves' reception, they'd be back to square one. The imposed peace would dissolve, allowing the darkness to flourish. *There'd be no stopping it, and we need unity now more than ever if we hope to save everyone's lives.*

"No," Cayden said. "The leaves must stay. It is for the good of everyone."

Leyna opened her mouth to speak, but she closed it when she realized Cayden stood prepared to sever their connection should she try to sway his thoughts. *I'm sorry,* he said, but she responded with silence. *You need to consider the implications, and you'll see that I am correct,* he thought, turning from his friends and walking alone into Stomatus.

***

Cayden wandered through Stomatus' maze-like streets, turning whenever he reached a crossroads. No one paid him the slightest bit of attention, and after an hour, he arrived near the base of the great tree, its branches now barren. It appeared smaller, less intimidating, without its mass of golden foliage. All roads lead to the tree, he thought.

Without deciding to, Cayden entered. He shuffled through the training hall where Astor had taken his first steps towards the hatred that would leave him injured or dead in his dungeon. He passed the bunk where he'd first met Tonius and Robinson. Finally, he stopped at the elevator leading to the tree's upper reaches, where the meeting hall holding the Perianth throne sat abandoned. At his command, the platform shot up beneath his feet.

In the abandoned hall, he stepped over the scattered chairs until he reached the metal throne. His reflection shone in its polished, golden surface, but the person staring back at him didn't look familiar. He reached out to touch the throne, finding it warmer than he expected against his chilled hands. All he'd done over the past year rushed into his mind at once, a jumble of decisions and experiences too unwieldy to process. I need time to think. Panic tightened across his chest, and the world spun around him as his breathing increased. No matter how quickly he inhaled, he couldn't catch his breath.

"What is happening?" he asked no one in particular. When his vision closed in, he sank into the nearest chair—the Perianth throne.

"It's uncomfortable, no?" asked a croaking voice from the shadows. Cayden sat up straight to see the beaten and tattered Perianth king.

"Are you doing this to me?" Cayden asked in between breaths. He's trying to kill me for what I did to him, he thought.

"No, not me. You're having a panic attack. There's nothing wrong with you, so don't worry. It'll pass in a moment." The king's mechanical knees groaned as he bent into a sitting position while he waited for Cayden to recover. After several minutes of gripping the edges of the throne so tightly his fingers turned white, the world stopped spinning.

"You survived the battle," Cayden said, gulping to force saliva into his dry throat.

"I've survived more battles than you can imagine, though I didn't expect to outlive my sister. I suppose I have you to thank for that." The last time Cayden had spoken to the king, during Jaffa's first attack a year ago, he'd judged the ancient man insane. Now, though an occasional shiver ran through his metallic body, the king appeared composed.

"I'm sorry I had to kill her," Cayden said, though when he searched for feelings of shame or remorse, he came up empty.

"Sorry you 'had to,' but not sorry you killed her, eh? No? Well, I don't blame you. She'd become a deplorable person."

"And you?" Cayden said, holding onto anger as his only means of coping. Rage helped push the remaining knots of panic below the surface. "You're as terrible as your sister, creating the leaves to control other people's minds and using your brother Lysander to rule the Perianth Empire. How many atrocities have you committed? How many have you killed?"

"I'd become as evil as my father, yes. I've had plenty of time to reflect during my tortures at the hands of Jaffa's witches. But my Perianth Empire allowed you to save us all."

"I want nothing to do with your Empire," Cayden said, disgusted. "All this death, and for what? So you could live two thousand years?

Well, good for you. Mission accomplished. You've managed to live while countless thousands have died in your petty wars. All while the true threat rampaged our world unchecked. You can have your throne back. I don't want it." Cayden stood.

"My throne?" The king snorted, the sound more metallic scratching than human laughter. "I've not come back to claim the throne, oh mighty and wise Airwalker. I'm no longer fit to rule my body, let alone an Empire."

"Then why come here at all?"

"To offer you my aid in your fight against my father. I'm the only one of his children left, aside from Dakota, Henrik, and the Alchemist. Dakota won't fight for others, while the Alchemist lacks a brain. Henrik is brilliant, but he's new to our predicament and is unfamiliar with our father's capabilities. But I know Sevron well enough to erase any doubt that his demise will benefit the universe."

Leyna, what should I do? Cayden asked, but Leyna didn't respond. *I know you can hear me.* Still, she withheld her thoughts from him. He pressed his fists against the throne as a headache throbbed behind his eyes. Cayden suspected the pain wouldn't subside even if he removed his consciousness from the body it occupied. So he sat on the throne and contemplated his future. *No matter what, I can't allow Sevron to retake our world.* The Seer had unleashed just the barest hint of Sevron's true power, and the encounter had taught him that, with his current knowledge, withstanding Sevron was unthinkable. He needed the Perianth king Adam's wisdom if any hope existed, for Dakota wouldn't lend his help. *Leyna, working with Adam will teach us what we need to know.* Still no response. *I am doing the right thing. I know I am.*

"You're doing the right thing, you know," said the former Perianth king, as an insane grin spread across his cracked face.

Other Books by Alexander Jacobs

Did you enjoy *The Ethereal Hand*? Visit AJWriting.com for a selection of Alexander Jacobs' other books!

The Other Side of Gold
First book in *The Ethereal Kingdom* Trilogy

Cayden's golden eye cast him as a dangerous outcast amongst the other children in his isolated village, and he spends his time daydreaming about a massive tree towering above a diamond city. Little does he know, the city is real. On a quest to discover the secrets of his past, he encounters men made of glittering metal, trees that float through the sky like blimps, and new friends who will help him bring balance to a world thrown into water.

The Ethereal Hand
Second book in *The Ethereal Kingdom* Trilogy

Cayden and Leyna race to unite the witches Perianths, and Sky People before a malevolent entity names Sevron consumes their world. Centuries of fighting and mistrust won't be easy to overcome. Meanwhile, the answers Cayden seeks may be held inside the mind of a young (yet very, very old) boy named Dakota.

His Ethereal Kingdom
Third book in *The Ethereal Kingdom* Trilogy

Years have passed. Leyna never forgave Cayden for his decision to follow Dakota's plan, and she seeks another solution on Earth. As

Sevron's unassailable power demonstrates the futility of even the best-laid plans, Cayden searches for answers that may exist beyond their reality.

The First Servant

After ten thousand years, the immortal ruler of the Defiant Empire begins slaughtering his citizens without explanation or obvious reason. Grey, a boy tortured by a maniacal demon, is swept up in a plot to overthrow the unstoppable tyrant - all while battling his own impulse to hurt everyone he encounters.

The Void

An obsessive Riverwalker priest convinces Birch, a dying man, that he is a reincarnated mythical icon destined to restore magic to a world in decay - but nothing is as it seems. Is the void's promise of immortality a blessing, or is it another Riverwalker lie? Birch spends his dying days on a journey that will transform the Riverwalkier religion forever.

www.ingramcontent.com/pod-product-compliance
Lightning Source LLC
LaVergne TN
LVHW050541160826
845677LV00011B/2129

* 9 7 9 8 3 6 6 2 1 2 2 0 5 *